D0888120

Almost a Serial Killer

Doreen Diller Humorous Mystery Trilogy, Volume 1

Margaret Lashley

Published by Zazzy Ideas, Inc., 2022.

Copyright

What Readers are Saying About Doreen Diller

"*A great plot, exceptional storytelling and a whole new cast of fun characters make this one a must-read.*"

"*What a delightful start to a new cozy mystery series by one of my favorite contemporary Southern authors!*"

"*Doreen Diller is pretty sure she didn't kill her boss. But, could the last few stressful days have turned her into a psycho-eyed homicidal maniac? Read it and find out!*"

"*I love books that grab me from the start, make me laugh and cry, and keep me glued to the end. This book is all that and more.*"

"*Ms. Lashley takes loads of quirky characters, a twisty mystery, a pinch of romance, and a heaping helping of humor to create this masterpiece!*"

"*This book is hilarious. I couldn't believe how funny Doreen is. The craziness in this story was such fun to read. Doreen is my new favorite character.*"

More Mysteries by Margaret Lashley

Available on Amazon in Your Choice of Ebook, Paperback, Hardback & Audiobook:

Doreen Diller Mystery Series (Ongoing)
https://www.amazon.com/gp/product/B0B2X3G3G7
Val Fremden Midlife Mysteries (Nine-Book Series)
https://www.amazon.com/gp/product/B07FK88WQ3
Absolute Zero (The Val Fremden Prequel)
https://www.amazon.com/dp/B06ZXYK776
Freaky Florida Mystery Adventures (Eight-Book Series)
https://www.amazon.com/gp/product/B07RL4G8GZ
Mind's Eye Investigators (Two-Book Series)
https://www.amazon.com/gp/product/B07ZR6NW2N

Chapter One

P eople in Hollywood don't lead normal lives.

Nowhere on Earth does the fine line between real life and the movies blur like it does in L.A. On any random day you could sit next to Jennifer Aniston in a restaurant. Or stand in line with Johnny Depp in a grocery store. Or pump gas next to George Clooney.

(I once hopped into a cab to find Betty White inside. Nicest, funniest lady ever. Highlight of my life!)

Anyway, because we live side by side with celebrities, news about them touches us deeper—like they're family. I always thought this was unique to Tinseltown. But I was about to find out the hard way that I was totally wrong about that.

The truth is, nobody *anywhere* leads a normal life. And that fine line between reality and fantasy? Well, it's one you cross at your own peril ...

• • • •

"I CAN'T BELIEVE YOU watch that crap," my roommate Sonya said, rolling her eyes as she tied the laces on her worn-out sneakers. "It's so lame."

"Are you *kidding*?" I said, aghast at her heresy. "Tad Longmire is a living god! Just *look* at him."

It was 7:30 in the morning, and I was in the middle of my daily "spiritual harmonizing" ritual. In other words, I was in my pajamas on the couch in front of the TV, gulping down a bowl of Lucky Charms, my eyes glued to Tad Longmire.

Tad played Dr. Lovejoy, the hunky heartthrob surgeon on my favorite daytime soap, *Days of Our Lies*. He was my yogi, messiah, and savior all rolled into one. I knew this because just one look at him made everything right with my world.

"Tad's not *that* great," Sonya said, crinkling her nose.

"Not that great?" I gasped, nearly choking on a mouthful of cereal. "Are you blind? He's tall, blond, and has those amazing, twinkling blue eyes. See how he moves? He's got the suave confidence of a top-shelf movie star. Tell me. What's not to love about him?"

Sonya tugged a gym jacket over her gray T-shirt. "Geez, Doreen. Sounds like you've got a crush on the guy."

I poised midway into shoveling a spoonful of magically delicious cereal into my mouth. "Maybe I do. Is that so wrong?"

Sonya laughed. "Last time I counted the candles, Doreen, you were thirty-nine."

"So?" I frowned and blew an errant lock of brown hair from in front of my eyes. "I'm never gonna give up on my dreams."

Sonya arched an eyebrow. "Good for you. Mine took a one-way bus to the Mojave years ago." She picked up her backpack and opened the front door. "I'm catching a ride to the studio with Derek. See you there. Don't be late. You know how Jared hates that."

"I know. I'll be there soon."

As the door closed behind her, I glanced at the time on my cellphone. My heart skipped a beat. Four days ago, Jared Thomas, big-time letch and small-time Hollywood studio director, had given me a new assignment. As usual, it totally sucked. But for once, my lousy job had an upside. It put me in the same production building as Tad Longmire. That meant in two short hours, there was a chance I might actually meet my dreamy soap opera surgeon face-to-face!

According to *The Hollywood Gossip Gal*, my favorite online blog, Tad Longmire was in L.A. working on the mid-budget action thriller, *Breaking Code*. As a longtime fan of Tad's, I knew in my gut the movie was going to be his big break—the role that would transform him from small-screen beefcake into big-screen dreamboat. And, as a longtime aspiring actress myself, I knew such breaks didn't come along every day.

If ever.

As for me, I was still waiting for my own ship to come in. I'd never admit it to Sonya, but lately I'd begun to fear my ticket aboard the cruise to fame and fortune had been eaten by a horny goat.

If that weren't bad enough, for the past week I'd been having this recurring nightmare. In it, the entire cast of *The Love Boat* waved from the bow as they steamed past me—while I sat in a leaky rowboat wearing a moldy life vest and bailing water for all I was worth. Every time I dreamt it, I'd wake up in a cold sweat, my sheet twisted around my neck like a noose.

That had to mean something, didn't it?

Anyway, today was going to be different. I could feel it in my bones. I put my cereal bowl in the sink, brushed my teeth, and pulled my wavy hair back into a messy bun. I was running late, so I tossed my cosmetics into a makeup bag. I'd have time to fix myself up properly when I got to work.

Being a Girl Friday at a Hollywood film studio might've sounded glamorous. But believe me, it wasn't. Besides the guy who cleaned the toilets, it was the lowest job on the studio rung. But it paid the bills—sort of—while I treaded water and waited for Captain Stubing to turn his blasted ship around.

Hopefully, he'd do it soon. I was starting to get wrinkly.

After fifteen years of acting lessons, dance classes, cattle-call try-outs, bit parts in low-budget community theater productions, bowing and scraping to studio bigwigs, and clearing my aura of karmic negativity, the biggest movie role I'd managed to land so far was stunt-double for a hooker found decapitated in a dumpster. Not exactly a cameo designed to make Hollywood casting directors sit up and take notice.

Jared Thomas had given me that gig six months ago. But only after I'd agreed to go out on a date with him. He'd promised that, if I played my cards right, he could get me a good part in his next project. The only problem was, Jared had been holding an ace the whole time—and it wasn't up his sleeve. Don't get me wrong. Like Jared, I believed in happy endings, too. Just not on a first date.

My failure to perform on demand had resulted in Jared giving the "good part" to a more willing starlet. In return, I'd vented my frustration by shoving a rotten banana down the front of Jared's pants in front of his film crew. After that? Well, let's just say my acting prospects had shriveled up faster than a spider in a microwave oven.

The only thing that had saved me from being fired outright was my SAG membership, which I managed to keep alive playing a random crowd "extra" in whatever low-budget movie would hire me. Because of it, Jared hadn't been able to can me on the spot. So instead, he'd settled for sticking me in a series of dead-end jobs that, I'd come to believe, were part of an evil, passive-aggressive crusade to make me so miserable I'd quit.

Jobs like my latest assignment—personal assistant to Dolores Benny.

Ms. Benny was a plump, googly-eyed actress in her late sixties. And even though she swore like a sailor, chain-smoked Virginia Slims, and looked like Jabba the Hutt in drag, I'd have done just about anything to be *her* instead of me.

Ms. Benny, like Tad Longmire, had made it to the big screen.

As her personal assistant for the past four days, I'd been responsible for attending to the odd-looking woman's every whim. That included hourly ego massages, landmine-filled hair and makeup sessions, death-defying wardrobe wrestling matches, and late-night ice cream-and-cigarette emergencies, which happened more often than you'd think humanly possible.

Most nights, grunt-workers like me and Sonya never even made it back to the flophouse apartment we shared in South Park with two other would-be stars. Instead, we usually took turns napping on the lumpy cots tucked away in a dark corner of the production studio. The ones reserved for "acting tryouts" and sleep-deprived underlings such as ourselves.

On a good night, we'd catch two or three hours of uninterrupted sleep before our cellphones rang, startling us into the next mad dash to the trailer of whichever star we'd been assigned to. On the bright side, the work was excellent acting practice. There was nothing quite like getting up at 3 a.m. to wax somebody's back hair or sort the blue M&Ms from a family-sized bag to help an aspiring thespian dig deep for an ingratiating smile or a cheerful attitude.

People like Sonya and me were the worker bees in a hive with too many queens. To cope, we swapped horror stories in the dark. And we dubbed ourselves the TTC—Trailer-Trash Crew. Why didn't we just quit? Believe me, we contemplated it daily. But there was one perk our jobs offered that made the demeaning tasks worthwhile.

Working there kept our studio passes active.

As long as we retained permission to roam the sacred grounds of a Hollywood production set, we wannabe-actors could still cling to the hope that fate would deliver us our own big break one day.

And with the chance of meeting Tad Longmire on the set today, *this* just might prove to be *my* lucky day.

. . . .

AS SOON AS I STEPPED out the door of the apartment, my carefully laid plans derailed faster than that horrific train crash in *Unbreakable*. In the movie, Bruce Willis had emerged from the wreckage unscathed. Whether *I* would survive my current catastrophe still remained to be seen.

First off, my car, a battered, drab-green Kia Soul I'll nicknamed The Toad, refused to crank. After opening the hood and beating the solenoid with a socket wrench, it finally coughed to life. But by then, I was running late. Really late.

When I finally got to the studio, I encountered my second glitch. Jared Thomas. The petty tyrant was storming through the studio warehouse on another one of his egomaniacal rampages.

Not willing to find out if I was the cause of or solution to his latest meltdown, I dived into a supply closet. After ten minutes of pressing my ear to the cheap panel door, the angry voices faded. The coast finally clear, I fled, makeup bag in hand, to Dolores Benny's trailer in the studio's back lot.

Escaping Jared's wrath might've saved me a chewing out, but it had cost me more precious time than I could afford. As I reached for Ms. Benny's doorknob, I checked my cellphone. It was nine o'clock on the dot. Today's filming would begin in half an hour.

Crap!

I was going to need every last remaining second to get Ms. Benny ready for her close-up with Tad—not to mention my own. Out of breath from running, I burst into the old woman's trailer. The horrors that awaited me inside made me let out an asthmatic wheeze.

Ms. Benny appeared to be engaged in a fight to the death with a full-body latex girdle.

I'd seen slasher movies that weren't that graphic.

"There you are, girl!" Benny grumbled. "It's about time you got here!"

I winced. "Sorry. Let me help you with that."

I flung my makeup bag on the counter and dived in, yanking at the flesh-squashing undies like the heroine in a low-budget sci-fi movie from the 1950s—*It Came from Planet Spanx.*

Eight minutes later, sweaty and exhausted, I'd managed to encapsulate Ms. Benny into her spandex chrysalis. But my work was only half over. I still had to turn her from a moth into a butterfly.

While she sat in front of the vanity mirror patting pancake makeup over her beet-red face, I opened Ms. Benny's wardrobe bag. Inside hung a purple sequined cocktail dress. It was a size ten—at least four sizes too small. (In Hollywood, "plus size" meant anything over a size two.)

God give me strength.

I slipped the dress off the hanger and unzipped it. "Step in," I said, holding the bottom of the dress open six inches off the floor.

"Gimme a minute," Benny said, snapping her powder compact closed. She set it on the vanity. Then, grunting from the effort, she stood. Gripping my shoulder for balance, she slowly shifted one bare-foot, pudgy white leg at a time into the opening of the dress.

"Good job," I said, tugging the sequined gown up the front of her ample torso. That part of *Mission Impossible* completed, I began stuffing her arms into the elbow-length sleeves.

"Cripes," Benny grumbled. "I look like a Liberace sausage in this getup."

"No way," I cooed. "You look gorgeous. Now let me zip you up."

I went around to the back of Ms. Benny. A long, silver zipper ran up the back of her dress from her butt crack to her neck. Against the dark purple fabric, it resembled a miniature railroad track. Unfortunately, just like in *Unbreakable*, the massive gap between destinations appeared tragically insurmountable.

"Here we go," I said, searching for the zipper pull. I found it protruding from the bottom of her buttocks like a stubby metallic tail. I grabbed ahold of it and tugged with all my might.

It wouldn't budge.

"Umm ... try holding your breath," I said gently.

"Ung," Benny grunted. "Fine. But don't bother holding yours."

"What?" I asked.

"Don't bother holding *your* breath," Benny repeated, letting her Jersey accent slip out. "Look, hun. I know you're not working this job for the perks. You wanna be a star, right?"

"Well, yes."

She shook her head. "Don't take this wrong, but I just don't see it happening."

"What?" I gasped, my fingers going limp on the zipper pull.

"You just ain't pretty enough for leading lady roles." Benny leaned in closer to the vanity mirror to touch up a fake mole on her puffy cheek. "Your only shot at the big screen is with character bits. Like me."

"Oh. I see. Thank you, Ms. Benny," I said. Wounded, I pursed my lips into a vice. If I wanted to see Tad, I needed to keep this stupid job. And to keep this stupid job, I had to keep my mouth shut and get Ms. Benny's zipper up.

I winced out a smile and tugged again with all my might. This time, the zipper shot up to her bulging waist.

"Watch it!" Benny said. Her reflection in the mirror glared back at me. "That pinches!"

"I am *so* sorry, Ms. Benny," I groveled. "Thank you so much for the advice about trying out for character-actor parts. Do you think you could recommend—"

The old woman's cackling laughter drowned out my pandering.

"You know, even landing a character role would take a miracle for you, hun. Your face is bland, girl. *Bland!* You got no *angle.* You got nothing to make you stand out. Those poor casting directors have to wade through a whole *sea* of headshots, you know? You gotta give 'em something to work with!"

Something to work with?

An odd combination of humiliation and rage surged through me. Remembering my acting classes, I *channeled the energy* into forcing the industrial-strength zipper past three rolls of spandex-covered back fat and up to the nape of Ms. Benny's mole-pocked neck.

I hooked the clasp at the top and tried to glean some bit of satisfaction from my Herculean solo performance. But who was I fooling?

As Benny hung earrings from her thick lobes, I studied my reflection in her vanity mirror. What *did* I actually have to offer? Unremarkable brown hair. Unremarkable face. Unremarkable ... *everything*.

Ms. Benny had been rude. But she'd also been *right*.

Crap.

Benny turned around to face me. Her dress was so tight it forced her to move in small, wobbly steps. My mind raced to an image of *ET the Extraterrestrial*—in cocktail attire.

"Face it, girl," Benny said, watching me inventory myself in the mirror. "You're a Plain Jane."

"Looks aren't everything," I said. "What about *substance*?"

Benny arched a drawn-on eyebrow. "Honey, the only *substance* anybody in L.A. cares about comes in pill, capsule, or powder form."

I frowned. "But—"

"How *old* are you, anyway?" She looked me up and down, her oversized eyeballs not quite following the same trajectory.

"Is that really relevant?" I asked, shriveling under her cockeyed scrutiny.

She chuckled. "*That* old, huh?"

I picked up a fake diamond brooch to pin to the front of her dress. Benny took it from my hand, then let out a series of clucking sounds that left no doubt as to what she thought about my prospects for stardom.

"I'll do it myself," she said, dismissing me with a wave of her hand. "I need coffee. Be a dear and go get me my usual, would you ... *Plain Jane*?"

My shoulders slumped beneath the weight of the old woman's casual death blow. "Yes, ma'am. Would you like your usual vanilla éclair to go with it?"

"Yeah. With extra filling. And hurry up. We don't got that much time left."

"Yes, ma'am," I said, reaching for the doorknob, my eyes brimming with tears.

Apparently, some of us never had any time to begin *with.*

• • • •

FIVE MINUTES AFTER having my acting prospects squashed like a roach by a pulsing larva in a purple dress, I was in the studio parking lot, dejectedly shuffling my way back to Ms. Benny's trailer. As I contemplated whether or not to add a few drops of arsenic to her double-shot, caramel, almond milk, iced-mocha cappuccino, a young woman burst from the trailer next to Ms. Benny's.

The stunning brunette steamed down the trailer steps and sprinted past me, leaving a trail of tears and curse words in her scorching wake. A second later, to my utter shock, Tad Longmire, my daytime daydream, appeared in the trailer's open doorframe.

He was shirtless.

I was speechless.

"Hey you," he called out, fastening the top button of his jeans. "Don't I know you?"

"Uh ... *me?*" I asked, my cheeks suddenly aflame. "No sir. But I definitely know *you*."

A corner of his mouth curled into an *of course you do* grin. "What's your name, sugar?"

I swallowed a lump in my throat. "D ... Doreen Diller."

Tad shot me a smile that melted the souls of my sneakers. "Ah, yes. I've had my eye on you."

"You *have?*" I gasped, nearly dropping Ms. Benny's cappuccino.

"Of course," he said. "Who wouldn't?"

"Wha—?" I fumbled, my tongue suddenly an uncooperative lump of meat in my mouth.

My hair was a mess. My makeup was still in a bag on Ms. Benny's countertop. Yet there he was, Tad Longmire, my secret crush, *hitting on me!*

This has to be a dream.

I wanted to pinch myself to be sure, but between the cappuccino and the éclair, I didn't have a free hand.

Then, while I stood there frozen like an idiot in shock and disbelief, *Days of Our Lies* heartthrob Tad Longmire spoke the ten words that would change my life forever.

"So, Doreen Diller," he said. "How'd you like to be a star?"

Chapter Two

If this were the movies, this is where I, Doreen Diller—the mousy but plucky little nobody—would be whisked away to makeup and wardrobe. In under an hour I'd reemerge virtually unrecognizable, transformed into a goddess worthy of gracing the arm of blond Apollo Tad Longmire.

Obscurity would no longer exist in my vocabulary. And, in a shower of rose petals, I'd wave goodbye to my fellow underlings as I rocketed to fame and fortune on a golden steed named Oscar.

But this *wasn't* the movies.

It was *L.A.*—the place where reality and fantasy collide to form strange bedfellows, indeed.

• • • •

AFTER TAD SHOWERED me with promises of glamorous work conditions, double my current salary, and introductions to Hollywood directors, I sprinted over to Dolores Benny's trailer and delivered that ridiculous coffee order of hers and told her politely (okay, passive-aggressively) to "break a leg."

Next, I pulled out my cellphone and pecked out a scathing resignation text to Jared that hinted (okay, spelled out) that his revolting personality was not the worst of his many "shortcomings."

I hit *Send* and laughed out loud. I could scarcely believe it! I was no longer at the mercy of that sexist pig! I was free at last not to merely follow someone else's rules, but to make my own!

No more napping on dirty studio cots. No more trailer-trash crewing. I, Doreen Diller, have graduated to the big leagues. Tad Longmire's going to make me a star!

Giggling with glee, I floated into Tad Longmire's trailer on cloud nine, ready to make my own, unique mark on Hollywood. I was going to set the new standard for what qualified as leading-lady material.

I would not kowtow to the Hollywood cliché and become a simpering, weak-minded, obscenely beautiful stick figure. No. I would forge the new face of femininity. Strong. Confident. And driven not by the external, but *internally*, by my own sense of justice.

Exhilarated by my newfound freedom, I sat down at Tad's banquette table to read over his employment contract. But I couldn't concentrate. Tad was only a few feet away from me. I couldn't help but keep sneaking furtive glances at him. I mean, who wouldn't?

My brain kept telling me to remain calm and hold onto my wits. But the rest of me wanted to jump his bones.

In a star-studded daze, I watched breathlessly as the handsome hunk slipped a crisp, white, button-down shirt over his smooth, perfect chest. He left it open, offering glimpses of his six-pack abs as he casually milled about in his kitchen—*humming a tune!*

All of a sudden, Tad reached up and took two crystal flutes from a cupboard. I held my breath as he bent over and took a bottle of champagne from his fridge...

Oh. My. God. I'm going to throw back some bubbly with Tad Longmire!

"I've had my eye on you," Tad said again, popping the cork. "You know, I think we could be really good together."

"You do?" I gulped.

"I do."

Tad's words echoed in my head like a bridegroom fantasy. As I envisioned him in a tux next to a big, white cake, he aimed his heart-melting, crooked smile my way.

"All signed, Dorey?"

I nodded, then hastily scrawled my name on the dotted line. Beaming, I held up the contract like a child showing Daddy her crayon drawing of a unicorn jumping over a rainbow.

"All done!" I squealed.

Tad grinned. "Perfect."

I sighed.

Yes, Tad. You totally are.

Mesmerized, I watched as Tad's strong, beautiful hands filled two sparkling crystal flutes with expensive-looking bubbly. With grace and elegance, he swept up one of the slender glasses and shot me a gleaming, toothpaste-commercial smile.

I nearly swooned.

Then, for the second time in under an hour, Tad Longmire said something that would change my life forever.

He nodded toward the trailer door and said, "Get out."

I nearly fell out of my chair. "What?"

"Come back in an hour," he said. "And bring me an In-N-Out Burger, animal style. Large fries." He turned away and took a sip of champagne.

"What?" I gasped as he brushed back his signature blond bangs, admiring his reflection in one of the huge mirrors lining the walls.

"You heard me," he said.

"But Tad, I don't underst—"

A quick rap sounded on the trailer door.

It flew open.

A gorgeous redhead with boobs bigger than her head came flouncing into Tad's trailer. She grinned at him lasciviously, not even bothering to acknowledge my existence.

My face dropped four inches.

"Oh."

The word tumbled out of my mouth like a bitter marble. I grabbed my contract and scrambled from the banquette. Then I slunk past the woman and out of the trailer like a scolded dog.

Outside, in the parking lot, anatomically incapable of kicking my own ass, I settled for biting down hard on my bottom lip.

"What an idiot!" I hissed at myself.

Once again, I'd fallen for the L.A. fairytale—hook, line, and too-good-to-be-true *stinker*.

Stupid, stupid, stupid!

I flopped my butt down on the hard curb and checked the time on my cellphone. According to Andy Warhol, Tad Longmire had just tricked me out of nine of my allotted fifteen minutes of fame.

I hung my head in shame.

Why do I keep falling for the bad guys?

As I sat there commiserating my own idiocy, a brown tabby cat came ambling toward me. A chunk was missing from his left ear. Apparently, I wasn't the only one having a rough life this time around.

The skinny feline rubbed its threadbare chin against my shin and purred. I sat up a little straighter. "You're right," I said. "Strays like us need to stick together."

I stroked its tawny head. It purred louder. I set my jaw determinedly and looked into the kitty's jade-green eyes.

"Tell you what," I said. "You show me where I can get some cat turds for my new boss's lunch, and I'll bring you back a tuna sandwich. Deal?"

The cat winked.

It was on.

Chapter Three

It's a well-known fact that anyone who says they've never fantasized about killing their boss is a liar. Possibly pathological.

After just four days of being Tad Longmire's personal assistant, I was ready to act on my newly revised fantasy about the handsome but lecherous hunk. Instead of dreaming of hitting the sack with Tad and rocking his world, I was ready to hit him over the head with a sack of rocks, then hold his face down in a dirty toilet bowl until his spirit left this world.

Other than that, things had been going relatively well.

Since being hired on Sunday, I'd spent my time alternating between helping Tad rehearse his lines—and then making myself scarce so he could have sexy time with the boobalicious redhead he'd been boinking almost non-stop since I slithered out of his trailer with a contract, but no champagne.

During my "get lost" breaks, Tad had kept me busy running out to get him coffees, smoothies, and In-N-Out Burger takeout. How the man could eat burgers and fries every day and look like he did was a discussion I was saving for when I met God in person. On the flip side, at least I didn't have to wrestle Tad into a girdle. And, I had to admit, Tad was a great actor.

He'd certainly fooled me.

Since Monday, my hunky new boss had been hitting his cues on *Breaking Code* like a superstar. So when I returned to the set on Thursday with Tad's emergency organic acai-and-blueberry green energy smoothie, I was surprised to find him engaged in an intense conversation with a short, hairy, red-faced man. It took me a minute to recognize the guy as the movie's director, Victor Borloff.

"What's going on?" I whispered to the camera guy.

He muted the mouthpiece on his headset, then turned to me and said, "Artistic differences."

"What kind of artistic differences?" I asked, watching a shirtless Tad back away from the director until his broad, tan shoulders were pinned against a wall.

"The 'director's cut' kind," the camera guy said.

I frowned. "What do you mean? Are they arguing about Tad participating in extended scenes?"

He smirked. "I guess you could say that."

I frowned. "I don't get what all the fuss is about. I'm sure—"

The cameraman cocked his head and shot me a smirk. "You know that big-boobed redhead Tad's been porking?"

"Uh, Bonnie? Yeah."

He wagged his eyebrows. "She's Borloff's wife."

My gut flopped. "Oh. My. God."

Dumbfounded, I watched in stunned horror as the director's right arm angled backward, then lunged forward. In a flash of red-knuckled fury, Borloff's fist smashed into Tad's once-perfect nose like an angry jackhammer.

"And there it is," the cameraman snorted. "The director's right cut."

• • • •

BACK AT TAD'S TRAILER, my philandering new boss was standing by the sink, holding an icepack to his swollen nose. I was seated at the banquette, holding his studio contract to my bespectacled eyes, reading through the fine print.

"I can't believe Borloff canned me," Tad grumbled.

I shook my head. "I can't believe he was savvy enough to include 'boning director's wife' as a cause for immediate dismissal. Didn't you even *read* this contract before you signed it?"

Tad rolled his gorgeous blue eyes. "Nobody reads those things, Dorey."

I grimaced.

Touché.

"I know," Tad growled. "I'll sue him for punching me!"

I shook my head. "Can't. The contract clearly states 'boning of said wife in Article 14-A entitles director to one face punch to the offender, any resulting damages of which are to be covered solely by said actor/actress.'"

Tad frowned. "Crap. Directors think of everything."

"At least you have three days to vacate the trailer," I said, reading Article 15. "I think you should use the time to try to mend fences."

"Like some groveling ranch hand?" Tad laughed. "Yeah, right." He flung the ice pack into the sink, grabbed a bottle of Jack Daniels from the countertop, and stormed out the trailer door.

I thought about trying to stop him. But what chance did I have against a raging god? Tad was a head taller than me and outweighed me by at least eighty pounds. Besides, while a broken nose on Tad's face would most likely be viewed as "adding character" and land him more tough-guy roles, a broken nose on *my* face would be deemed an "insurmountable flaw" and destroy whatever slim chance I had left of landing a decent part.

So I didn't run after Tad.

Instead, through the open trailer door, I watched him march across the parking lot toward the production warehouse, chugging whiskey straight from the bottle.

I knew Tad Longmire was no heroic, white-hatted cowboy. But I had no idea just how determined he would be to set himself out to pasture—*permanently*.

· · · ·

CAUGHT IN A TRAP OF his own making, Tad had gone ballistic.

Fueled by whiskey and emboldened by lack of self-reflection, Tad Longmire did *not* take my advice and mend fences. Instead, he set about burning every bridge he'd ever built in Hollywood.

While I cowered in Tad's trailer scouring my contract for a loophole to get out of working with him, news of his exploits buzzed my cellphone like tiny kamikaze pilots. Texts came in hot and heavy from Sonya and other members of the Trailer-Trash Crew.

> *Tad released a cageful of rats on the film set!*
> *Tad peed all over the catered lunch buffet!*
> *Tad kicked dents in the director's Lamborghini!*
> *Tad took off in the studio owner's Tesla—with his wife!*

I sat back and groaned.

Kill. Me. Now.

As Tad's personal assistant, I knew I'd be labeled guilty by association. My reputation in Tinseltown—if I ever *had* one—was officially toast.

Not swanky, chic, avocado toast.

Burnt toast.

Burned-beyond-scraping-the-black-stuff-off toast.

Even worse, according to my contract, I still had eleven months, three weeks, and three days left to serve as the personal assistant to a drop-dead-gorgeous madman.

Chapter Four

Since moving to L.A., I'd lived through plenty of highs and lows. But until now, I didn't know how truly nasty Hollywood gossip could get. Apparently, however, my longsuffering roommate Sonya *did.* Yesterday, after she found out about Tad's tornadic tirade, she'd come home bearing a gift to cheer me up.

"I don't know if this is any good or not," she said, handing me a brown paper bag. "But at this point, it can't hurt."

"What is it?" I asked. "A pack of cyanide capsules?"

"I wish," Sonya said. "I've looked around. Nobody sells those. This is the next best thing."

I opened the bag, anticipating a cobra to pop out and bite me on the neck, allowing me to end my life in a final act worthy of Cleopatra. Instead, inside was a pocket-sized book. Its cover was the yellow-orange color of a caution light. The title read, *Hollywood Survival Guide.*

"It's supposed to have tips on how to get through any occasion or situation," she said. "It says so right there on the cover."

"Geez," I said. "Does it cover how to survive your boss's career-suicide?"

My cellphone buzzed.

Sonya winced. "There it goes again."

I groaned and reached for my phone. For the last day and a half, calls and texts about Tad had been blowing up my phone like a string of Black Cat firecrackers. Some had been helpful. Most had not.

"Somebody says they spotted Tad at the Lost Property Bar," I said, reading the text.

"Better hop to it, then," Sonya said. Then she added sarcastically, "Don't forget your smile."

• • • •

AS I PULLED UP TO THE Lost Property Bar in my rusty Kia, I got another text saying Tad had moved on and was now making a ruckus at Tramp Stamp Granny's. After coughing and sputtering my way there in The Toad, a text came in saying Tad Longmire had just left the building.

Crap! Where the hell are you, Tad?

I was about to drive back to the studio and ram The Toad into Tad's trailer when yet another text came in saying he was drunk and disorderly at a bar called Sunset & Vinyl.

By the time I got there, Tad was gone again.

I slumped my head onto the steering wheel. I was exhausted. I'd been white-knuckle driving all night trying to apprehend Tad before he committed a felony. But no matter how fast I'd driven, I'd remained one step behind my boss's wanton trail of destruction.

I was out of leads and nearly out of gas when, at a few minutes to midnight, my phone buzzed again. This time, I recognized the number immediately. It was the In-N-Out Burger on Venice Boulevard.

As one of Tad's daily nutritional requirements, I'd put the fast-food restaurant on speed dial. But the image lighting up my cellphone screen wasn't their late-night burger menu. It was a picture of Tad. Pants down. Passed out in a restroom stall.

The accompanying text read, *"U got 20 minutes. Then I call the cops."*

I ditched The Toad, grabbed a taxi, and made it there in eighteen.

After convincing the restaurant manager not to press charges, I shoved one of Tad's business cards into his palm and promised to pay for any damages. His ruffles soothed by the news, the manager helped me shove Tad's drunken carcass into a taxi. I used my last twenty-dollar bill to bribe the cab driver into helping me drag Tad into the studio trailer and onto the bed.

While Tad lay sprawled out snoring like a sea lion, I spent the early morning hours trying to figure out what the hell to do next. As I fished through my purse for a much-needed chocolate bar, I spotted the little yellow book Sonya had given me. I grabbed it and thumbed through the pages.

According to the *Hollywood Survival Guide*, Tip #2 was: *Always have an escape plan.* (Tip #1 was: *Never trust an actor whose lips are moving.* But it was way too late for that.)

Yes! An escape plan was *exactly* what I needed.

I wonder if Prince Holland Cruise Lines is still hiring. I hear Siberia is nice this time of year.

I glanced over at Tad. His head was snuggled against a goose-down pillow tucked inside a 600-threadcount Egyptian cotton pillowcase. After laying waste to his career and possibly mine, the drunken sailor was smiling as if he didn't have a care in the world.

Jerk!

My jaw clenched. My hands balled into fists. I wanted to punch Tad's lights out. But they were already out. Besides, if I killed him, I'd be out of a job. Then I'd *never* get my big break in showbiz.

I flopped down onto the couch and chewed my thumbnail.

As I sat there wondering how I was going to get Tad out of the trailer by noon and back to his place, I realized I had no idea where Tad actually lived. We'd never discussed it. I rifled through his wallet. It was stuffed with credit cards, slips of paper with hearts and phone numbers on them, and VIP club passes. But no driver's license. And nothing with an address.

Perfect. What the hell am I supposed to do now?

Chapter Five

Tad's terroristic tour of Tinseltown had pretty much assured the number of friends he had left in Hollywood was exactly zero. Unfortunately, my contract as his personal assistant made it my responsibility to "manage" the colossal mess he'd made.

I didn't know what to do. The few friends I had left, I didn't want to call. If I dragged them into this, they might also end up blacklisted by association.

At four in the morning, I gave up searching for help and picked up my contract with Tad. There had to be some way out of it. But after reading through the whole thing, I hadn't spotted a single loophole. The attorney who'd put it together was good. I found his name at the bottom of the last page.

Ralph B. Steinberger, Esq.

Desperate and out of options, I google-searched the attorney's number, then rang him up. To my shock, Steinberger actually answered. Then I remembered the guy was *Tad Longmire's* attorney. He was probably used to late-night emergencies.

"Sorry to call at this early hour, Mr. Steinberger," I said. "I'm Tad Longmire's personal assistant, and this is kind of a crisis."

"Yes," he said wearily. "It always is."

"Uh ... I was wondering ..."

"If there's any way to get out of your contract?"

I winced. "Well ... yes."

Steinberger let out a sigh, then spoke as if he'd memorized the lines by rote. "There are exactly three sets of circumstances by which you can be released from your legal obligation. One, by mutual agreement to end said contract. Two, if Mr. Longmire fails to pay you. Three, if either party dies."

"Thank you," I said. "Any chance he won't pay me?"

"Doubtful. His trust fund is still loaded. And you're set up for direct payments."

My right eyebrow rose an inch. "Tad's forty years old. He's still a trust-fund baby?"

"There's no age limit on arrested development."

You aren't kidding.

I chewed my bottom lip. "What would it take to get Tad to mutually agree to release me from the contract?"

"Are you having sexual relations with him?" Steinberger asked.

"What?" I gasped. "No!"

"Good. My advice? Don't. Find a replacement who will. It's your best hope."

I frowned. "Unless he dies."

"Excuse me?" Steinberger said.

"Nothing."

"I thought so. Good luck, Ms. Diller."

"What about if I—" I said, but I was talking to a dial tone. Steinberger had already hung up.

I glanced over at Tad. He was splayed out on the bed like a sculpture carved by a drunken Michelangelo. I shook my head.

I've either got to find a hot-to-trot replacement, or make a run for it, change my name, and live in a mud hut surrounded by wild dogs.

As appealing as the mud hut was beginning to sound, I knew it wasn't really a viable option. If I left Tad, my dream of a movie career would go with it. At my age, and with Jared Thomas as my only other reference, I wouldn't get another chance in Hollywood. Not even as a personal assistant.

I wracked my brain. What else could I do? All those years of acting lessons had left me virtually unemployable in the real world. And, apparently, in Hollywood, too.

I couldn't sing like Tina Turner. I couldn't dance like J. Lo. I couldn't tell jokes like Margaret Cho. The only true gift I had was my ability to keep my closetful of festering feelings bottled up inside while wearing a fake smile and projecting a false sense of giving a crap.

In other words, I was perfectly suited to working in retail.

Crap!

I chewed my bottom lip. Whether I liked it or not, my star was firmly—and legally—hitched to a broken wagon named Tad Longmire.

I glanced around the messy kitchen in his trailer. At least cleaning it up would be someone else's problem at noon. Even so, I couldn't control myself. I picked up an empty bourbon bottle and threw it into the trash. As it slammed into the bottom of the can, the cold, hard truth hit me. If either one of us was ever going to have another shot at the silver screen, I was going to have to get Tad back on the wagon, and *keep* him there.

I caught my reflection in one of his many wall mirrors. The look on my face said it all.

Yeah, right. Good luck with that.

• • • •

AT EXACTLY 9:37 A.M., after taking a taxi to recover my car, I returned to Tad's trailer in The Toad, ready to set the rest of my freshly hatched escape plan into motion.

Steeling myself, I took a deep breath, gulped my last sip of coffee, and climbed out of the Kia. I stuck my chin in the air, tugged the hem of my jacket for good measure, and marched determinedly into Tad's trailer.

The lout was still in bed, unconscious, just as I'd left him. I let out a huge sigh.

Dammit. How could a drunk jerk who hasn't bathed or shaved in days still look so infuriatingly sexy?

"Wake up, Tad," I said, leaning over the bed and shaking him on the shoulder.

Tad cracked open a bloodshot eye. "Wha?"

"I said, wake up."

His eye clamped shut. "Go away."

I frowned. This wasn't exactly how I'd envisioned my escape plan playing out in my head. It was nearly ten o'clock. Somehow, I had to get Tad's drunken butt up and out of this stupid trailer in less than two hours.

"Please?" I asked, gently jogging his side.

"Why?" he grunted.

"Because your phone keeps ringing."

It was true. Ever since I'd hung up with Mr. Steinberger at 4:15 this morning, Tad's phone had been buzzing like a masochistic moth in love with a sadistic bug zapper.

"Huh?" he grumbled, opening his eyes. They didn't quite focus on me. No doubt he was still lit from his three-day bender.

"What's your phone code?" I asked, holding up his cellphone.

"Why?" Tad groaned and tried to sit up. Only then did he finally notice that I'd tied both his hands to the bedposts.

Yes. *Bondage* was part of my newly hatched plan to get Tad sober.

The way I figured, Tad couldn't drink if couldn't reach a booze bottle. I squeezed the balled-up pair of gym socks concealed in my left hand. They were at the ready to stuff into his mouth if he started yelling.

"Hey," Tad said, tugging playfully on the nylon leggings I'd used to bind his wrists to the posts. A crooked smile broke the crusty corners of his mouth. "Kinky, Dorey. Me *likey*."

"Phone code," I said, sitting down on the edge of the bed beside him. "Somebody's been calling you all morning."

"So?"

"Come on, Tad. Cough it up. You made me give you mine."

Tad grinned lewdly. "Okay, Mistress Dorey. It's T-A-D-1."

I stifled an eye roll.

TAD-1. Of course *it's TAD-1.*

I punched the code into the phone.

"Hey, I need a Jack and Coke," Tad said, trying to sit up again. "Hair of the dog, you know."

"Yeah. Not happening. It's time your dog learned some new tricks."

"Yeah?" He shot me a lascivious leer. "Now we're talking. Bring it, Mistress Dorey!"

I hesitated for a second. I mean, how often did a gal like me get a chance to have her way with a gorgeous movie star? But then my self-preservation gene kicked in.

I really hated that gene sometimes.

I gritted my teeth, looked away, and hit the button to play Tad's voicemail over the cellphone speaker.

"Hello, Mr. Longmire?" a woman's voice said. "I'm Kerri Middleton from Sunshine City Studios. We're interested in having you audition for an upcoming television series we're putting together. Please contact us at your earliest convenience."

I nearly dropped the phone. "Tad! Someone's calling about a job offer!"

Tad didn't appear quite as excited. Actually, he was passed out cold again. I fought the urge to punch him where the sun didn't shine, and shook him awake again.

"What?" he grumbled.

"Be a good boy and listen to this. If you do, I'll go get you a latte. Okay?"

That perked him up a bit. "With bourbon?"

"No bourbon. Now listen!" I tried to replay the voicemail, but screwed it up. A second message played instead.

"Hi. This is Kerri Middleton calling again. We'd really like to hear from you as soon as possible, Mr. Longmire. We think you'd be perfect for the leading role in our upcoming project. Please contact us as soon as possible."

"Did you hear that?" I nearly squealed. "A job you're *perfect* for!"

Tad frowned. "What kind of perks are they offering?"

I fought back the urge to throttle him. The guy was so drunk he couldn't remember his name, but he remembered to ask for perks. "I don't know, Tad. Probably good ones. Should I call them back?"

Lines creased Tad's beautiful brow. "If they don't include free booze and burgers, I'm not doing it."

My face turned to stone. "Look, Tad. You've basically Blitzkrieged both of our careers. You'll do this audition or I'll ... I'll ..."

My train of thought derailed. Tad was shooting me that sexy grin again. The one that, six days ago, had nearly melted my tennis shoes. While his come-hither smile still made me catch my breath, in view of recent events its effect on me had cooled considerably.

Tad smirked. "Or *what*, Dorey? What are you gonna do?"

I steeled myself, then glanced around the room for something to threaten my new boss's life with. A pair of manicure scissors lying on the nightstand caught my eye. I snatched them up, then sat back down on the edge of the bed.

Tad laughed. "What are you gonna do, Dorey? Trim my cuticles?"

I leaned over Tad's prone body until our faces were inches from each other. "You'll audition for this role, Tad Longmire, or I'll cut your bangs off like that guy in *Dumb & Dumber*."

Tad gasped. "You wouldn't!"

"Try me."

I clicked redial on Tad's phone, praying someone at the studio worked on Saturdays. The phone rang once, then someone picked up. "Sunshine City Studios. Kerri Middleton speaking."

"Oh ... uh ... hello," I said, caught off guard. "I'm Doreen Diller, personal assistant to Tad Longmire."

"Oh. Hello!" the woman said enthusiastically. "Thanks so much for getting back to me. I've been calling for days. I thought Mr. Longmire might not be interested in the part."

Days?

I shot Tad an angry glance. He opened his mouth to speak. I held up the miniscule scissors and savagely cut the air with them like a psychotic barber. He shriveled.

"No, Mr. Longmire is *very* interested," I said. "Could you please email me the terms and audition script?"

"It would be my pleasure, Ms. Diller. Auditions begin on Monday. Does that work for you?"

"Auditions?" Tad grumbled. "Why should I have to—?"

I jabbed the tiny scissors toward his groin, Tad grimaced and drew up his knees.

"That should be no problem, Ms. Middleton," I said cheerfully.

"Excellent! I'll put you down for 3 p.m. on Monday. I'll email the script and terms to you right away. I'm so sorry, but I'm afraid you'll have to find your own accommodations in town. We're running on a tight budget. But we'll reimburse Mr. Longmire if he gets the part." Ms. Middleton's voice lowered to a whisper. "And between you and me, it's a done deal."

Feeling fifteen thousand pounds lighter, I said, "That's fine, Ms. Middleton. But could you keep this on the down-low?"

"Certainly. We'll be filming on a public beach. We'll have enough drive-by gawkers as it is."

"Thank you," I said. "We'll be there."

"Perfect!" she said. "May I recommend The Don CeSar Hotel?"

My left eyebrow rose an inch. "I've never heard of it. What part of L.A. is it in?"

Ms. Middleton giggled. "Oh. We're not in L.A., Ms. Diller. We're in St. Petersburg, Florida. See you on Monday!"

Chapter Six

Well played, Kerri Middleton.

I had to give her this—the woman from Sunshine City Studios had chutzpah. She'd hung up before I could respond to her hidden bomb that her film studio wasn't in L.A., but in St. Petersburg, Florida.

I shook my head. I wasn't sure I could get Tad out of this stupid *trailer* by noon today, much less get him to *Florida* by the day after tomorrow.

But the bigger question was, was it even worth the effort to try? My L.A. peeps always said nothing big ever came out of anywhere but Hollywood. But then again, Tad was nothing big here anymore, was he? And at this rate, I never *would* be.

Crap.

I sighed and glanced over at Tad. The guy was incredible. Despite having both hands bound to the bedposts, he'd fallen asleep again. There he was in all his glory. My fantasy crush reduced to a dirty, drunken ape tied to a mattress in an aluminum-clad cage.

And they say Tinseltown has lost its glitter ...

• • • •

ON MY WAY TO THE COFFEE shop to pick up Tad's cinnamon mocha, dark-roast Honduran, iced oat-milk latte, I google-searched St. Petersburg, Florida. If memory served, one of my mother's relatives used to live there.

I'd never met whoever it was. But I vaguely recalled catching glimpses of the postcards Ma occasionally got in the mail. Sometimes she would show me the picture on the front. A baby alligator. An orange tree. Old people on green benches.

Based on that, I expected my google search to reveal a collage of shabbily dressed seniors waiting for a bus to catch the early-bird buffet. Instead, the images I found surprised me. White-sand beaches. Sunlit street festivals. Thriving downtown food and entertainment scenes. St. Pete looked like a mini L.A.—without the choking smog or the celebrity snobs.

Intrigued, I looked up Sunshine City Studios. It was one of a handful of small, independent production houses in the area. Online, the studio had decent ratings from several local businesses who'd hired them for what I assumed were TV commercials and recruitment videos.

Huh. I wonder what kind of project they have in mind for Tad.

• • • •

I PICKED UP TAD'S ORDER at the coffee shop. As I walked back, I sipped my cappuccino and began to warm to the idea of a trip to Florida.

I mean, what would be the harm?

As I reached Tad's trailer, my phone pinged. It was the email Kerri Middleton had promised. I set Tad's iced coffee on the front steps and glanced around to make sure no L.A. spies were watching. Then I sat down beside his frosty latte and opened the email.

To my surprise and delight, Tad's pay and terms were much better than I'd expected. The project, on the other hand, was much worse. Kerri's studio was shooting a pilot for a new TV series apparently aimed at drunken beach bums. Its working title was *Beer & Loathing in F.L.A.*

My nose crinkled.

I scrolled through the sample script and groaned. It read like a cross between *Two-Headed Shark Attack* and *Dude, Where's My Car?*—without any of that annoying plot stuff.

I blew out a disgusted breath.

Beer & Loathing was more of the same mindless, misogynistic rubbish that made women like me—of a certain age and IQ—abandon all hope for the evolution of mankind. It was exactly the kind of crap I'd made my goal in life to eradicate, once I made the bigtime.

If I made the bigtime.

I closed my eyes and let out a huge sigh.

The script was totally wrong.

But Kerri Middleton was totally right.

Tad Longmire was absolutely perfect for the role.

. . . .

"I DUNNO," TAD SAID as I finished reading him the studio's proposal.

After making him promise to behave, I'd freed his right hand. Tad was sitting up on the edge of the bed, calmly sipping his iced latte through a straw—as if being tied to the bedpost happened to him *every* Saturday.

Yuck. Maybe it did.

"What do you mean, you don't know?" I asked, hiding my frustration under an ever-thinning veneer of syrupy sweetness. "This is an excellent offer!"

Tad shrugged, his dirty blond hair sticking up like a cockatoo's crest. "TV again? I'm not so sure it's a good career move."

My face went slack.

And boning the director's wife was?

I plastered on the extra-special personal assistant smile I kept in a jar for emergencies. Seeing as how Tad had destroyed my other prospects, I *had* to keep in his good graces. He was the only life raft I had left.

If Tad went down, I went with him.

The way I saw it, I could either stab a hole in the raft, or get busy inflating Tad's ego. I chose the latter, but kept the little cuticle scissors handy, just in case.

"Look, Tad," I cooed. "You were fabulous as the heartthrob doctor on *Days of Our Lies*."

He shrugged. "I know. But it was just a daytime soap opera for old ladies."

My eyebrows shot to my hairline. "I watched it all the time!"

"Hey, if the orthopedic shoe fits, wear it," Tad said with a smirk.

I'm younger than you, *you philandering jerk!*

I was about to give Tad a piece of my mind when I remembered *Hollywood Survival Guide* Tip #3: *If all else fails, start slinging compliments like an angry chimp at the zoo.*

I reset my attitude and cleared my throat. "Look. *Days of Our Lies* got you a lot of great exposure, Tad. Don't forget, George Clooney got his big break after doing that TV show *ER*. And you have to admit, the salary for this project is pretty generous."

Tad took a sip of latte and shrugged. "Yeah. But—"

"Come on, Tad. It's just three weeks of shooting. Think of it as a little vacation from L.A. You know. Time to work on your tan and let things cool down a bit."

"Cool down?" An indignant line creased the brow of Tad's impossibly handsome face. "What exactly are you implying needs to 'cool down'?"

I gritted my teeth into an Emmy-worthy smile.

Your nuclear meltdown, perchance?

"Give them time to miss you," I said smugly. "Make them come crawling back."

Tad nodded slowly, a sly grin formed on his lips. "Hmm."

"The show is set on the beach," I said in the kind of voice mothers used to woo kids into eating strained peas. "Doesn't that sound like fun? It'll be filmed on location in a quirky little beach shack."

Tad frowned. "A shack?"

"I meant *cottage*."

"Uh-huh. What's my role?"

You play a drunken, burned-out, misogynistic dirtbag. I know it'll be a stretch. But with your magnificent acting talents, I think you can handle it.

"The lead, of course!" I said brightly.

Tad nodded and chewed the straw sticking up from the lid on his latte. "I gotta think about it."

We've got to be out of this freaking trailer in 30 minutes. We don't have time for you to think about it, you pompous, pampered, freak of nature!

I took a deep breath. It was time to sell this idea like my life depended on it. I leaned in closer and played my ace in the hole.

"Did I mention that you'll be surrounded by gorgeous beach bunnies in teeny-weeny bikinis?"

Tad licked his lips.

I winked and grinned. "Say yes and I'll untie your other hand."

Tad smiled. "Okay, Dorey. Yes."

I clapped my hands. "Excellent decision, Mr. Longmire!"

I reached over the bed and used the manicure scissors to cut the nylon legging binding Tad's left hand.

"Now, mister," I said. "*You* get in the shower and clean yourself up. *I'll* make all the arrangements for Monday."

"Okay, Dorey." Tad's freed hand landed on my waist. He glanced up at me with those bedroom eyes of his. "What would I do without you?"

I swatted his hand away. "Just about *anything*, I'd say."

Tad studied me for a second, then laughed. "You're probably right."

A tentative smile curled my lips. "You made the right decision, Tad. Now be a good boy and scoot!"

"Okay. But call a limo for me. I'm not going anywhere in that butt-ugly car of yours."

"Yes, sir."

As Tad yawned lazily, then slowly stood, the seconds we had left before Jared had us forcibly thrown from the trailer ticked off in my head.

Apparently, Tad wasn't bothered by such minutia. He continued to languidly stretch his beautiful torso for what seemed like half an hour. Then, finally, he dragged himself off to the bathroom like a teenager heading to the principal's office.

As soon as the bathroom door closed behind him, I snatched up my phone and got busy dialing.

Phase one of Escape Plan A is complete. Now, all I have to do is get Tad to Florida and under contract before they find out what a jerk he is. If that fails, I'll resort to Escape Plan B.

I'll drown Tad in the Gulf of Mexico myself.

Chapter Seven

Traveling with Tad Longmire was like holding onto the leash of an irresistibly adorable, but totally untrained puppy. Every woman old enough to drive stopped to gush over him—but those who lingered too long were in danger of getting their legs humped.

It was Monday morning, and I'd been in Tad's employ for exactly one week. Yesterday, at his ultra-fabulous apartment, he'd proven to be quite the hands-on boss. Even so, I'd followed Tad's lawyer's advice and thwarted my new boss's flirty advances.

Thank goodness there'd been a lock on the guestroom door.

Actually, I was fairly certain Tad was enjoying the conquest challenge I presented. He probably considered me a shag to save for a rainy day. But now that I'd discovered the charming puppy was actually a rabid wolf, it would take a typhoon to get me under the sheets with him.

During the five-hour flight from L.A. to Tampa, I kept Tad out of trouble by going over the audition script for the pilot episode of *Beer & Loathing*. All was going well until nature called. When I returned from the bathroom, I discovered a star-struck flight attendant slipping Tad her phone number—along with a little something extra in his Coca Cola. By the time we landed in Florida, Dr. Jekyll was displaying telltale signs of Mr. Rye.

Totally not good.

"I can't believe all the women that keep throwing themselves at you," I whispered as Tad downed his fourth Coke, which I was certain had been spiked with bourbon.

He grinned. "Can I help it if I'm irresistible?"

Can I help it if I want to punch you in the gonads?

Given how much he'd drank, a normal person would've probably needed a wheelchair to get off the plane. But professional drunken letch that Tad Longmire was, he managed to stagger his way through the terminal with me, drag his luggage off the carousel, and tumble into a cab under his own steam.

"Downtown St. Petersburg," I said to the cabby as I climbed into the backseat with Tad. "How long is the ride?"

"Twenty, maybe twenty-five minutes."

Crap. It's already 2:25. Thanks to Tad's inebriated bumbling, we're cutting it way too close.

"Thank you," I said to the driver. "We're supposed to be downtown at three o'clock. Can you make that happen?"

The cabbie eyed me in the rearview mirror. "I'll do my best." He smiled and hit the gas pedal, sending me tumbling into Tad's lap.

"*Now* we're talkin, Dorey," Tad said, grinning at me lewdly.

"Ugh," I grunted, scrambling out of his arms. I rifled through my purse for something that might sober up my drunken disaster of a boss. I figured mace would only aggravate him. And unfortunately, I'd left my Taser at home...

"Here, eat these," I said, pulling out a bag of airline peanuts.

"Kiss me, first," he said.

Any other time I'd have probably gone for it. That's how infuriatingly hot the guy was—even with a nose still swollen from Borloff's right-handed punch. But, as usual, my timing was impeccably bad. If I didn't get Tad under control and pronto, my last chance at a career in showbiz would go right down the toilet along with his.

"Settle down, hotshot," I said. "Now, be a good boy and open up for a peanut."

"Make me." Tad pursed his lips and giggled like a naughty child.

"Zoom zoom, here comes the peanut train," I said, wishing I had a vise to crack his nuts with. Tad grinned and let me pop a peanut into his baby-bird mouth. "Good boy."

"Ooo, water," Tad said, crunching the peanut and gawking out the cab window. I glanced out and realized we were crossing a long bridge over what I assumed was Tampa Bay.

"Yes. Pretty," I said, nodding at the shimmering water. But I didn't really see it. I was too busy praying the peanuts would work a miracle on Tad's blood-alcohol and render him coherent enough for the impending audition.

Tad put a hand on my thigh. I let out a sigh.

Geez. I'm totally not getting paid enough for this crap.

. . . .

EITHER MY PRAYERS HAD been answered, or Tad was a bigger pro than I'd given him credit for. By the time the cabbie pulled up to the address I'd handed him, Tad was sitting up straight. He'd also regained control of nearly all of his facial muscles.

"This is it," the taxi driver said.

Tad shot me a confused look. "Where are we?"

Oh. Dear. Lord.

"I hope you're joking," I said, grabbing him by the shoulder and yanking him out of the cab. "Please. For the love of God, try to act sober, would you?"

As the taxi drove away, I realized we weren't in a warehouse district, like I'd expected. Instead, Tad and I stood in front of an unassuming, faded red door attached to a two-story brick building. There was no placard on the door. Uncertain, I checked the address Kerri Middleton had given me. The numbers matched.

"This must be it," I said. "Sunshine City Studios."

"You sure?" Tad asked.

No, I wasn't. Oddly, the building was on Central Avenue, in the middle of an old-fashioned, main-street type area. To either side of the studio stood an eclectic mix of small, glass-storefront boutiques, trendy coffee shops, and mom-n-pop diners. My stomach sank. Was this place a dive? Had I just made a huge mistake?

Then I remembered *Hollywood Survival Guide* Tip #4. *Never EVER look back. Especially on a first date.*

"Of course this is the place," I said, straightening Tad's tie. "Now, smile."

I knocked on the door, half expecting it to be answered by some shuffle-footed, dirty-haired Millennial with a nose ring and tat sleeves. But I was wrong—again.

"Welcome to Sunshine City Studios," said a tall, slender, elegantly dressed woman in her mid-fifties. She opened the door wide, then beckoned us in with a graceful swoop of her hand. "You're right on time. I'm Kerri Middleton."

"Oh! Hello," I said. "We're—"

"Hurry. Don't let the mosquitos in," Kerri said, tucking a lock of silver hair behind her ear.

"Come on, Tad," I said, grabbing him by the arm and scurrying inside.

Kerri shut the door behind us, then assessed us with sharp, hazel eyes. "You must be Tad," she said, skimming over him quickly before turning her attention to me. "And you must be Doreen Diller."

"Yes," I said. "We're glad to be—"

"Is this where we'll be filming?" Tad asked, crinkling his swollen nose hard enough to make him wince in pain.

"No. Just the auditions," Kerri said. "We do most of our filming on site. Please, follow me."

Kerri turned and marched down a hallway, her shiny, kitten heels clicking on the hardwood floor. She led us to a room with exposed brick walls and a cozy sitting area furnished with a teal couch and two white leather chairs.

"Have a seat. I'll let Marshall know you're here. Would you like something to drink?"

"Yeah," Tad said. "I'll take a—"

"Coke, if you've got it," I said. "Two Cokes?"

Kerri's eyes crinkled as she offered us what appeared to be a genuine smile. I wasn't sure, having not seen one since I moved to L.A.

"Coming right up," she said. "I won't be long."

As soon as Kerri left, I shot Tad a death-ray glare. "No more drinking! Not until you've got the part. Don't ruin this for us!"

"*Us?*" Tad laughed. "I thought this was *my* audition."

"It is, but—"

"Who's Marshall?" he grumbled.

I took a deep breath and fought the urge to hit Tad over the head with my purse. "Marshall Lazzaro. He's the director of the project you're auditioning for. We've been over this a dozen times! Now, what are the rules?"

Tad's handsome head cocked to one side. "Rules? I don't know about—"

I thrust my hand two inches from his face and made scissoring motions with my first two fingers. Then I grabbed a lock of my bangs with my free hand and used my finger scissors to cut the hunk of hair off at my scalp.

Tad blanched. "Okay already. The rule is, no drinking."

"Right. *And?*"

"No boning the director's wife."

"Good boy." I patted his leg. "Play nice and land the job, okay? It'll be fun. You'll see. Like a beach vacation."

Kerri returned holding two cans of soda. She noticed my hand on Tad's knee. I jerked it away and took the Coke she offered.

"You look just like your headshot," she said, handing Tad his can of Coke. "Except for the nose."

Tad frowned at his soda. She hadn't opened it for him. "Yeah, well—"

"Just allergies," I said, cracking the tab on my can of soda. I quickly switched it with Tad's before he could make a fuss.

"I see," Kerri said. "Well, I think we can work around it. Actually, Tad, why don't you go on in? Marshall is eager to meet you."

Tad stopped mid-slurp. "Huh? Oh. Okay."

"He's just through there," Kerri said, motioning toward a solid oak door.

"Thanks for the soda," I said, standing up to join Tad.

Kerri put a hand on my shoulder. "Just Tad. For now."

"Oh. Okay." I shot Tad a thumbs up. "Show them what you've got, superstar!"

"Right-O, Dorey." Tad wagged his eyebrows. "I'll knock 'em dead."

I turned my worried cringe into a smile, then watched Tad amble casually toward the door, my entire future riding on his wobbly steps.

You'd better knock 'em dead, Tad Longmire. Or I'll kill you myself.

Chapter Eight

"So," Kerri said, turning to face me as Tad disappeared behind the director's door at Sunshine City Studios. "How did you get tangled up in this mess, anyway?"

"You mean showbiz?" I asked.

"I mean Tad Longmire."

I blanched. "You ... you *know* about Tad?"

Kerri's left eyebrow arched. "Anybody with an internet connection knows about Tad Longmire. Why else do you think we figured we had a chance at hiring him?"

I grimaced and fiddled with the tab on my Coke can. "Well, I think the whole story about him going ballistic was blown out of proportion. You see—"

"Loyalty," Kerri said, cutting me off. "I like that. But listen, sister. You can save the excuses. I'm a big girl. I know a player when I see one. Tad and Marshall? They're two of a kind. They'll get along fine. It's the people like us—the ones who do the actual *work*—who need to watch each other's backs."

I stared up at her, wide-eyed. Kerri Middleton didn't play around. That was fine by me. I was used to blunt. But was there a chance she was actually sincere as well? That she actually played fair?

I thought back to something I'd read in my *Hollywood Survival Guide*. Tip #6: *Nothing is fair in love, war, or movie making.*

I chewed my lip, wondering whether to trust Kerri. She was in movie making, but then again, this wasn't Hollywood. It was St. Petersburg. Maybe the rules were different here. Plus, there was something about Kerri that drew me to her. I just couldn't quite put my finger on it ...

"So, what's the real score with Tad?" Kerri asked.

"Honestly?"

Kerri smirked "Of course. Aren't you *always*?"

I blushed. "I have to admit, when it comes to being frank, I'm a bit out of practice. L.A. stands for Liars Anonymous, in case you didn't know."

"Really." Kerri smiled. "I always wondered about that."

"You've never been?"

"No. But I'd like to visit a Hollywood studio someday. It's on my bucket list."

"Well, don't bother," I said. "Whatever you might have imagined goes on behind the scenes of making a movie, add to it a horny, hairy-backed director, a bowl of cocaine, and—god help me—a bubble machine."

Kerri laughed. "Yet you somehow managed to survive with some integrity intact."

I stared at her, stunned, as if I'd just been blessed by the Dali Lama. "Why do you think I have integrity?"

"Easy," Kerri said. "You can still blush."

"Oh." I let a smile curl my lips. "Thanks." Then, all of a sudden, it hit me. That was it! That odd thing about Kerri I couldn't place. She'd just named it herself.

Integrity.

Kerri seemed to have it. Off the bat, I couldn't think of another person in my life who did. Quite possibly not even *me*—not much, anyway. I decided right then that Kerri Middleton deserved to know what she was getting into by hiring Tad, warts and all.

"Okay, here's the honest truth," I confessed. "Tad Longmire is gorgeous, obviously. And he's actually a really decent actor. But when it comes to discretion? Forget it. Tad puts the 'pro' in inappropriate."

"What do you mean?" Kerri asked.

"He can be demanding. Whiny. Hot-tempered. And most of all, lecherous. But he's not all that horrible unless he drinks. Then? Well, all bets are off."

Kerri's eyes narrowed. "Does he use hard drugs?"

"No," I blurted. "Well, I've only been his assistant for a week. So, none that I'm aware of. As far as I can tell, his main weaknesses are brown liquor and red-headed bimbos."

Kerri pursed her lips and nodded slowly. I steeled myself for rejection. Good thing I'd purchased flexible return tickets. I sighed. This time tomorrow, I'd be back in L.A., resuming my pathetic life as a stand-in for headless dumpster-hookers.

"Okay," Kerri said. "I can work with that."

"Really?" I said, nearly springing from my chair.

"Yes, really."

"Oh! Thank you, Kerri!" I squealed, shaking her hand. "I promise I'll do my best to keep Tad on track."

"Good. Now, one final question." Kerri locked eyes with me. "How do you feel about the project, based on the sample script?"

Aww, crap! The script was total kaka. Another idiotic, shiftless beach bum who—for some inexplicable reason—is a magnet for hot beach babes. What a crock of ...

I swallowed hard, recalling the sage advice in the *Hollywood Survival Guide*. Tip #7 read: *The path to stardom is lined with lies—fling them around like pavers.*

I could feel Kerri's hazel eyes scrutinizing me. "I ... uh ...," I fumbled.

Come on, Doreen! Just say you like the stupid thing and the job is in the bag. JUST DO IT!

I hesitated, looking for a clue in Kerri's face. The woman could've won a national poker playoff.

Screw it.

"Honestly, Kerri?" I said, mentally pulling my bags off the luggage carousel back in L.A. "Nothing personal, but the script is infantile rubbish. *Beer & Loathing* is just the kind of sexist crap that makes me want to stab the author in the gonads."

Kerri snorted—something I'd never have expected from someone who looked so proper and elegant. "You certainly don't mince words, do you?" she said.

"I'm sorry," I said, wanting to kick myself. "I thought that—"

Kerri held her palm out, a signal for me to stop talking. "No need to apologize, Doreen. I appreciate your candor. So I'll be frank, too. Marshall wrote the script himself. I agree, its total garbage. But he's the boss. His father bought him this studio, along with all the assorted toys and gadgets. So, like it or not, Marshall has final say on the project."

I sighed. "Just like Tad."

Kerri smiled tiredly. "In a lot of ways, it's still a man's world, isn't it?"

"Yeah. As much as I'd like to change that."

"I would, too." Kerri pursed her lips, then locked eyes with me again. "So, can I count on you to keep a good attitude, even though the project is a boatload of crap?"

I let out a short laugh. "Believe me, if L.A. has taught me anything, it's how to steer my gondola through a sewer and still belt out a love song."

Kerri grinned. "I can believe that." She cocked her head. "I'm curious. Why do you stay with Tad if he's such a lout? Are you two, you know...?"

"No!" I said. "Nothing like that. I ... I stupidly signed a twelve-month contract as his personal assistant." I smiled sheepishly. "Only fifty-one more weeks to go."

Kerri winced. "Ouch. Why'd you do it?"

I shook my head and sighed. "Tad promised to make me a star."

Kerri's bright hazel eyes dulled. "Just like in the movies."

"I know," I groaned. "I should've known better, for crying out loud. I'm 39 years old and I'm still a total sap. It's just that ... it's hard to give up on your dreams, you know?"

"Yes," Kerri said. "Believe me, I know exactly how you feel."

The convincing tone of her words made me sit up straight.

"Okay," I said. "You know why *I'm* here. Let me ask you the same question. You seem like a smart, well-put-together woman. How'd *you* get tangled up in the production of something called *Beer & Loathing*?"

Kerri shot me a tired smile. "Someone in the room has to be the designated grown-up."

My eyebrows rose an inch. "Excuse me?"

Kerri sat down in the leather chair next to mine. "I'm here as a favor to an old friend. Marshall's mother and I were best pals before she passed away seven years ago. Marshall was just sixteen. His father, Dave Lazzaro, well, he kind of left Marshall to run wild."

I fidgeted with my can of Coke. "Oh. I'm sorry to hear that."

"Thank you. Anyway, after Marshall flunked out of college last year, Dave set him up in this studio. He was hoping to give his son something productive to focus on. Dave hired me to help keep an eye on both Marshall and his own financial investment." Kerri shot me a wry smile. "So, basically, my job is to make sure Marshall doesn't swing naked off a cliff and take Dave's bank account down with him."

"Wait," I said. "So this whole studio is just some privileged brat's *hobby*?"

"No. I didn't mean that at all," Kerri said. "We aim to make a serious go of it. We've already filmed several commercials and training videos for local businesses. *Beer & Loathing* will be our first stab at a real production, though."

"So, no one here has any experience?" I asked, trying not to groan.

Kerri shook her head. "No, that's not correct. We have a decent cameraman on salary. And we hire professional staff on a temp basis. You know, for makeup and set production, that kind of stuff."

"But with a 23-year-old kid directing, how—"

Kerri locked eyes with me. "Just so you know, Dave didn't hire me for my mothering skills. I've never had children of my own. What I bring to the table is direct industry experience, along with tons of local connections."

"Oh," I said. "What did you do before?"

"I was the co-anchor for Channel 22 news for 15 years. But like an idiot, I had the audacity to age." She shook her head. "Last year, the powers that be decided I'd gotten a bit too old for the job. They handed me a silver parachute to match my hair. You know how it goes."

I sighed. "Yeah, I do."

Kerri's perfectly glossed lips formed a wistful smile. "Funny thing is, my male co-anchor is ten years older than me. Paul looks like a walrus in a cheap suit, but he's still on the air and going strong."

"They were fools to let you go," I said. "You're so beautiful. And ... *elegant.*"

"Thank you," Kerri said. "But to be honest, this job at Sunshine City Studios suits me fine. It's fun. There's a ton less bureaucratic bull to deal with. And there's no pressure to look like a plastic supermodel all the time." She grinned and leaned in closer to me. "Want to know a little secret?"

"Uh, sure," I said.

She winked. "Carbs are delicious."

I laughed. "Yes. They *totally* are."

Kerri sat back and sighed. "I only wish this project Marshall wants to do was less ... what would you say?"

"Sophomoric?" I offered. "Neanderthal?"

Kerri laughed. "Exactly."

The door to the director's office flew open. Tad and Marshall came tumbling out, slapping each other's backs like they'd just won the NFL playoffs.

"Looks like we've found our leading man," Marshall said, beaming at Tad.

Tad wagged his eyebrows at me mischievously and said, "I'll drink to that!"

Chapter Nine

"That takes care of the paperwork," Kerri said, handing me a red folder. Inside were two copies of the contract Tad had just signed with Sunshine City Studios. "We start shooting the pilot in the morning."

"So soon?" I asked, winking at Kerri.

At my request, she'd convinced Marshall to agree to the ultra-quick start, arguing it would save money on production. While that was true, the real reason was my need to keep Tad in check. By beginning filming tomorrow, my wayward boss wouldn't have enough time to get into any real trouble—fingers crossed.

I smiled at Tad. "Well, this is exciting! I guess we should get over to our hotel and rest up for the big day tomorrow. You've got lines to rehearse."

"What?" Marshall objected, his freckled, college-boy face aghast. "Don't you want to see where we'll be filming? It's right on the beach!"

"That's right," Tad said as if he'd just remembered we were in Florida. He high-fived Marshall. "I'm in. Let's go!"

"Well ..." I hesitated, feeling a bit like Tad's parole officer.

"I'll drive," Marshall said. "How about that, Doreen?" He slid a pair of expensive-looking aviator sunglasses from atop of his strawberry blond head and onto the bridge of his suntanned nose.

I grimaced. "Well, it's just that—"

"Come on," Marshall said. "It's not far from where you're staying at the Don CeSar. I'll drop you there afterward. I promise. It'll be fun!"

I glanced over at Kerri. She shrugged. The corners of her mouth crinkled upward, betraying a stifled grin. I was about to object again, but suddenly my feet lifted off the floor.

"Lighten up, Dorey," Tad said, sweeping me up into his arms. "Marshall, you get the luggage. I've got the girl."

Marshall grinned. "Tad, I bet you *always* get the girl."

Tad squeezed my thigh and winked. "You better believe I do."

• • • •

TAD AND MARSHALL HOOTED like frat boys as we cruised down Central Avenue in his shiny red Mercedes convertible. Florida's tropical sun beamed warmly on our faces. The guys were stretched out in the front seat. I was crammed into the tiny afterthought of a backseat. Tad had unceremoniously dumped me into it after I'd opted out of sitting in his lap. Kerri had opted out of the trip.

Well played yet again, Kerri Middleton.

As we sped along, the wind whipped my shoulder-length brown hair around like a palm tree in a hurricane. "How far is it?" I asked, swiping at an errant lock of hair flitting around my eyes.

"Not far," Marshall said. "Relax, Dorey. Enjoy the ride."

"It's *Doreen*," I said.

Marshall appeared confused. "But Tad calls you—"

"Tad writes my paycheck," I said, cutting him off. "When *you* do, you can call me whatever you like."

Marshall's back stiffened. "Yes, ma'am."

I winced. "Except for *ma'am*."

Marshall's brow furrowed. "No? What should I call you, then?"

"Sorry," I said, softening my tone. "It's just that I hate ... never mind. How about just calling me *Doreen*?"

Marshall nodded. "You got it, Doreen."

"Geez," Tad said. "Chill out, Ms. Minion. Boss's orders."

"Jerk," I muttered to myself, sinking lower into the narrow wedge masquerading as a back seat. I glanced in the rearview mirror. The small cluster of high rises that made up downtown St. Petersburg were fading farther and farther from view as we followed the sun westward.

After a few miles, the colorful, renovated shops and storefronts of St. Pete's Grand Central District gave way to generic, neglected strip centers. The startling contrast had me wondering how long the shiny new façade of friendship between the two men in the front seat would last.

Tad was nearly twice Marshall's age. On the other hand, just as Kerri had hinted, the two men shared something in common with each other *and* the section of town we currently traveled. They all appeared to be suffering from the same problem of arrested development.

"Ooop!" I blurted as we sped across a small bridge. Flying over the span had, for a second, sent the Mercedes airborne—along with my stomach.

"Welcome to Treasure Island," Marshall said, beaming proudly. He gestured toward the right side of the road.

I glanced that way and spied a lifesize cutout of an old-timey pirate. Dressed in full regalia—from feathered hat to peg leg—the swashbuckler stood astride an open treasure chest full of orange citrus fruits.

"Treasure Island," I whispered to myself. A vague memory played hide-and-seek with my brain. "Cute," I said, as an unexpected smile tugged at my lips.

We crossed another bridge and the west-bound lanes abruptly dead-ended. Marshall pulled up to the stoplight and said, "Doreen, let me be the first to welcome you to the best beach in the whole entire world."

"What? Where?" I asked. Then I spotted it. Straight ahead. Peeking out from behind the 1950's-era Thunderbird Hotel, the sparkling Gulf of Mexico twinkled like blue diamonds in the golden sun.

"Not L.A., but pretty nice," Tad said, glancing around as we waited for the light to turn green.

"It's *better* than L.A.," Marshall said, ribbing Tad with his elbow. "Wait till you see the tiki bars!"

Tad grinned. "*Now* we're talking. Carry on, my wayward son."

Marshall hooted, then turned the convertible left onto Gulf Boulevard. As the sun beat down, we cruised south along a strip of low-rise hotels, funky gift shops, and kitschy restaurants catering to the tourist trade.

The sidewalks lining both sides of the road were filled with a steady procession of deeply tanned people dressed mainly in bathing suits and beach cover-ups. Many of them dragged small canvas wagons behind them, laden down with beach chairs, umbrellas, and coolers.

I'd seen Elvis movies set in beach towns like this. But I'd never believed they really existed. Growing up in the Pacific Northwest, our beaches were cold and gray and dangerous. If you weren't careful, you'd be swept out in a fast-rising tide. Or crushed between huge, water-soaked logs.

The only danger I spotted on Treasure Island was getting sunburned.

The thought made me touch my nose. It was warm and tender. I was just about to ask Marshall to stop and let me buy a sunhat when he turned right onto a small side road. He drove a couple of blocks past a few condos and houses, then pulled the tiny red convertible up to a small bungalow that could've been plucked from a fantasy in my mind.

The adorable cottage was painted turquoise blue. Its high-gabled roof was clad in sheets of tin. Lemon-yellow shutters lined the large, sunny windows. A set of wide French doors opened onto a front porch that ran the length of the cottage. In the shade of the porch, wicker loungers beckoned invitingly, each fitted with comfy-looking cushions in pastel tropical prints.

"What do you think?" Marshall asked, cutting the ignition on the Mercedes.

"What do I *think*?" I asked. I caught a glimpse of myself in the rearview mirror. My nose was red, but I was grinning from ear to ear. "I *think* this will do just fine, Marshall."

We climbed out of the convertible. I was dying to take a peek inside the cottage, but Marshall led us away from it and toward the beach.

Across a wooden boardwalk flanked by sea oats lay a wide expanse of sugar-white sand and the glistening shore of the Gulf of Mexico.

I had to stop and admire the contrast. Treasure Island was the polar opposite of the beaches I'd grown up with along the Washington coastline. Here, the sand was warm—and gleaming white. The tide was calm and playful. And instead of tangles of deadly driftwood waiting to drag you to your death, countless seashells dotted the sand like confetti, as if inviting you to a non-stop party.

As I took in the gorgeous view, I spotted a huge, pink, castle-like building along the shoreline a mile or so south of us. I recognized it from the internet. It was the famous Don CeSar, our destination for the night. Tad had insisted on first-class accommodations. From what I could see, the hotel certainly fit the bill. Suddenly, the urge for a warm shower, clean cotton sheets, and sushi delivery overwhelmed me.

"The location looks great," I said to Marshall. "But we should get going. We need to check into the Don CeSar. It's been a long day and I'm exhausted."

"Can't we just stay here at the cottage?" Tad asked. He pointed to a thatched-roof structure a few doors down. "Look. There's a beach bar right over there!"

Marshall chewed his lip, then shrugged. "Well, I guess so. Sure. Why not? But I gotta warn you. There's not much in the fridge. And there's no room service like you're used to in L.A."

"Sure there is," Tad said, draping his arm across my shoulder. "I've got Dorey right here."

Chapter Ten

Sometime around ten o'clock, I left Tad and Marshall swapping war stories from their barstools at the Crooked Conch. That was the kitschy name of the open-air tiki bar Tad had spotted when we'd first arrived at the beach cottage late that afternoon.

Thankfully the bar was only a hundred yards or so down the beach from the little turquoise bungalow where we were staying. And even though I was dragging tired from jet lag when I'd set off alone, I enjoyed the peaceful walk back to the cottage.

The feel of the soft sand on my bare feet. The warm salt air in my lungs. The starry sky overhead. The absence of Tad and all the other L.A. noise. They all intertwined to soothe me like a lullaby.

With Marshall babysitting Tad, I was finally free to let my guard down a little and relax. And I knew exactly how I wanted to spend my "me" time. I brushed my teeth, washed my face, slipped into my pajamas, and snuggled into the fluffy feather bed in the guest room.

Ahhh!

The last thing I remember was picking up Marshall's script, reading the first line, and then promptly nodding off to sleep.

• • • •

WHAT IS THAT WEIRD noise?

I cracked open an eye. Faint bluish morning light was peeking through the slits between the bedroom-window blinds.

The strange noise repeated itself.

Mwack. Argk. Yark.

It sounded like a cat coughing up a hairball. I got up and padded into the kitchen, looking for a wayward beach kitty. What I found instead was a tomcat named Tad.

He was dry-heaving into the kitchen sink.

Lovely.

"Morning," Marshall said, startling me.

I whirled around to find the young director sitting at the kitchen table sipping a can of energy drink and snickering.

"Gotta excuse Tad," he said. "He had a rough night."

I shot a worried glance at Tad. "What did you do to him?"

"Tequila shots. My bad. I thought he was a pro."

I grimaced. "Tad is. He's just ... not as young as you are."

"No kidding," Marshall said. "From here on out, I promise to go easier on the old man."

"Old man!" Tad grumbled. "I'm not—" But he couldn't finish his thought. Interrupted by another wave of nausea, he doubled over the sink again and imitated coughing up a mouse.

"What are we going to do?" I asked Marshall. Bright-eyed and grinning, apparently he'd bounced back from a night of drunken debauchery like a shiny rubber ball. "Don't we start filming any minute?"

Marshall shrugged. "No worries, Dorey. I mean, *Doreen*. Look. The opening scene is just Tad in bed, hungover."

"I guess that's not too far a stretch," I said, glancing over at Tad.

"No stretch at *all*," Marshall said. "Actually, the way he looks now is *perfect*. Tad won't need makeup or a wardrobe. And he's already got a wicked case of bedhead." He smirked at me. "You know what, Doreen? You should be paying *me* for doing *your* job."

I smiled wryly. "I would, but I don't think you'd be impressed with the wages."

Tad groaned into the sink. "A little help here, please?"

Marshall laughed. "I'll get the old guy in bed. You get him some coffee. I already got a pot going."

"Oh." Surprised at not having to deal with Tad for a change, Marshall's offer was one I couldn't refuse. I grinned. "Okay. You got yourself a deal."

• • • •

AFTER TUCKING TAD IN bed with some aspirin and a cup of coffee, I joined Marshall back in the cottage's cozy kitchen for my own badly needed cup of java.

"Good thing all Tad has to do is lie in bed with two girls," I said, pouring coffee into a bright yellow mug. "Inside scoop. It's one of his specialties."

Marshall laughed. "I *bet* it is. He does all right for an old guy."

I thought about telling Marshall to stop calling Tad *old*, but I was getting way too much enjoyment out of how it made Tad wince.

"I started reading your script last night," I said, dumping cream into my coffee.

"And?" Marshall asked.

Crap.

I mentally kicked myself for bringing it up. From what I'd read so far, the freckled frat boy's screenplay was a jumble of mismatched ideas. A heap of incoherent crap. I winced, shoveled a spoonful of sugar into my coffee, then forced a smile and turned to face Marshall.

He was leaning back in his chair, sporting a smug expression that told me he was bracing for an avalanche of compliments. While I *did* feel like unloading on him, compliments weren't exactly what I had in mind. I bought myself a few seconds to think by stirring the sugar into my coffee.

"Well?" he asked.

"Uh ... to be honest, I don't exactly get the plot, Marshall," I said, joining him at the table.

His head cocked slightly. "What don't you get about it?"

Cornered, I stared into the swirling void of my coffee. "Well, Tad shags a bunch of women, all of whom end up getting eaten by a shark."

"Right."

"I don't see the connection. The only thing that kind of makes sense is the ending. You know, where he winds up in a gutter alone, clutching his Teddy bear."

"Oh, man," Marshall said. "Haven't you seen that movie *Inception*?"

I looked up at him. "With DiCaprio? Of course. I'm from L.A. I've seen every movie ever made. But I—"

"It's just like *that*, only different." Marshall's eyes gleamed with creative spark—either that or depravity. L.A. had taught me the two were surprisingly close bedfellows. "You see, in *Inception*, DiCaprio can't tell if he's in a dream or not. So he keeps a dreidel in his pocket. If he can spin the top, he knows he's awake."

"Uh ... okay. But what's that got to do with *your* project?"

"Don't you see?" Marshall said. "Tad spins a beer bottle to see if he's dreaming or not. But whoever it lands on ends up dead. Did he kill the girls? Or did the shark get them? Then Tad wakes up in a ditch clutching his childhood Teddy bear, thinking it's all been a dream."

My nose crinkled.

Don't you mean nightmare?

"Err ... has it been?" I asked. "A dream, I mean?"

Marshall grinned, then winked. "Who knows? Tune in next season to find out."

"Think *Inception* meets *The Beach Bum* meets *Jaws*," a familiar voice said behind me.

I turned in my chair to see Kerri Middleton standing in the front hallway. She was wearing a crisp, cotton sundress and clutching a white paper sack that read *Fray's Donuts*.

My eyebrow shot up. "Okay," I said. "But the script reads like a patchwork of disjointed ideas."

"Kinda," Marshall said. "But I want *Beer & Loathing* to do something that's never been done before."

"Uh ... so did Dr. Frankenstein," I said. "And see where that got him?"

"Oh!" Marshall said. "That's *it*, Doreen! We could add a monster!"

Kerri shot me a pained glance and put a finger to her lips. I got the message.

Don't add more nuggets to the flaming poo poo platter.

I dropped the topic, and Kerri dropped the bag of donuts on the table. "Hey," she said. "If there's an audience for *Sharknado V*, there's bound to be an audience for *Beer & Loathing,* right?"

I cast a concerned eye at Kerri. "Uh, sure. But all those films you guys are referencing are movies. This is a *TV series*. It's a whole different animal."

"In what way?" Kerri asked as Marshall dug into the bag of donuts.

"Well ... in just about *every* way," I said. "Story length. Continuing story threads. Audience expectations. Even distribution channels. I mean, how do you plan on marketing this to the major networks?"

"Kerri's got connections," Marshall said, as if that answered everything. Then he bit into a powdered donut.

"I'm working on that," Kerri said. "If all goes to plan, I think I have a fairly good shot at convincing the local station manager at Channel 22 to switch out reruns of *Gilligan's Island* for *Beer & Loathing* in the 2 p.m. time slot."

I caught my mouth before it fell open. Was Kerri serious? In show-biz, "small potatoes" didn't come any smaller than that.

"Uh ... Tad won't be happy about that," I said.

Kerri's lips pressed to a white line. "Look, Doreen. We're not paying Tad to be happy. We're paying him to draw an audience. As you know, the only thing that talks in this industry is money. I know for a fact that Channel 22's ad revenues are down. *Way* down."

"So?" I said.

"*So,* if I can convince them that Tad Longmire can increase their viewership, Channel 22 will get the audience numbers they need to justify an increase in the rate they charge their advertisers for that time slot. Tad gets paid. You get paid. We get paid. The station makes money. Everybody wins."

I nearly dropped my coffee cup. Not only was Kerri smart. She was as shrewd as a circling shark. But hell. Maybe she really *could* make this garbage scow of a show float. Anyway, that was *her* job, not mine. Why should I care one way or the other?

"You're right," I said, feeling the pressure ease from my shoulders. "Like you said, everybody wins."

"I hope the station manager is as easy to convince as you were," Kerri said, her back to me as she fixed herself a cup of coffee. "But I can't even begin the negotiations without a decent pilot to show them."

"Hey, don't sweat it," Marshall said. "We're gonna start working on it today, like you wanted."

"I know," Kerri said. "But I have some pressing news. I spoke with an old friend at Channel 22 last night. One of the execs decided to take a vacation next week. So yesterday they moved up the planning meeting to schedule the summer rerun lineup."

"So?" I said.

Kerri nervously tapped a manicured nail on her coffee mug. "So, that means that if we're going to have a shot at being considered, we've now got to have the pilot episode filmed, edited, and available for their review by tomorrow at three."

I nearly spewed my sip of coffee. "You're *kidding*!"

Kerri sighed. "I wish I was. But I'm not. So, I guess that means we'd better get busy, eh? Any more questions before we start setting up for filming?"

"Nope," Marshall said, springing up from his chair. "I'll go wake up Tad."

"Uh ... I have a question," I said to Kerri after Marshall disappeared down the hallway. "If by some miracle we actually get this thing filmed, the station approves it, and it bumps Gilligan off his 2 p.m. timeslot, does *Beer & Loathing* really have a chance at boosting Channel 22's revenues? I mean, who'll be watching at that hour?"

Kerri shrugged. "I don't know. Probably just unemployed deadbeats, stay-at-home moms, and little old ladies."

"Then how can it—"

"Look," Kerri said, cutting me off. She glanced around, then whispered, "I just said all of those things to boost Marshall's morale. Whether any of this actually works out or not, we'll just have to wait and see. There's no guarantee on any of it. But does it really matter to you? Tad gets paid one way or the other."

"Sure, that's true," I said. "But for your sake, I'd like for it to be a success, just the same."

Kerri shot me a pained smile. "Thanks. I appreciate that. So, will you help me? Will you work with me and do what you can to help make that happen?"

"Of course!" I chewed my lip. "But we have to make one change right away."

"What's that?"

"I noticed in the script that Marshall is using the cast's real names. We can't have Tad's character actually be named Tad Longmire in the show."

"It's not," Kerri said. "It's Tad *Love*mire."

"Oh." I picked up my copy of the script again. "I must've missed that. Still, it's a little on the nose, isn't it?"

Kerri sighed. "Marshall's an on-the-nose kind of guy. But take my word for it. Letting the cast keep their real first names is going to make filming a whole lot easier."

"It is? Why?"

Kerri smirked and shook her head. "Let me put it this way. Marshall didn't pick these people for their Mensa scores."

"Morning, Kerri!" a man's voice called out.

I looked up to see a slim, bald man in his mid-thirties walking into the kitchen. In his left hand he carried a gray metallic case. A camera tripod was slung over his right shoulder.

"Doreen, this is Tommy Bigelow," Kerri said as he joined us. "Our cameraman and editor extraordinaire."

Tommy grinned at me. "Thanks, but I think Kerri meant *debonair*."

Kerri laughed. "Tommy, this is Doreen Diller. She's Tad Longmire's personal assistant."

"Oh." He grimaced. "My condolences."

I smirked. "Hey. *Somebody's* got to lead the glamorous life."

The three of us shared a brief laugh, then Kerri handed Tommy the bag of donuts.

"Thanks," he said, fishing out a cruller. "We're setting up in the bedroom, right?"

"Yes," Kerri said. "The opening scene has Tad in bed with two women."

"Of course it does," Tommy said, shaking his head. "From Marshall, I would expect no less."

Chapter Eleven

The opening scene was Tad *"Love*mire*"* waking up in bed with a pair of beach bimbos named Candy and Honey. By the time we finished filming, I realized Kerri hadn't been joking about the actors' IQs. While the two young women were indeed knock-outs, they were so ditzy I'd have bet good money the pair thought Grape Nuts was an STD.

"Hold that pose," Tommy directed Candy, her lips puckered on Tad's cheek. The canned overhead spotlights glared off the cameraman's bald head as he slowly panned his equipment out for a wide-angle shot of the cozy threesome propped up on bed-pillows. "Okay! I think that'll do it. Cut!"

"Yes! It's a wrap," Marshall said. "Great job, everyone!"

"You're the best, Marshall," Candy Liebowitz (aka Candy Lipps) cooed. The irritatingly gorgeous young redhead climbed out of bed wearing a thong bikini that would've been declared illegal in most un-developed countries.

I sighed and took consolation in the fact that, according to the script, she would be the first to die.

"Yeah, thanks, Marshall," Honey Thompson (aka Honey Potter) said. She'd played the blonde bombshell occupying the left side of Tad's bed. Tad leered at Honey's taut, skimpily clad butt as she stood and ran a tanned hand through her long, golden tresses.

What did I care? I knew Honey was destined to be the second bimbo to become fish food for an inflatable shark. I smirked.

I wonder if plastic sharks like silicone ...

"You girls were great," Marshall said as the twin bombshells cornered him and simultaneously kissed him on either cheek, lifting a leg like pinup models. "You two take twenty, then meet us out at the beach in your bikinis."

"Ah, break time," Tad said, flashing his blue bedroom eyes. "So, which one of you two lucky ladies wants to come join me for a sleepover?"

"Hold on, Romeo," I said to Tad. "We've got a tight schedule to follow."

"Yeah, so do *I*," Tad quipped, smiling appreciatively at Honey's derriere.

"Sorry, Tad," Marshall said. "Doreen's right. Let's forget the break. Everybody into wardrobe, then out to the beach in five. It's time to feed Candy to the shark!"

• • • •

I WALKED WITH MARSHALL toward a tent set up on the beach, listening as he eagerly discussed the next shot. In it, Candy was to get crushed in the jaws of a Great White.

I had to admit, the thought had me excited, too. I'd planned to argue that Great Whites weren't in the Gulf of Mexico. But a quick Google search had set me straight. According to a marine research group, there were currently nine Great Whites circling the Gulf of Mexico, the largest of which weighed in at 2,076 lbs.

So much for my plans for a quick dip after lunch.

"And then she sinks under the water in a bloody cloud," Marshall said. "What do you think?"

"Uh, groovy," I said, having missed half the conversation due to rewriting the scene in my head. "Question. Do implants float?"

"Trevor! Blake!" Marshall shouted toward the tent, apparently not hearing my question. "How goes it with the star of the show?"

Under the shade of a large blue canopy, two hot young men in tropical print swim trunks were wrestling with something large and rectangular. As we got closer, I realized it was a cardboard carton containing an air pump.

"Not so good, Marshall," the taller of the two men called back. "How're we supposed to get the box open?"

"With the box cutter I left you," Marshall said. "It's right over there on the table behind you."

"Oh. Yeah," the other guy said, picking up the blade. "Okay, dude. We're on it!"

I stifled an eye roll. "Where'd you find *those* two?"

"Longtime friends," Marshall said. "They're not too bright, but they're always up for a good time. And best of all, they work for beer."

"Ah." I watched the two stud muffins slice open the carton. "That explains so much."

Apparently the smartest member of this cast is from China—and arrived in a box labeled Super Monster Fish Killer Shark ...

"So," I asked, "What can I do to—"

"Somebody help me!" a woman shrieked. I turned to see Candy Lipps, the beautiful redhead, holding a hand over her nose as if it had just been cut off.

"Could you see what's up with her?" Marshall asked. "She's kind of high maintenance."

You think?

"What's wrong?" I asked, sprinting over to Candy. She was on her knees in the sand, wringing her free hand while the other covered her nose.

"I think I feel a pimple coming on," she whined. "My nose feels all hot and stuff."

"Oh. Well, maybe you should put some sunscreen on it," I offered.

"That stuff makes me all itchy," she said. Candy glanced over at Marshall, then pulled me to the side and whispered, "Does this bikini make me look fat?"

"Seriously?" I had more fat under my chin than she had on her entire body. "You look fine," I said. "But the sun's hot today. Let's get you into the shade before your makeup melts."

I led Candy over to the canopy. Trevor and Blake were gone. In their place, Marshall and Kerri were trying to attach the air pump hose to the inflatable shark's posterior region.

"There! Got it," Marshall said. "Let's fill it up."

Kerri flipped the switch on the air pump. The plastic beast began to inflate. We all stood and watched in amazement as the apex predator of the ocean took shape. Unfortunately, it only took a couple of minutes to become painfully apparent that *Super Monster Fish Killer Shark* wasn't quite living up to the hype.

The label on the side of the carton displayed the image of a menacing man-eater with a mouthful of razor-sharp teeth. In reality, the plastic shark was about as scary as a Disney princess.

Instead of the promised mouthful of lethal, slashing incisors, the shark's balloon-like teeth formed a hokey, cartoonish smile reminiscent of Donkey in *Shrek*. What were supposed to be black, menacing eyes were as goofy as ... well ... *Goofy's*.

If that weren't bad enough, the inflatable shark's dorsal fin drooped like a bad comb-over. And the end of its nose was concave, as if it had just lost a bar fight with Mike Tyson. To be honest, I hadn't seen a monster prop this bad since *Attack of the Eye Creatures*.

"Aww, crap," Marshall grumbled. "This stupid shark looks bogus, doesn't it?"

I pursed my lips. *Bogus?* More like *ridiculous*. The only believable way that shark could kill someone was if they died laughing at it.

I stifled a snicker. "Er ... can't you get the nose to inflate?"

"I'm trying," Marshall said. "But I think Trevor and Blake must've cut a hole in it when they sliced open the box. Crap! What are we gonna do now?"

"Yeah," Candy whined. "I can't work with that thing. I'm a professional!"

My eyebrows rose an inch.

Wow.

Marshall kicked the shark in the side. It squeaked like a dog toy and rolled belly-up in the sand. "Man, this really sucks!"

Kerri chewed her lip. "I'm sorry, Marshall. If we're going to get this over to Channel 22 tomorrow, we don't have time to order another one."

"Yeah," I said, rubbing my index finger across my bottom lip. "Anyway, I don't think another one of those things is the answer."

"Then what *is*?" Marshall asked, his normally happy-go-lucky face red with anger and frustration. "We need a solution. *Now!*"

"He's right," Kerri said. "It's almost noon. We've only got the rest of the day to get this done or we miss our chance."

"I *know*," I said, chewing my lip. "Hey. Wait. I've got an idea. Why don't you just have a *person* kill Candy?"

"A person?" Kerri asked, as if she'd never heard of such an outrageous idea.

"Like, who?" Marshall asked. "We don't have anybody on cast who looks like they could be a killer."

"Then how about a *secret* killer," I said. "One you won't reveal until the end of the season?"

Marshall kicked the sand. "Yeah. Maybe." He looked up at me. "But for it to work, we'll need somebody *weird*. You know, somebody who really stands out in a crowd."

"You mean like a hunchback?" I asked.

"Or someone with a scarface?" Kerri offered.

"No," Marshall said. "I was thinking more like somebody with super-huge ta-tas."

My lips pursed into a sour line. "Of course you were. But where—"

"I know!" Marshall said. "I'll call Angel Santos!"

"Is that an escort service?" I asked sarcastically.

I bet the kid has it on speed dial.

I rolled my eyes. A pain shot through my left socket, making me wince. "Ouch!"

"Did you get sand in your eye?" Kerri asked.

"No." I wiped my watering eye. "I think my contact lens got hung up in the socket."

"I didn't know you wore contacts," Kerri said.

"Only one," I said, trying to hold open my burning eye. "Kerri, could you take a look, see if you see it up in there?"

"Sure."

Kerri peered into my face. Suddenly, she gasped.

Then Marshall gasped.

When Candy screamed, I knew they'd all seen it.

The secret I'd kept hidden since I was old enough to talk.

I blew out a long breath.

Great. Now I'll never get a job in Hollywood.

Chapter Twelve

"What's going on with your eye?" Kerri asked. "Should I call an ambulance?"

"No," I said, squeezing my left eye shut. "I have *Heterchromia iridum.*"

"Wicked!" Marshall said. "Is it contagious?"

"No," I grumbled, both angry and slightly afraid. The secret I'd tried to hide under a contact lens for nearly 40 years was finally out in the open.

"I was born with one brown eye and one pale blue one," I explained. "It's a family genetic trait."

"Oh," Kerri said. "Does it hurt?"

"Not normally," I said. "Only when my contact lens decides to take a trip up inside my head."

Candy's beautiful face puckered in horror. "Gross! Your eye looks so creepy! I think I'm gonna throw up." She grimaced and turned away.

I ground my teeth and thought about all the times my mother had warned me about the cruelty of ignorance. What would someone like Candy know about imperfections? The girl was flawless.

Ma had been right to homeschool me until I was old enough to tolerate a contact lens. People could be stupid. And cruel. And complete ass-wipes. Up until now, I'd been able to escape the trauma wrought by uncaring idiots. But now, the gig was up. Thankfully, I was mature enough to handle it—I hoped.

"Sorry if my eye disturbed you," I said to Candy. I tried to put my hand on her back. She squealed and shrank away from my touch like I was an escapee from a leper colony.

"Well, I think your eye is cool as hell, Doreen," Marshall said.

"What?" I asked, blinking up at him. "You think my milky white eye is *cool*?"

"Yeah!" He stared at me. A grin spread across his freckled face. "Oh, man, you look freaky! Like you're possessed or something."

"Thanks," I said sourly. "I'm glad you find me so entertaining." I turned to go. I really needed to find a washroom so I could coax the contact lens out of my eye socket and back onto my cornea. "I'll be back in a few minutes."

"Wait!" Marshall said. "That's it!"

I turned around. "*What's* it?"

Marshall grabbed me by the shoulders. "Doreen, with those eyes of yours ... you'd make the perfect psycho killer for *Beer & Loathing*!"

Kerri, who'd been staring at me like a concerned mother hen, suddenly burst into an enthusiastic smile. "Marshall's right!"

"No way," I said, jerking away from Marshall. "Kerri, please. Come with me back to the cottage and help me get this contact lens back in the right place."

"Aww, come on, Doreen," Marshall whined as Kerri put an arm over my shoulder. "Be our killer. Please? Pretty please?"

"It would solve a world of problems for us," Kerri whispered in my ear. "And we'll pay you for the bit."

The bit.

Kerri's words transported me back to Ms. Benny's trailer, and the words of wisdom the googly-eyed woman had dropped on me like a ton of bricks. *"Your only shot at the big screen is with character bits, like me."*

I stopped in my tracks. Maybe I should give up on the idea of trying to live up to society's idea of beauty and perfection. Maybe I should embrace my shockingly weird left eye. Maybe it's not a flaw holding me back, but the *angle* that could propel me forward!

Maybe I was born to play the bit of a crazed psycho killer!

"You okay?" Kerri asked.

I nodded, then gently pulled Kerri's arm from my shoulder. I glanced around the beach for Tad. What would he think of the idea of me taking the role?

I spotted my boss across the sand over by the makeup tent. His wandering hand was on the thigh of the giggling blonde named Honey. A petite brunette with a pixie haircut eyed Tad with disdain. I recognized her as Leslie, the makeup woman Kerri'd hired for the project.

I nearly groaned with disgust.

Screw Tad. I don't need his permission.

"You know what?" I said, whirling around to face Kerri. "Sure. I'll play the part. Why the hell not?"

"Woohoo!" Marshall hooted. "Now we're just gonna need a body double."

"For what?" I asked.

Marshall cocked his head like a confused puppy. "For the boobs, of course."

I shot Kerri a sideways *WTH* glance.

"Marshall," Kerri said. "I think we may need to make a few concessions. Doreen's saving our bacon here. Can't she do it with a pair of 36Cs?"

They're 34Bs, but what the heck.

"Sure," Marshall said, looking me up and down. "I guess I can roll with that."

• • • •

IT TOOK A PAIR OF TWEEZERS and a whole bottle of Visine to retrieve the wayward contact lens from way up inside my eye socket, but it was finally out. When I emerged from the bathroom triumphant, Kerri and Marshall were at the table eating lunch, busily working on rewriting the script.

"Got you a tuna on rye," Kerri said. "Hope that was okay."

"Fine," I said. "I'm starved!" I sat down at the table and tore into my lunch bag. "So, how's it going?"

"We're a bit stuck," Kerri said. "The shark didn't have any lines."

"Only Candy screaming at it," Marshall said.

"We need something to leave them wanting more," Kerri said. "What we need is some kind of twist at the end."

Marshall started to speak. Kerri shut him down. "And I don't mean a twist of the knife, Marshall. Having a woman killing off our characters is unusual, but not exactly innovative."

"Kerri's right," I said, munching a mouthful of sandwich. "What about if the killer spoke?"

"Earth to Doreen," Marshall said. "I think that's been done before."

"I know," I said, wracking my brain for ideas. Then I remembered *Hollywood Survival Guide* Tip #8: *If all else fails, tell a joke.*

"Hey," I said. "What if the killer was a wiseass?"

"Huh?" Kerri and Marshall uttered in unison.

I took a sip of soda to wash down the sandwich. "Hear me out. Instead of just stabbing the victims, what if we gave the psycho killer a few lines to say? It could add a kind of macabre humor to the end of each episode. You have to admit, it would be totally unexpected, right?"

"Uh ... I guess," Marshall said.

"Like, what did you have in mind?" Kerri asked.

I picked up a carrot stick and held it like a knife. "Picture this. What if, when the killer stabs Candy, she says something corny like, 'Revenge is sweet, Candy.' Then the killer lets out a sinister laugh and says, 'Looks like I got you *good and plenty.*'"

Kerri snickered. "God, that's bad."

Marshall laughed. "It's so bad it's great! I love it!" He set down his soda. "So, like, what would you say for Honey Potter?"

I grinned. "How about, 'Bee brave, Honey. This might sting a bit.'"

Marshall hooted and high-fived me. "Now *that's* what I'm talking about!"

Kerri's face lit up. "Yes! It's brilliant! And given the ridiculousness of the rest of the characters, by the end of each episode, the viewers might actually *be rooting* for the serial killer."

I smirked. "I agree the motivation is definitely there."

"This is perfect," Kerri said, shooting me a big smile. "It takes care of the shark problem, and we can continue shooting the rest of the pilot today." She leaned over and hugged me. "Thank you! You're a lifesaver!"

"Well, that's rather ironic," I quipped, "considering you just hired me to *take* lives."

Marshall and Kerri stared at me for a second. Then the joke hit home. As we all shared a chuckle, a thought hit me.

"Wait," I said. "There's a problem. If we film my face—I mean the face of the *killer*—the viewers will know it's not Tad, and there won't be any surprise reveal at the season finale."

"She's right," Marshall said. "Hey, wait. What if you wore some kind of mask? You know, like Jason did in *Friday the 13th*? Then all people would be able to see is those crazy eyes of yours!"

Kerri chewed her lip. "That could work. But what about the voice? They'll know the killer's a woman and not Tad."

"I know," Marshall said. "We could use an *electronic* voice. You know, like Siri. That way, the killer could still be Tad, or another dude, or even a woman. And if it all turns out to be a dream, the electronic voice would just make everything even weirder."

"Okay," I said, a conflicted smile crooking my lips.

Geez. I finally get a real role in a production and they don't want my face or my voice on the screen. Awesome.

"This is good stuff," Kerri said, making notes on a pad. "We'll save the reveal of the killer's face for the final scene of season one."

"Yeah," Marshall said, turning to me. "Then we blast the viewers with your face with those crazy eyes of yours! Oh! And instead of ending up in a ditch, we can make Tad go spinning down the drain in your pale blue eye!"

"Perfect!" Kerri said, scribbling in her pad.

I wasn't quite sure what either one of them was talking about, but I figured we'd work it all out along the way.

"Works for me," I said.

"Great. Now all we need is a name for our killer," Marshall said, slapping me on the back. "How about Doreen *Killigan*!"

I glanced over at Kerri. The smirk on her face made me burst out laughing.

So bad it's good? From Marshall's lips to God's ears.

• • • •

IT WAS TIME FOR THE after-lunch shoot, and I couldn't find Tad anywhere. He was integral to the shot, as it was the bar scene where he was to spin the beer bottle, thus marking Candy for certain death.

After scrambling around the beach, the prep tent, and the Crooked Conch, I was just about to panic when I spotted him lying on one of the loungers on the front porch of the cottage. As I ran toward him, I realized he was drinking a bottle of beer he'd actually opened himself. For Tad, that practically counted as a DIY project.

"There you are," I said, too excited to even be mad at him for day drinking.

"You found me," he said. "Damn."

"Get up," I said, grinning down at him. "It's time for the shoot. By the way, you're looking at the newest member of the cast."

Tad's smirk lost a bit of smugness. His brow furrowed. "They gave you a role?"

"Yes. As the killer."

He snorted. "Ha! You gonna wear a shark-skin suit, or what?"

"No. We changed the killer to a person."

"Oh." He looked me up and down. "So you're gonna kill me, are you?"

I shrugged. "That depends."

"On what?"

"On whether you keep drinking on the set. Remember, you're under contract."

Tad frowned. "You told me this project was just a piece of crap, and we were really on holiday."

"I know." I frowned and fidgeted. "But now ... well, this might actually end up being something good. Don't blow it. Please?"

Tad eyed me like a predator toying with its prey. "I see what you're doing here. You think this little sideshow is gonna make you a star, don't you, Dorey Diller?"

"No," I protested. "I'll be in a mask. Nobody will even know it's me. Look, Tad. Kerri should be coming by with my contract in a few minutes. You don't see any issues with me doing it, do you?"

He shrugged. "I guess not. Just so long as you keep my smoothies and lattes coming. And you help me rehearse my lines. And don't bust my balls over a beer."

"Okay. Anything else?"

"Yeah. Don't let this gig go to your head and get all dreamy on me."

I shot him a facetious smile. "Why? Jealous I might make it into a movie before *you* do?"

Tad snorted. "Me? Jealous of a *woman*? Now I *know* you're dreaming, Dorey."

Chapter Thirteen

After Tuesday's filming finished at sunset, Tommy and Marshall took off like stray bullets. They had a long night of editing ahead to transform the raw footage they'd shot today into a pilot worthy of showing to Channel 22 executives tomorrow.

Despite our best efforts, we'd run out of daylight before we could film the final scene. The guys said they'd be back at the beach cottage at the crack of dawn tomorrow to shoot it, then hightail it to the studio to edit it into the first episode and get it to the station by three o'clock.

For once, I was glad I had *my* job instead of *theirs*.

As they climbed into their cars to go, I wished them luck. They were going to need it. Then I snuck back to the cottage to call my mother. I wanted to share my news about my bit part in *Beer & Loathing*. Lord knows, she'd waited long enough for news I'd finally landed a role.

I wasn't a celebrity yet, but it was a start.

Funny, since moving to Hollywood over 15 years ago, I'd grown accustomed to people comparing everyone to celebrities.

"That guy's got crazy eyes like Jack Nicholson in *The Shining*."

"He's got a frizzy red fro like Jon Heder in *Napoleon Dynamite*."

"She laughs like Julia Roberts in *Pretty Woman*."

Granted, the resemblances weren't always spot on—but you got the gist of what they meant in a second, and in a way no amount of words could adequately convey.

As I dialed Ma's number, I lay back on the feather bed and took a deep breath to brace myself. You see, my mother, Maureen Diller, was the spitting image of Chloris Leachman in *Young Frankenstein*. But in pretty much all other ways, Ma channeled Roseanne Barr in *She Devil*.

She was cautious, plotting, and paranoid. As her child, I'd always felt like an inconvenience—a dim-witted, bumbling, sidekick she'd had to watch like a hawk to keep me from sticking a fork in a light socket or drowning in the rain.

"Hi, Ma," I said.

"Who is this?"

"Doreen. Your offspring."

"Oh. I'd given you up for dead."

"I called two weeks ago."

"A lot can happen in two weeks."

"I know."

Sensing a chance to detour from our usual dead-horse soundtrack, I blurted, "I got a new job!"

"What? The studio fired you?"

Not exactly...

"No. Ma, I got a role in a new TV series!"

"You're kidding."

"I'm not. And it's an *important* role, too."

"Huh. What is it?"

"I play a killer."

"Oh. What kind of killer?"

"Uh ... the kind that kills people?"

"More than one, huh?" Ma grunted. "So, a serial killer."

I hadn't thought about it, but yeah. "Yes."

"Lemme guess. You showed them your crazy eye."

I gritted my teeth. "It was an accident. Anyway, what's the big deal?"

Ma let out a sigh that could've been heard from Snohomish without the phone. "So you're a psycho killer now. I'm so proud. Where are you?"

"St. Petersburg."

"*Russia?*"

"Florida. It's so nice here—"

"Your Aunt Edna lives there," Ma blurted. "Have you seen her?"

"No. Why would I—"

"You should contact her while you're in town."

"But you told me she was dead."

"I never said that."

"Then Aunt Edna's still alive?"

"Of course she is," Ma said. "If you weren't so caught up in yourself all the time, you'd know that. Now be a good person and take an hour out of your *busy acting career* and go visit her. It's time. Here's her phone number, 7-2-7—"

"Ma, I can't write it down right now. Could you text it to me after we hang up?"

She sighed. "I suppose. I have to do *everything* around here. Hey. So these people flew you to Florida for this gig?"

"Well, sort of. I came here with Tad Longmire. I'm his personal assistant now."

"Tad Longmire?" my mother gasped. "Dr. Lovejoy on *Days of Our Lies?*"

I smirked. "The very one."

"Why would *he* be hanging around *you?*"

My smirk vanished. "I was the one who convinced him to take the starring role in the project here in St. Pete. We're fellow cast members now."

"Why didn't you tell me this before?"

"It all happened kind of last-minute. We just got here yesterday. We've been busy filming ever since."

"Uh-huh."

I could hear my mother's devious mind whirring on the other end of the line. I didn't want to be around for what finally came flying out. "I gotta go, Ma."

"Hold your horses, Dorey. I heard about Tad's blowout in Tinsel-town."

I gulped. "You did?"

"Of course. It was all over the tabloids. So I get why he was available on short notice. And you? Well, you've had an empty dance card since you left Snohomish."

"Is there a point to this, Ma?"

"Yeah. Why were there these openings in the first place?"

"What do you mean?"

"I mean, who were the two suckers cast for the roles before *you two* suckers replaced them?"

Arrgh!

"I gotta go Ma."

"Don't be rude. Call your Aunt Edna," I heard her yelling as I clicked off the phone.

A few seconds later, Ma texted me a phone number. I stared at it blankly. I'd never met my Aunt Edna. And if she was anything like Ma, with any luck I never would.

Chapter Fourteen

Wednesday arrived way too early, and stayed way too late. Between keeping up with Tad's whims, keeping his hands off the beach babes, and keeping my chin up through eleven takes of the pilot finale featuring yours truly as Doreen Killigan, the whole harried morning melted into a frenzied blur.

Except for two things.

One—being startled awake by an old man in a bingo cap. And two—being jolted by a blast of ice-cold seltzer water to the face.

The day had started off with a knock on my bedroom door. Before I could rouse myself to total consciousness, the lock began to jiggle. Then the door cracked open and an old man stuck his shriveled head inside.

"What the!" I yelled, pulling the bedcovers to my chin.

"It's me," the old man said. "Marshall." Then, like a scene out of *Total Recall*, he pulled off his face. He'd been wearing a gnarly rubber mask.

"Marshall!" I gasped. "You nearly scared me to death!"

He shrugged. "Sorry. I was testing a theory."

I sat up in bed. "What are you talking about?"

"Our killer needs a mask, right?"

"Uh, yeah."

"So, what do you think of this one?" Marshall stepped inside my bedroom and held up the latex head like the victor in a rubber sword fight to the death.

I squinted at the severed rubber head. It was as pasty-white and wrinkly as an albino raisin. A pointy, hook nose protruded from above a wide slit of a mouth. A pair of flabby ears stuck out on each side like jug handles. Deep, sunken eyeholes stared blankly at me from beneath a ball cap that read, *I Love Bingo*.

Still half asleep, I didn't know what to think. I chewed my lip and stared studiously at the mask, buying time while my mind scrambled to recall something I'd read in the *Hollywood Survival Guide* about just such a situation. Ah, yes! Tip #9: *When stuck for an answer, ask, "What's the concept?"*

"What's the concept?" I asked.

Marshall grinned. "Think about it. What's the opposite of an attractive, but scary-looking woman? A harmless, ugly old man."

Attractive? You think I'm attractive?

I shot him a smile. "You know, that whole irony thing could work."

"All right!" Marshall said. "I was hoping you'd say that. Now get up. We've got a scene to shoot!"

· · · ·

THREE HOURS OF FRENZIED filming went by in a flash. Before I knew it, we were on the 11th take of my killer's last scene. My arm was tired from all the stabbing, and I was beginning to feel like Bill Murray in *Groundhog Day*—except I kept killing the same dummy over and over again ...

"Action!" Tommy yelled.

The camera zoomed in. I plunged the eight-inch collapsible knife into the bulbous, bikini-clad chest of Candy Lipps. Right on cue, Leslie, the makeup woman, squirted fake blood from a squeeze bottle onto both of us. Candy began screaming, and I made googly eyes at the camera through the holes in the old-man bingo mask covering my head.

This was usually the point where Tommy yelled, "Cut. Let's do it again." Then we'd all race around like mice, trying to get cleaned up for another take.

But this time, Tommy yelled something different.

"Yes! It's a wrap, folks!"

Marshall followed with a hearty, "Woohoo!"

"All right!" I joined in, tired, but elated. I pulled off the sweaty rubber mask and ran a hand through my damp hair. Suddenly, cold water spurted onto my forehead and ran down my nose.

Marshall had shot me in the face with a seltzer gun.

"What the?" I said, water dripping from my chin.

Marshall laughed and handed me a towel. "It's supposed to be good luck."

I laughed. But still, I eyed him suspiciously.

Good luck? I hadn't read anything about that *in the* Hollywood Survival Guide.

After the hit-and-run filming session, Tommy and Marshall took off like lightning bolts. It was already past 11 a.m., giving them precious few hours to edit the final act into a pilot worthy of showing Channel 22 at three o'clock.

After they left, Kerri gathered her things to make a hasty getaway. "I need to supervise those two," she said, climbing into her Jaguar. "And I've got to prep for the meeting at three."

"Good luck," I said, squeezing her shoulder.

"Thanks. Keep your fingers crossed. And take the rest of the day off. You earned it!"

· · · ·

WITH NOBODY ELSE LEFT at the cottage but Tad, I took him to lunch at the Crooked Conch. I felt like celebrating my first real action shoot, but Tad decided to be a spoilsport and refused to even raise his beer to the toast I'd made for the success of the project. Disgusted, I left him at the bar with his beloved bourbon and bimbos.

Fine by me. I can think of better ways to spend my time than babysitting Tad's humongous, fragile ego.

As I shuffled along the beach on my way back to the cottage, my cellphone chimed a funny ringtone. It was the special ring Sonya and I used for gossiping with each other back at the Hollywood studio. We'd nicknamed the tone, "Drama Alert."

I checked my phone for her text.

News flash! Boobie Bonnie's husband sent her packing from the set today.

I texted back.
What happened???

Borloff caught her in the supply room with one of the camera grips. Her punishment? A vacation in Miami. Geez. Where do I sign up for that life?

Seriously. Some people have all the luck.

How's it going in St. Pete?

Actually, pretty good. Tad's being a jerk, of course. But get this. I actually got a role in the production. A good one, too! I get to kill bimbos!

Wow! Good for you! So what you're saying is that for us to get a job in the movies, we have to leave Hollywood?

It would appear so.

Life is too weird to contemplate, D. Must drink wine and consume massive amounts of air-popped popcorn.

Got to watch that figure.

Always. Later!

It was almost 2 p.m.—nearly deadline for the guys back at the studio editing their butts off. I didn't want to bother them, but I just had to know if we were going to make the time crunch. I hit speed dial for Sunshine City Studios.

"How's it going?" I asked Marshall when he picked up.

"Thanks to Tommy's perfectionism, we got some excellent footage," he said. "Like he keeps saying, 'Better a good take than a bad fake.' But let me tell you, Doreen, the real magic happens in editing."

"Right," I said. "Is there anything I can do to help?"

"Yeah. Pray for magic."

I grimaced. "Uh ... okay. Will do."

Chapter Fifteen

A thunderstorm kicked up the wind last night. Tucked safely inside the downy womb of my soft, goose-feather bed, I'd drifted off to sleep to the sound of thunder and ocean waves tumbling onto shore. When I awoke this morning, the sky had cleared. I hoped it was a portent of good things to come.

I sat up and thought about the conversation I'd had with Kerri yesterday afternoon.

"Hey, Kerri. How'd the meeting go?"

"Well, they didn't say no, so that's good."

"What *did* they say?"

"Well," Kerri had hesitated. "They were impressed we'd gotten Tad Longmire to star in it. So be sure and thank Tad."

"Uh ... I will. He's not here right now."

"Oh. Well, anyway, they said they'd let me know as soon as they made a decision. The meeting for that is at 2 p.m. tomorrow. They won't call before then. So we can all quit holding our breath."

"Hard to stop," I'd said.

"Agreed. Look. We're all exhausted here at the studio. I told Marshall and Tommy to take tomorrow morning off. We're too nervous to work, anyway. Sleep in and I'll call you tomorrow. Okay?"

"Okay," I'd said. "But I'd like to see the pilot if you don't mind."

"Oh! Sure. I'm sorry. It slipped my mind. I'll arrange something for tomorrow and let you know."

I yawned and stretched. Tomorrow was now today. A jolt of nervous energy surged through me. Today I'd get to see the pilot episode of my first official acting gig! I pressed my eyes closed and giggled excitedly.

So this is what it feels like to be a movie star!

I lay back in bed for another moment, planning my lazy morning ahead. First, as a treat I'd have breakfast somewhere I could dig my toes into the sand. Then I'd stroll the beach collecting shells, thinking up punchlines for upcoming episodes, and keeping my fingers crossed Channel 22 would give us the green light.

My stomach gurgled. Daybreak was peeking through the blinds. The room was so quiet I could hear the clock ticking on the nightstand. I breathed in deep and drank in the silence. No car horns beeping. No tires squealing. No roommates bumbling around in the kitchen. No Tad barking orders at me.

Tad!

I sat up and checked my cellphone. Somehow, it had switched itself off. I powered it back up and stared at the screen.

Messages from Hollywood directors? Zero.

Messages from Tad? Eighteen.

Eighteen!

I leapt out of bed. Hazy memories of yesterday afternoon pinged in my brain like drips from a leaky faucet. After filming had wrapped up yesterday morning, Tad and I'd shuffled over to the Crooked Conch for fish tacos. He'd tried to turn it into a drinking match. Disgusted, I'd left the jerk to fend for himself.

All afternoon and evening.

And Tad had been calling me over and over ever since!

What has he done now? Geez, I hope it doesn't involve the police!

"Tad!" I hollered, then scurried out of my room and ran down the hallway like the cottage was on fire.

When I got to Tad's bedroom, the door was open. The bed was still made. Tad was nowhere in sight. Panic shot through me. An image of Tad in an orange prison jumpsuit flashed in my mind. I shook my head like an Etch-a-Sketch to clear it away.

"Tad!" I yelled down the hallway. "Tad! Where are you?"

I raced through the cottage. He wasn't passed out on the bathroom floor. He wasn't dry-heaving into the kitchen sink. He wasn't sprawled face down on the living room sofa.

OMG. This is so not good!

In a few hours, we'd know the fate of *Beer & Loathing*. And while everyone else had been working their butts off to make that happen, I'd gone and lost the leading man!

I flung open the French doors and ran outside. Two steps onto the porch, I nearly tumbled over a pile of stuff heaped up near the front door.

"Ouch!" a voice sounded from somewhere under the jumble of pillows and cushions.

"Tad?" I asked.

"Who else?" he grumbled. A hand emerged from the pile and pulled a chenille throw-blanket from his face. Sometime between yesterday's lunch and now, Tad had acquired a black eye.

"Dear lord!" I cried out. "Are you okay?"

"You missed it," Tad said, his lips pouting above his unshaven cleft chin.

"Missed what?" I asked. "The ambulance?"

"No. The party."

"Tad, there's only so much tequila a girl can take. What happened to you? How'd you get the shiner?"

"Shiner?" he asked. "I dunno. I fell down, I think."

I groaned. "Why didn't you come inside last night?"

Tad frowned at me. "The door was locked. You didn't answer your phone. I didn't have a key."

I winced.

Oops.

Tad yanked back the blanket, revealing his complete asset package.

"Why are you naked?" I gasped, unable to stop myself from staring.

"I always sleep in the raw, Dorey." He rubbed his forehead. "My head hurts. Help me up."

He reached a hand toward me. Sensing a trap, I hesitated.

"And have you pull me down into your naked lair? I don't think so."

Tad laughed. "Eh. It was worth a try."

"Geez, Tad. Look at you! Get up. We need to get you showered and shaved. Then we've got to cover up that shiner."

"You're no fun," he said, hauling himself up. "All work and no play will get you nowhere."

"So will all play," I countered.

Tad's brow furrowed as if trying to think made his head hurt.

That would explain so much ...

He stumbled to his feet. Then he reached out and hugged me, pressing all six feet of naked man-hunk against me. My mind screamed "NO!" But despite everything I knew about the jerk, my traitorous body screamed, "YES! YES! YES!"

Thankfully, Tad himself came to my rescue. He opened his mouth and extinguished my libido with six little words.

"Dorey, get me a latte. *Now.*"

My cellphone rang. "Hold on, Tad. It's Kerri."

"Doreen, hey, it's Kerri. If you're interested, I wanted to invite you and Tad to the studio at one o'clock to see the finished pilot reel. Then we can sit around and chew our nails off until the callback from Channel 22 at two."

Tad frowned. I cut the air between us with my finger scissors.

"That sounds fantastic, Kerri. We can't wait!"

• • • •

SOBERING UP TAD AND concealing his black eye took most of the morning. By the time he was washed, fed, and fit to be seen in public, it was time to hail a limo to Sunshine City Studios. But at the last minute, Tad backed out, saying he had other things to do.

I wasn't about to argue. I'd simply said, "Fine," and left without him.

I arrived at the studio a minute after one o'clock. The faded red door was unlocked. As I stepped inside, I heard people talking. I followed their voices to the conference room. There, Tommy and Marshall were seated across from each other at a large, rectangular table. Both were staring at a large TV screen mounted on the wall.

"Doreen!" Marshall said, turning to face me when I walked in. "Where's Tad?"

"Uh ... I left him at the beach ... in the care of a local redhead."

I'd wanted to add, "Sorry about Tad. Not sure if he's an asset to the project or just an ass." But from the look on Marshall's face, he was figuring that out all by himself.

"Come have a seat," Marshall said, pulling out a chair for me. "We're getting ready to watch the pilot reel again."

"Awesome." I slipped into the chair next to Marshall. Kerri poked her head in the door and joined us.

"Any word from Channel 22?" I asked.

"Not yet," Kerri said, chewing a fingernail.

"Why do you think we're watching this thing again for the fourth time?" Tommy asked.

"Anyway, it's too soon," Kerri said, glancing at a clock on the wall. "They're probably still reviewing the pilot. After that, they'll consider what to offer us."

"*If* they like it," Tommy said.

"Right," Marshall said. "If they don't, well, it's done."

Suddenly, the conference landline jangled. The four of us jumped as if a bomb had gone off.

"You gonna get that?" Tommy asked, eyeing Marshall with trepidation.

Marshall glanced at me, then snatched up the receiver. "Hello?"

"Is it Channel 22?" Kerri whispered.

Marshall shook his head. "Pizza guy. I left the door open for him. Somebody closed it."

"Sorry," I said. "That would be me."

"Well, at this point," Kerri said, "Let's hope no news is good news."

Chapter Sixteen

While Tommy let the pizza guy in, Marshall and I grabbed some sodas from the breakroom at Sunshine City Studios and microwaved some popcorn. With the fate of *Beer & Loathing* in the hands of the Channel 22 gods, we decided to blow off some steam and watch the pilot episode in style.

"Okay, here goes," Tommy said, clicking the remote as we all settled into our chairs around the conference table.

The big screen flickered on. Bongo-beat tropical music played as the words *Beer & Loathing in FLA* appeared against a beachy backdrop. The camera panned to an outside view of the idyllic beach cottage.

Suddenly, the scene shifted to an unshaven Tad Longmire, nose still red from Borloff's special director's right cut.

Tad leered at us drunkenly from his bed. On either side of him, two mysterious lumps under the duvet moved from his groin area up toward his head. The faces of two gorgeous women popped out from under the covers. A blonde and a redhead.

I closed my eyes and prayed it would get better from there.

It did not.

After twenty minutes of Tad horn-dogging women around the beach and into his bed, Marshall elbowed me out of my disgusted stupor.

"Here it comes," he said. "Your killer scene!"

I sat up straighter. The camera honed in on a close-up shot of Candy Lipps. Her bronze, bikini-clad body lay sleeping, uncovered, atop the bed. She clutched a Teddy bear.

I stifled a groan.

I guess I should be grateful she isn't sucking her thumb.

Suddenly, the wrinkly, rubber chin of the bingo man mask appeared next to her ear. "Revenge is sweet, Candy," my digitized voice whispered.

A jolt of horror-movie soundtrack jabbed the silence, making me jump. A flash of light stabbed my eyes. Suddenly, a hand jutted into the air, gripping a gleaming knife. It plunged downward savagely. When it rose again, the blade and the killer's hand were completely soaked in stage blood.

I'll admit it. I gasped.

The next shot was of Candy's lifeless eyes staring into space. (I figured she conjured up the look by trying to multiply 347 by zero.) Candy's once-nubile chest was now a bloody pool of multiple stab wounds.

Let's hope she didn't spring a silicone leak.

The camera panned over to my character, Doreen Killigan. Dressed in black from neck to toe, it was impossible to tell whether I was a man or a woman. I stood over Candy, the bloody bingo man mask concealing my identity.

Suddenly, the camera zoomed in close on the mask. Behind the rubber eye holes, my brown eye was hard to see. But my pale blue one was as visible as the moon in a cloudless sky—and was darting around like a paranoid schizophrenic.

A chill went up my spine. I finally saw myself like everyone else did.

I shivered in my seat.

In the midst of the macabre scene, a sinister laugh cut the silence. My digitized voice followed, landing the final line, "Looks like I got you good and plenty."

The screen faded to black.

Marshall hooted. "Wicked, man! I'm telling you, that's wicked with a capital W!"

As a movie buff, I'd seen a crap-load of films. So, in all honesty, I had to admit I'd seen worse. To his credit, Tommy's camera work was surprisingly good. So was the acting, considering how disjointed both the script and the filming had been.

I sat back and smiled. If I were a movie critic, (a kind one) I'd have written that "*Beer & Loathing* could best be described as the beachside prequel to *Idiocracy*—with a dash of *I Married an Axe Murderer.*"

"Well?" Marshall asked, his eyes eager with anticipation. "What do you think, Doreen?"

Knowing this moment would come, I'd already plucked a gem from the *Hollywood Survival Guide*. Tip #22. *When at a loss for words, you can't go wrong with "interesting."*

"Interesting," I said. "And, I have to admit, unexpected."

"In a *good* way, right?" Marshall asked.

"Totally," I said, improvising.

"God, I wish Channel 22 would call already," Tommy said, wringing his hands. "The suspense is killing me. I'm gonna take a walk to calm my nerves."

"Good idea," Kerri said. "Mind if I join you?"

I was relieved when Tommy left the conference room. He'd drummed his bitten-to-the-quick fingers on the table during the whole viewing. If the guy didn't let out some nervous tension soon, I was afraid he might next start pulling out his eyelashes.

As soon as Tommy and Kerri left, I grabbed my chance to be alone with Marshall. "So, I wanted to ask you something."

Marshall leaned back in his chair and locked his fingers behind his head. "Sure. Shoot."

"I ... I guess I'm just curious about something. When did you first write *Beer & Loathing*?"

"Oh. Last year. Why?"

"No reason really. I just thought, you know, given the last-minute casting, that it was a recent project. You only cast Tad for it four days ago. That doesn't seem like Kerri Middleton's way of doing things."

Marshall smirked. "But it *does* seem like mine, huh?"

I shrugged and smiled. "Well, kind of."

"Look," Marshall said, unoffended in the slightest. "I know everybody thinks I'm just a kid. And maybe this project isn't the greatest story ever told. But everybody's got to start somewhere, right?"

"Sure. I didn't mean—"

"And to answer your question, we *did* have another guy lined up for the role before Tad."

Crap. Ma had been right. I hated it when she was right!

"So what happened?" I asked.

Marshall shook his head. "I don't know. Brent—my high school buddy, Brent Connors? He was all stoked up about doing it."

"So, what happened?"

"Like I said, I'm not sure. After the audition, he met with Kerri to sign the contract and the next thing I know he'd dropped out of the project."

My eyebrows knitted together. "Did Kerri say why?"

"No. She was as baffled as I was."

"Why baffled? Everybody's entitled to change their minds."

"Sure," Marshall said, lowering his hands to the armrests. He leaned in close to me. "But not everybody just disappears off the face of the earth afterward."

I blanched. "Brent *disappeared*?"

"Yeah. He won't return my calls. His car isn't at his apartment. He used to come to the beach every day. I haven't seen him since he quit."

"When was that?"

"Last week. Wednesday or Thursday, I think."

Whoa. Kerri Middleton is smart and ambitious. But is she smart and ambitious enough to throw Brent under the bus? Or to get rid of him for good when she found out Tad was available for the leading role? No. That couldn't be possible. Could it?

I needed more information from Marshall. "What about—"

The conference door squeaked open. I dropped my thought as Kerri stepped in, looking excited but worried.

"So what have you two been talking about?" she asked.

Oh, nothing. Just whether or not you might be a two-faced murderer ...

Marshall pursed his lips. "We were just—"

"Discussing the pilot," I interjected. "You think we have a chance with Channel 22?"

"All I can say is, it's in their hands now," Kerri said, heaving a sigh. "But based on their reactions, I'd say they liked it."

"Really?" Marshall asked, fishing for a compliment. "Which part did they like best?"

Kerri smirked. "I believe it was the part about the audience numbers Tad's been generating for *Days of Our Lies.*"

• • • •

TOO NERVOUS AND WOUND up to go home, at 4:30 Marshall, Kerri, Tommy and I were still sitting around the conference table in the studio downtown. We'd been killing time re-watching the pilot episode of *Beer & Loathing* and wafting pros and cons back and forth about whether or not we'd get the nod to be in the summer time slot on Channel 22.

After watching Kerri the whole time, I decided she couldn't have harmed Brent. But then again, I used to think Tad was a dreamboat.

"Enough gabbing already," Kerri said. "We can wish and pray all we want. But the decision about *B&L* boils down to Bob Johnson, the guy in charge at 22."

"*B&L*?" Marshall asked.

"Oh. That's Johnson's nickname for the series. I did my best to persuade him. Geez. I promised him everything but the moon."

"Let's just hope he didn't think you were full of cheese," Tommy quipped.

"That's funny," Marshall said. "Hey, Doreen, you should have the killer say something like that."

"I could," I said. "But I've already worked out the lines for the rest of the bimbos."

"Oh yeah?" Tommy said. "Let's hear them."

"Yeah," Marshall said. "What's the line for Penny Nichols?"

I sat up and tried to imitate the digital version of my voice. "I cents it's time for a change, Penny. But I can see you're already spent."

Kerri laughed. "I love it! What about Cookie Baker? What do you tell her when you're stabbing her to death?"

I smirked and gave them my best Mae West. "So long, sugar Cookie. Let the chips fall where they may."

"Wicked," Marshall said. "That just leaves the season finale bimbo. What do you say to Fanny Tight?"

I opened my mouth.

The conference phone rang.

The three of us jumped like victims in a horror movie.

Kerri was the first to un-freeze. She snatched up the handset on the conference landline.

"Kerri Middleton speaking." Her eyes grew wide. "Oh, hello, Mr. Johnson. Yes. Now's a good time. Actually, I and the other studio principals were just finishing up a meeting. Shall I put the call on speaker? Very good, then."

Kerri eyed us wildly, then mashed the speakerphone button.

"Hello," Johnson's voice boomed through the speakerphone. "I don't exactly know what to call this thing you've all made. It's quirky. Kind of like *Baywatch* meets a female *Dexter*."

"We call it a daytime serial," I said, then cringed and wanted to kick myself.

Johnson laughed. "You! You're the voice of the mysterious serial killer, aren't you? I love that dry sense of humor of yours."

"Uh … thank you, sir," I said, still cringing.

"Are those eyes real?" Johnson asked. "I mean, brrr! Really spooky special effects!"

Kerri shot me an apologetic grimace. "So, Bob. Don't keep us in suspense. All joking aside, we're dying to know. Is it a 'go' or is it a 'no'?"

"Like I told you in the meeting, Kerri. I can't answer that until you tell me whether *B&L* is ready for airtime."

"Right," Kerri said. "Hold on a second. Let me get the latest update from production."

Kerri leaned over and jabbed the speakerphone button to shut it off. Her eyes darted from Tommy to Marshall and back again. "Listen, guys. In the meeting? I ... I *lied* to Johnson."

"What?" Marshall said.

Kerri winced. "I had to. I thought he was about to greenlight us. Then, all of a sudden, he sideswiped me with this requirement to have five complete episodes ready before he could approve it."

"What do you mean?" I asked.

"What I mean is, for *B&L* to be considered for a timeslot, we have to have five episodes ready to air. Anyway, the thing is, I panicked and told him a lie. I said filming was finished on all of them, and production was nearly complete." She turned to Marshall and grimaced. "I'm sorry. It was either lie, or the project was dead in the water. I should have—"

"What's the harm?" Marshall said, putting a hand on her shoulder. He glanced over at Tommy. "We can crank them out pretty quick, right?"

"Yeah, sure!" Tommy said. "We've got the prototype done!"

"So we're agreed?" Kerri asked.

Marshall nodded. "Agreed."

Kerri clicked the speakerphone back on. "Mr. Johnson? Don't worry. We're very close to finalizing the project," Kerri said.

"Hmm," Johnson growled. "How close?"

"Um ... we just have to finish editing the last episode. My production team sees no problem with it. In fact, everything should be in the can and ready for airtime by tomorrow afternoon."

"I see," Johnson said. "In that case ... it's on."

A collective gasp filled the conference room.

"What was that?" Johnson asked.

"Nothing," Kerri said. "A faulty air-conditioner vent."

"Oh," Johnson said. "Okay. Listen. I'll clear that spot at 2 p.m., like we discussed. We'll air the first episode on a Friday, and let the media buzz build over the weekend. If it's good, we'll run the first episode again on Monday to catch more viewers. The remaining four episodes of *B&L* the following Tuesday through Friday."

"That's fabulous," Kerri said. "Which Friday are you thinking of to air the first episode?"

"*Friday* Friday," Johnson said. "As in *tomorrow*."

Kerri gulped. "Um ..."

"Is there a problem?" Johnson asked.

"No problem at all, sir," Marshall blurted.

"Good. So tell me," Johnson said. "Do we have a deal?"

We glanced around at each other, then nodded like a collection of bobble-head dolls.

"Bob?" Kerri said. "We have a deal!"

Chapter Seventeen

After promising the moon, it was my new friend Kerri and I who were left seeing stars. As the only two bona fide grownups on board the *B&L* ship of fools, it was up to us to figure out how to produce four episodes in under four days.

At 7 a.m. Friday morning, she and I were already hard at work at The Frog Pond diner, trying to slap together a production schedule between panic attacks.

I nervously drummed my fingernails against my coffee cup. "How are we going to wrangle Tad and a bunch of pouty, pampered starlets into cramming two weeks' worth of filming into what basically amounts to one long weekend?"

"First things first," Kerri said, downing half a cup of coffee like it was a shot of whiskey. "We need to fix the scripts. They need more dialogue."

"Are you sure?" I countered. "Given the cast, the less they have to say, the faster filming will go."

Kerri's face grew serious. "You've got to help me, Doreen. I have a reputation in this industry. I really didn't think Marshall's project would get this far. But now that it has ..." She looked away and shook her head. "My *name's* going to be associated with this."

I grimaced. "What can I do?"

Kerri locked eyes with me. "You've seen the scripts. Help me fix this disaster before it happens."

Over coffee and croissants, we did our best. Mainly, we beefed up Marshall's skimpy plots with more tongue-in-cheek dialogue from Doreen Killigan, my murderous alter ego.

To be honest, by the time we were done, my character had practically become the star of the show. It was a little embarrassing and self-serving. But I had to admit, it was also a bit of an ego rush. I, Doreen Diller, was single-handedly ridding the world of five hapless bimbos.

"Okay, that's the last one," I said. "Fanny Tight is finished."

"Good lord," Kerri said, glancing at her watch. "We better get a move on. The entourage should be arriving at the beach cottage any minute now."

I motioned for the waitress to bring the check. When it arrived, Kerri snatched it up.

"This is on me," she said, relief returning a bit of sparkle to her hazel eyes. "I owe you, big time. The load of zingers you wrote almost makes up for the idiocy of the rest of the script."

"Almost?" I asked.

Kerri smirked. "That's what I said, didn't I?"

Chapter Eighteen

As they say in Hollywood, time flies when you're killing bimbos. From Friday to Sunday, in four frenzied days of filming, I'd stabbed three additional starlets to death with a butcher knife the size of a hothouse cucumber. As gruesome as that sounded, I'd enjoyed every second. It beat lying headless in a dumpster any day.

My fledgling acting career wasn't the only thing looking up for me. Other than catching Tad with some mysterious redhead at the beach cottage when I got home from the studio on Thursday night, I'd managed to keep Tad on mark with his lines and out of any major trouble.

Believe me, accomplishing this had required every spare second I had between film takes. Tad Longmire was such a diva that his idea of "roughing it" was lukewarm French fries. Despite Tad's numerous attempts to woo Kerri to his boudoir, she'd remained completely immune to his smarmy charms. I loved that about her.

And now, here it was. Monday morning. The last day of filming. After the past three 15-hour days, I was exhausted before I even climbed out of bed.

Despite feeling that my limbs were made of lead, the sound of tires crunching on the gravel outside the beach cottage sent me springing up out of the covers for a peek through the blinds. I spotted Kerri's silver Jaguar pulling up to the front porch.

She rolled down the window and waved.

I blanched.

Can she see me?

Then I realized she wasn't looking at me. She was waving toward the front of the cottage. My mind raced. It was barely daybreak. The sun was just coming up. Who could be out there at this hour?

OMG! Tad! Had he slept on the front porch again—naked?

I shot out of my bedroom and down the hallway. But it was too late. Through the French doors, I could see Tad's firm, meaty buttocks glowing in the pink rays of dawn. He was standing on the porch steps grinning and waving at Kerri.

God. Give. Me. Strength.

I bolted out the French doors, grabbed a pillow from a lounge chair, and placed it strategically over Tad's loins.

Calmly, Kerri climbed out of the Jag carrying a cardboard tray of Starbucks coffees. "Good morning, you two," she said, walking up and handing me a coffee.

As she passed by on her way toward the French doors, Kerri cocked her head and took a good, long look at Tad's naked ass. She didn't even smirk.

Man, that Kerri Middleton had poise.

• • • •

"SORRY AGAIN ABOUT TAD," I said.

Kerri and I were sitting on the porch sipping our coffees, waiting on the rest of the crew to arrive. "I do my best to keep an eye on Tad, but I'm not a machine. I have to sleep sometimes."

"I understand," Kerri said. "Perhaps staying at the cottage was a bad idea. We'll get you into the hotel when we wrap up filming today."

"No," I blurted, then caught myself. "Uh ... what I mean is, I actually like it here. And since you're renting it for the production anyway, it's a lot cheaper than us staying at that fancy hotel, right?"

"You're right about it being cheaper," Kerri said. "But we're not renting the cottage. Marshall's father owns it. So it's not actually costing us anything."

"Really?" I said, nearly choking on a sip of coffee. "The guy must be *loaded.*"

"There's no 'must be' about it," Kerri said, laughing. "Actually, if you want to stay a few extra days, I don't think he'd mind. Want me to arrange it?"

"I'd love to," I said. "But Tad can't wait to get out of here. I've already got our flights booked back to L.A. tomorrow morning."

"He doesn't like the beach?" Kerri asked, frowning. "I know we've been pushing him hard, filming the whole series in under two weeks. But he still gets his full pay. I thought he'd be pleased."

"It's not that," I said. "It's just that ... well, St. Petersburg isn't L.A."

"Really? What's L.A. got that we don't?"

"Something vital to Tad's quality of life," I said.

Kerri's eyebrow arched. "What?"

I leaned closer to Kerri. "There's no In-N-Out Burger."

She laughed. "I see."

I rolled my eyes. My contact lens slipped again.

"Ouch!" I muttered. "Stupid contact lens! Can you help me out?"

"Sure," Kerri said. "Then we'd better tell the emperor to put on some clothes. It's time to get this last day of filming in the can."

Chapter Nineteen

With the clock ticking down to D-day, everyone was scrambling around the set like fire ants trying to rebuild a kicked-in nest. Everyone *except Tad*, that was.

As usual, the "star of the show" had demanded every last one of his contractual perks and breaks—including his In-N-Out Burger substitute—a Wendy's shake, a Burger King Whopper, and a supersized McDonald's French fries.

But as it turned out, it wasn't Tad who'd ended up being the biggest pain in the butt on our final day of marathon filming. That distinction fell to the final femme fatale of the series, Fanny Smith—aka Fanny Tight. She was every bit the prima donna Tad was, with one exception.

Fanny was abysmal at acting.

After screwing up her line, she'd nearly ruined her makeup by spritzing herself with coconut water. I'd rushed to Fanny's aid with the special organic blotting tissues she'd demanded. While tamping her petulant forehead, Fanny spotted my pale blue eye, screamed, and shouted she was going to call 9-1-1 and report a zombie invasion.

Yeah. That really happened.

By the time the other crew members got her calmed down, I was pretty certain the only real assets Fanny had brought to the table were those 38 double-Ds in her bikini top.

Her part in the final scene couldn't have been simpler. Fanny was supposed to scream, then lie there while I stabbed her and delivered my punchlines. In my mind, it should've taken all of fifteen minutes to film. But even though the woman only had one line (a scream, no less), she kept screwing it up by breaking into a giggling fit.

We were now on hour four of shooting—and tempers were starting to flare. At 3:00 p.m., Marshall angrily announced that if we didn't get the shot completed within the next ten minutes, we were going to miss the deadline to deliver the four remaining episodes of *B&L* to Channel 22 by five o'clock today.

According to Marshall, if we didn't deliver on time, the project was dead. All I knew was that if I didn't get out of that sweltering old-man mask soon, *I'd* be dead as well.

Frustrated, I was ready to kill Fanny with my bare hands if she giggled again. I wasn't the only one for whom Fanny had lost her luster. Tommy and Marshall had stopped staring at her chest and begun glaring at her face. I took it as a sure sign the apocalypse was at hand.

"Come on, people, we can do this," Kerri announced, trying to inject some calm into the stormy set. She glanced at her watch and gulped.

"Are we too late?" I asked through the mask.

"Maybe," Kerri said. "Maybe not."

Fanny giggled.

"Dammit, Fanny!" Marshall hissed. "This isn't funny!"

"Look," Kerri said. "It's past three. Channel 22 just finished replaying the same pilot episode that aired Friday. At this point, they're pretty committed to running *B&L*. I'm going to call Bob Johnson and beg for an extension. I mean, what can he say?"

"Good idea," Marshall said.

"Good luck," I said as Kerri scurried out the door.

While Kerri begged for leniency, we kept filming. And, infuriatingly, Fanny kept giggling.

Talk about your incentive to murder someone ...

I think Marshall was about ready to stab Fanny himself when he was interrupted by Kerri's return.

"Bob's agreed to give us more time!" she beamed.

"Yes!" we all cheered.

"Don't celebrate just yet," Kerri said, holding up a finger. "The extension is based on one condition. Bob said that as long as the three new episodes we've finished are delivered to Channel 22 by five today, he'll give us until five tomorrow to deliver the final episode."

"You've got wicked negotiating skills, Kerri!" Marshall said, patting her on the back. "You saved us!" He turned to Fanny. "That should be no sweat, *right?*"

Fanny smiled sheepishly. "Sure." Then she giggled.

I gritted my teeth and glanced out the window. The sun was setting outside. We were all exhausted. Would this dingbat woman ever quit giggling like an idiot and give us a freaking break?

"Come on, crew," Tommy said. "This is the final scene for the series. Let's nail it with this next take, then go celebrate, okay?"

We all mumbled in agreement and took our places on the set. Fanny lay on the bed. I stood over her with the collapsible knife. But as soon as I raised my hand to stab her, Fanny giggled.

Again.

For the millionth time.

"Once more, from the top," Marshall said wearily.

I contemplated asking Marshall for a real knife. Then I recalled a nugget of the wisdom I'd gleaned from the *Hollywood Survival Guide*. Tip #39. *When you're ready to stick a fork into another cast member's eye, channel your rage into character inspiration.*

I envisioned Fanny lying headless in a dumpster.

"You know, Fanny dear," I said, raising the knife above her ridiculous, bulbous breasts for the umpteenth time. "You can be a *real* pain in the ass."

Fanny's lips began to curl into a smile. Before she could giggle again, I ripped off the rubber bingo-man mask and leaned over her until my bare, sweaty face was mere inches from hers. I glared into her mascara-laden peepers with my ghostly, pale-blue eye and hissed like a snake.

Fanny gasped. And I don't think she was acting.

Like a lightning strike, I raised the fake knife and plunged it into her chest. Tommy zoomed his camera in for a close-up of the action. I turned my face to the camera and let out a maniacal laugh, whirling my weird, mismatched eyes for all I was worth.

Suddenly, something cold and wet spurted across my face. Right on cue, Leslie the makeup girl had squeezed a rubber ketchup bottle full of fake blood at me. It splatted across my face in a perfect line.

"Yes! Yes! Yes!" Tommy screamed. "It's a wrap!"

"Wicked!" Marshall yelled. He rushed over and hugged me, getting fake blood on his expensive Hawaiian shirt.

"Sorry about ripping the mask off," I said. "But I figured we already had enough takes of it the other way. All we needed was to get the final shot without Fanny giggling like a deranged hyena."

"Great save, Doreen," Tommy said. "I don't think we could've gotten through this without you."

"What about me?" Tad said from his comfy chair in the corner. He was sipping an organic shake, his arms folded across his chest. "*I'm* the real hero here."

"Of course you are," I said, barely containing my disdain. "*Everyone* knows that."

"Here you go, *hero*," Leslie said, then shot Tad across the chest with the fake blood.

I smirked. I guess I wasn't the only one fed up with my boss's holier-than-thou crap.

"This is silk!" Tad growled. "The dry cleaning is coming out of *your* paycheck."

"It was worth it," Leslie said, and squirted Tad again.

"Uh, okay," Marshall said, grabbing Leslie by the arm. "We're all beat. Let's go home and get some rest."

"Fine by me," Tad grumbled.

He shot the two young girls a lewd look. They turned to each other, fake-gagged, and headed for the door. On their way out, I heard Leslie whisper to Fanny, "What a pig."

Marshall turned to me, grinning from ear to ear. "We got some great footage that time, Doreen." He leaned in and whispered in my ear, "Fanny may be a pain in the ass, but she really brought out your killer instinct! Your face on that last take was a real money shot!"

Uh, okay...

I glanced over at Tad, expecting him to be happy that I'd done so well. Nope. His face was the color of a ripe pomegranate. Or was that a ripe grenade?

Geez. I just survived a marathon filming session and now I have to soothe Tad's ego? This is bull hockey!

"I was merely the sideshow," I said loud enough for Tad to hear. "We all know the *real* star is *Tad*."

Tad sneered.

Seriously? Ugh. Grow up!

I turned to Kerri. "When you talked to Bob, did he mention anything about last Friday's audience numbers for the pilot?"

"Yes he did," Kerri said. "He said they weren't bad. But coming from Bob that could mean anything."

"Oh." I suddenly felt deflated. Kerri must've noticed.

"Chin up, Doreen," she said. Then she leaned in and whispered in my ear. "Johnson told me that if the audience gathers steam by the time the final episode airs this Friday, he may decide to run the whole serial again. Maybe even pick it up for another season."

My eyebrows rose an inch. "Seriously?"

"Yes, seriously. But keep that under your hat for now." Kerri turned and spoke loud enough for everyone else to hear. "You know, it wouldn't hurt for us to try and create some publicity for the show."

"Like what?" Tommy asked.

"Whatever might get us some traction on social media. Any ideas?"

"Yeah," Tad said, eyeing me angrily. "We could kill off Dorey."

"What?" I hissed. Anger shot through me. "How about we kill off *you*!"

"We need Doreen for next season," Marshall said, stepping between us. "If we get picked up, I mean."

Tad's eyes narrowed. "Won't you need *me*, too?"

"Of course," Kerri blurted. "That goes without saying."

I shot Kerri a *maybe it's time for you to get out of here* look. She got the hint. She reached out and shook Tad's hand. "Thank you for everything, Mr. Longmire."

Tad sighed. "Whatever."

Kerri turned to me. "We best be going. We've barely got more than an hour to get those episodes over to the station."

"I wish you luck," I said, the words catching in my throat. I'd been so busy the last three days I hadn't had time for the realization to sink in that the job with Sunshine City Studios was over. Most likely, I'd never see any of these people again. Except Tad, of course. I couldn't get rid of the jerk even if I wanted to. Life really could stick it to you sometimes.

"It's been great working with all of you," I said.

"The pleasure was ours," Kerri said. "I'm sorry to see you go."

"Yeah," Marshall said, handing me a beer. "I planned an after-party to celebrate tonight. I thought we'd be finished. But as long as we don't get too wasted, we should have enough brain cells left to finish editing the final episode tomorrow and get it to the studio by five, right Tommy?"

Tommy nodded. "Yeah, sure."

"So we'll see you and Tad at the Birchwood rooftop downtown for the party, right?" Marshall said. "Say, nine o'clock?"

I cringed. "I'm sorry. We can't. I glanced over at Tad. He was checking his cellphone and chugging a beer. "Uh ... our plane leaves for L.A. in the morning. I need to get Tad back to the cottage. We've got a long day of travel ahead."

"Of course," Kerri said. "We'll clear out of here and let you two get some rest." She took my hand. "Thanks again for convincing Tad to take the role. And for helping make the project a success. Let's stay in touch. I mean it."

"Okay," I said.

She shot me a friendly, maternal smile. "Have a safe journey home." She hooked Marshall by the arm. "Now we better go deliver those three episodes to Channel 22!"

"Get going, you two," Tommy said, then walked up and placed a hand on my shoulder. "Nice working with you, Doreen. I'm just gonna get a few shots of the outside of the cottage at sunset and I'll be out of your hair." He turned to Marshall and Kerri. "I'll see you at the Birchwood."

"I'll be out of reach most of tomorrow," I said as the three stepped off the porch and headed for their vehicles. Oddly, I already missed them. "But I'm available for a video meeting on Tuesday," I called out like a spinster hoping for a second date. "I'd love to preview the finale. I can't wait to see how it ends!"

"Wouldn't it be great if this turned out to be a hit?" Marshall yelled as he climbed into the passenger seat of Kerri's Jaguar.

I grinned. "It sure would."

Tad snickered behind me. "That load of crap? I wouldn't get my hopes up."

"Hush," I hissed.

"It sure would be great if it was a hit!" he said, mocking my voice. "You're such an ass kisser, Dorey."

I pursed my lips. "It's called *caring*, Tad. You should try it some time."

"Ha ha," he sneered. "Oh, by the way, speaking of *caring*, Dolores Benny cared enough to call me a couple of days ago."

My face went slack. "Ms. Benny? What did she want? She didn't accuse me of stealing something, did she?"

"No." A cruel smirk curled the corners of Tad's handsome mouth. "The crazy old bat asked me if I'd recommend you to play some stupid part in *Breaking Code*."

My mouth fell open. "What?"

Tad let out a sharp laugh. "Yeah. I told her you weren't interested. You were too busy doing your silly serial-killer side gig."

"You *what*?" I screeched.

Tad snorted. "Come on, Dorey. You're not big-screen material. You should be grateful Marshall wanted you for that lousy bit part in his TV series."

"That's not fair!"

"Isn't it?" Tad's ice-blue eyes cut through me. "Isn't that exactly what you told *me* to get me here? Isn't that why I'm in this stupid town filming this piece of crap?"

Insulting *me* was one thing. Insulting my friends and my acting career was quite another.

"Tad Longmire, I could *kill* you!" I screamed.

I raised my hand in anger, then realized the fake knife was still in it. I plunged the collapsible blade into his chest, almost wishing it were real. "You're a first-rate jackass! You know that?"

Tad laughed and grabbed my arm. "At least *I'm* first rate at *something*. Doesn't look like *you'll* ever be."

A car horn beeped. I glanced into the yard. Kerri's silver Jaguar was halfway down the drive. Marshall hung his head out the passenger window and yelled, "Everything okay over there?"

I fake-smiled and waved. "No," I muttered under my breath. "Not by a longshot."

Chapter Twenty

Screw the *Hollywood Survival Guide*. Sometimes when you've got nothing left to lose, you just freaking lose it.

After ripping into Tad with everything I had, he snatched my rubber knife from my hand. I jerked free of his grip and ran toward the beach. Halfway to the shoreline, I began frantically dialing Dolores Benny, hoping it wasn't too late to audition for the part she'd talked with Tad about in *Breaking Code*.

Two hours later, she hadn't returned any of my 38 messages.

I was so mad at Tad Longmire I could barely breathe.

For Kerri and Marshall's sake, I'd worked hard to keep my dirtbag boss in line. But filming was over. And so was my patience. Tad could now officially fall off a cliff for all I cared. I thought about Brent, the young man who should've had the role in *B&L*. Where was he now? Geez. Even if Kerri Middleton had chopped him into little pieces, I'd still think she was a better human being than Tad.

Still fuming, I marched over to a nearby convenience store and bought a bottle of wine to try and dull my anger. Afterward, I skulked back to the cottage, locked myself in my bedroom, packed my bags, and set the alarm for 6 a.m.

I tried calling Ma again, to let her know I was heading back to L.A. She didn't answer. I didn't leave a message. Instead, in desperate need of a good friend and a better mood, I surfed through Netflix until I found my old standby, *Bridget Jones' Diary*. I settled into bed and hit play.

Then, my good buddy Renee Zellweger and I downed a bottle of cabernet sauvignon and commiserated about men until I passed out cold.

• • • •

BUZZ.

I groaned.

Go away.

BUZZ BUZZ.

I rolled over in bed. My brain thumped against my skull.

BUZZ BUZZ.

I leaned over and slapped the little travel alarm clock until it finally shut up. I groaned again, then rolled over onto my back. My head throbbed with every pulse of my heart. To distract myself from the pain, I stared up at the ceiling and counted the tiles. Thirty-eight. That done, I did a bit more math in my head.

I didn't like the outcome.

I still had eleven months and eight days left to serve on my sentence as Tad Longmire's personal assistant.

Crap!

I sat up in bed. My head pounded as if it had just been slugged with a rubber mallet.

Ugh. With any luck, the plane to L.A. will crash and put me out of my misery ...

In a hangover daze, I got up and stumbled to the kitchen for some much needed coffee.

Why on earth hasn't someone invented a coffee IV bag already?

As I fumbled with the coffee filters, I noticed it was 6:15. Mercifully, there was still plenty of time to let the aspirin do its work before Tad and I had to catch the limo to the airport. It was scheduled to arrive at 7:30.

For ten minutes, I sat at the kitchen table, my head in my hands, and let the coffee and pain relievers kick in. Feeling slightly better, I shuffled over to Tad's bedroom door in my fuzzy slippers.

"Get up, Tad," I shouted through the door. "It's time to get going!" Not my most brilliant move. Yelling at him had set off the throbbing in my head again.

Through the door, Tad muttered something I couldn't make out. Knowing him, it was an obscenity. I leaned an ear against the door and listened to be sure. I heard a grunt. Then a woman giggle. My teeth began to grind.

You've got a girl in there? You've got to be kidding me!

"Wrap it up in there," I said. "We have to be out of here in an hour."

"Unbelievable," I muttered over and over as I took a quick shower. I dreaded the trip back to L.A. with Tad. The guy couldn't keep his hands to himself if his life depended on it. And what a control freak! If I had my way, I'd dress for today's travel day in comfy yoga pants and a t-shirt. But as Tad's assistant, he insisted I always appear "professional and sexy," so as not to tarnish his image as a player, I guess.

I begrudgingly pulled on a pair of slacks, a silk shirt, and strappy heels. After fixing my hair and applying the minimal obligatory amount of eyeliner and lipstick, I closed my suitcase and dragged it out into the living room. That done, I glanced over at the coffee I'd set on the kitchen counter for Tad. He hadn't touched it.

Geez Louise! What a turd!

I marched back to Tad's bedroom in a fury. The grunts and groans emanating from behind his door could've made the perfect soundtrack for a porno film. Disgusted, I raised my fist and banged on the door. It swung open.

Cringing, I hazarded a peek inside, hoping I wouldn't get an eyeful of something I couldn't un-see. Tad was still in bed, moaning and sighing. Mercifully, the covers were pulled up over him, so at least I didn't have to un-see *that*.

Anger surged through me anew as I wondered which of the beach bimbos he'd lured into his bed *this* time. My money was on Fanny Tight, the big-boobed pain in the ass. She was a dye-job redhead and dumb as a box of rocks.

Perfect Tad bait.

"Get up, Tad," I grumbled. "You've only got a little over half an hour left to get ready."

He didn't respond. I glanced over at the TV. A dirty movie was playing. I gritted my teeth.

The stupid jerk is pranking me!

"Ha ha. Very funny," I spat. "I get it. The joke's always on me. Now get up. We've got a limo to catch!"

I jerked back the duvet. Tad stared up at me, a stupid, googly-eyed expression on his face. His hands were wrapped around the handle of the fake knife, which he pretended was stuck in the middle of his chest.

"Seriously, Tad?" I growled. "This isn't funny. If you're not ready when the limo comes, I'm leaving without you. I'm serious!"

Tad just stared at me, that stupid grin on his face. Then I saw it. The blood-soaked sheets underneath him.

"Tad!" I screamed. "Tad! Are you all right?" I tried to loosen the knife from his hands and pull it out of his chest. But Tad's hands were cold and stiff. The knife wouldn't budge.

Oh. My. God! This is real!

Panic shot through me like ice water.

Someone's murdered Tad! Are they still here?

Am I next?

I gulped against the hard knot in my throat and slowly backed out of the room. The second my backside hit the doorjamb, I turned and fled down the hall, my heart pounding in my ears like an underwater drum solo.

I gotta get out of here! I gotta call someone!

With the last grain of wits I had left about me, I grabbed my purse off the kitchen table and bolted for the French doors.

I never made it.

Three steps from safety, I slammed into a dark figure in the living room. He grabbed me by both arms and wouldn't let go.

Chapter Twenty-One

"Let me go!" I screamed as I struggled with the unknown intruder in the dim light of the beach cottage's living room.

"Calm down, lady!" the man said, holding me by the wrists as I squirmed, trying to break free.

"Please!" I pleaded. "Don't kill me!"

"Kill you?" the man said. "Come on, my driving isn't *that* bad."

"Wha??" I asked, confused and on the verge of hysteria.

"I'm the limo driver," he said. He released one of my wrists from his vice-like grip. As I stared at him like a stunned sheep at the slaughterhouse gates, he reached into his jacket. I flinched, expecting a gun or a knife. Instead, he pulled out a business card.

"I'm Darryl Fin. From Florida Limos. Somebody called about a ride to the airport?"

I nearly fainted from relief. "What are you doing here so ... so *early?*"

"Trying to beat rush-hour traffic," he said. "The door was open. I thought I might come in and get some coffee while I waited. But then I heard someone screaming bloody murder, and you came running at me."

"Oh. Sorry." I felt both stiff and limp at the same time—as if I couldn't move, but might collapse on the floor any second.

The driver let go of my other wrist and I nearly toppled over. "You okay?" he asked. "Wait. What's all over your hands?"

I looked down. It was blood. My hands were covered in Tad's blood.

"Help," I whispered, suddenly unable to breathe. "Call the police. Somebody murdered my boss."

The driver eyed me as if I might be deranged. "Where?"

"In the bedroom."

"Uh ... stay here. Don't move." He slipped past me and cautiously made his way down the hall to Tad's bedroom. I watched, frozen in place, as he took a peek inside.

"Holy hell!" he yelled. "I'm calling 9-1-1!"

* * * *

DARRYL THE LIMO GUY stayed with me until the police arrived. He stood beside the limo, nervously smoking one cigarette after the other. I sat on the front steps of the cottage, shivering and blinking back tears as I watched the sun rise on a new day without Tad Longmire in it.

After what seemed like forever, two police cruisers came racing up the driveway. A tall, slim black man in a blue uniform jumped out of the lead car.

"Where's the victim?" he asked.

"He's in there," I said weakly, pointing to the French doors.

The cop looked me over for a moment, then sprinted inside the cottage, gun drawn. The second cop stood guard over Darryl and me, his hand at the ready on his revolver.

After a minute or so, the first cop reappeared on the cottage porch. "All clear, Rainy," he said to the other cop. "One DB. Second door to the left. Call forensics." He knelt down on one knee beside me on the steps. "What's your name?"

"Uh ... Doreen Diller."

"I'm Sergeant McNulty." He glanced at my hands. "Are you injured?"

"Uh ... no. I don't think so."

"Okay. Tell me what happened, to the best of your recollection."

I glanced over at Darryl. "Where do I start?"

"Rainy," McNulty said, shooting the other cop a stern look. "Take the driver's statement over by your patrol car."

"Yes, sir," Officer Rainy said, then led Darryl out of earshot.

Sergeant McNulty watched them go, then turned his attention back to me. "Do you know the man inside?"

"Yes. He's Tad Longmire."

"What's your relationship to him?"

"He's my boss."

"Can you explain what happened to him?"

"No. I found him like that this morning. I thought it was a joke."

"A joke?"

"You see, last night I was playing around with the knife. I told Tad I wanted to kill him. So when I found him I thought he was pranking me ..."

I stared at the blood on my hands and crumpled. "Can I go wash my hands? Please?"

"No. Not yet." McNulty took me by the arm and stood me up on the steps. "Come with me." He walked me over to his police cruiser and opened the back door. "Get in, Ms. Diller."

"Where are we going?" I asked.

"To the police station."

I cringed. "What for?"

His brow furrowed. "Lady, do you really have to ask?"

Chapter Twenty-Two

"So let me get this straight," Sergeant McNulty said, his knuckles ashen as they pressed against the metal interrogation table he was leaning across. "You're telling me you slept through a homicide that occurred in the bedroom right next to yours?"

"Well, yes," I said.

Technicians had already confiscated my purse, swabbed my hands, collected fingerprints, and stripped me nearly naked to check for fresh wounds and bruises. Then they'd photographed me both front and sideways for what I assumed were *not* new headshots for my acting portfolio.

After processing was done, I was carted off to a very small room that smelled of stale coffee, urine, and desperation. Still numb from the shock of Tad's death, I rubbed my trembling, purple fingertips together. To stop my thighs from shaking, I wrapped my ankles around the front legs of the hard, metal chair I'd been directed to sit on.

"How is it possible you didn't hear a thing?" McNulty asked.

I looked up at the police sergeant. "Well, you see, I'd been watching TV and ... uh ... drinking."

He blew out a breath. "What were you watching and drinking?"

"*Bridget Jones* ... and a very nice bottle of cabernet sauvignon."

A vein on McNulty's temple began to pulse. "Right. So you're saying you got drunk and fell fast asleep. Then what?"

"My alarm went off at six. I got up, made coffee, and took a shower."

"Not hearing or suspecting a thing."

I nodded. "That's right."

"So, did you stab Mr. Longmire *before* or *after* you took the shower?"

I blanched. "What? Neither! I mean ... that doesn't make sense. Why would I take a shower and wash off the blood only to get myself all bloody again?"

The corners of McNulty's mouth curled slightly upward. "So you took the shower to wash off the blood *after* the attack."

"No! That's not what I meant! I was only saying it makes no sense—"

The hard look on McNulty's face made my voice trail off.

"Look," I said. "When I first went to wake up Tad, I heard groaning. And a woman giggling. I thought Tad was having sex. He ... uh ... did that a lot. So I yelled through the door for him to hurry up or something like that, then I went and got a shower."

"Hurry up?"

"We have ... uh *had* ... a flight at ten this morning back to L.A."

McNulty eyed me carefully. "Ms. Diller, were you and Longmire lovers?"

I nearly choked. "He was my employer."

"That's not what I asked."

"No. We weren't lovers."

"Never? Not even once?"

I shook my head. "Not even once."

McNulty scrutinized me with his dark brown eyes. "I hear the guy is some kind of TV heartthrob. It must've been hard to resist his charms."

"Okay," I said. "I'll admit it kind of was. Before I met Tad, I had a crush on him for years. But that ended when I got to know him. He's actually a real jerk."

"What do you mean by 'real jerk'?"

"He's mean-spirited. Lecherous. And a philanderer. And yesterday I found out he cost me a big acting role back in L.A. It quite possibly could've been my big break!"

McNulty's tone sharpened. "So you were angry at him."

"Yes."

"Angry enough to stab him in the heart with a butcher knife?"

I stared, wide-eyed. "Come on. You don't really think—"

"I'm not sure *what* to think, Ms. Diller. "That's why we're having this conversation."

The way he was looking at me, I had a feeling McNulty already knew *exactly* what to think. And it didn't appear I was winning his vote for the Miss Goody Two-Shoes Award.

Backed into a corner, I desperately rifled through the *Hollywood Survival Guide* in my mind. Tip #67 popped up. *Before you dig your own grave, call a lawyer with a sharper shovel.*

"I ... I don't want to say any more without someone here with me," I said.

McNulty let out a disgusted-sounding grunt. "Are you requesting legal representation, Ms. Diller?"

"Shouldn't I?"

The cop's eyes narrowed. "If that's the way you want to play it."

"Play it?" I gasped. "I'm not *playing* anything! Hey, don't I get a phone call or something?"

"No."

"Why not?"

"Because you're not under arrest."

I blanched. "I'm *not*?"

"Not *yet*, no," McNulty said.

I frowned. "What's *that* supposed to mean?"

"It means you're free to go—for now, Ms. Diller."

"I am?"

"Unless you'd like to recant your request for legal representation."

I shook my head. "I don't know. I need to think about it."

"By law, that *is* your right." McNulty opened the door to the tiny room. "Thank you for your cooperation. I'd advise you not to leave town until we've cleared you to do so. I have a feeling we're going to need you for more questioning."

"Uh ... okay," I said, scrambling up from the chair.

McNulty handed me a business card. "We'll be in touch. In the meantime, you can reach me here if you have further information you'd like to share."

"What about my purse and my cellphone?" I asked as I brushed by him and out into the hallway.

"They should be done processing them by now. You can pick up your personal effects at the reception window on the way out."

• • • •

OUT IN THE HALLWAY, I stumbled into Darryl Fin, the limo driver. He was dumping the contents of a manila envelope into his hands. Out tumbled his wallet, a watch, and his cellphone.

"I see they took *your* phone, too," I said.

"And my black shirt I needed for work." Darryl pulled at the tight black T-shirt he'd worn underneath his other shirt. "They confiscated it for evidence. It had your bloody handprints on it."

"Oh. Sorry," I said. "Do they think you're a suspect?"

He grimaced. "If they don't, they sure left me wondering. How about you?"

"Yeah. I feel the same. Guilty until proven innocent."

"Tough break for us," he said. "Hey, if you ever need another ride, do me a favor and *don't* give me a call. The last one totally wasn't worth it."

"Geez!" I said. "I totally forgot. I need to pay you for the ride to the airport."

He shot me a pained smile. "Don't sweat it. Send me a get-out-of-jail-free card instead, and I'll do the same for you."

• • • •

AS I WAITED IN LINE to pick up my cellphone, Kerri walked into the station. I nearly leapt for joy at seeing a friendly face.

"Kerri!" I called out. "You came!"

She saw me, winced out a smile, and came rushing over, her arms open wide. "It's so awful about Tad. I came as soon as I heard."

"Thanks. I ... I don't know what happened. But I'm pretty sure the police think I did it."

"Seriously?" Kerri said. "Why?"

"Who's this?" a voice sounded behind me. I turned to see Officer McNulty eyeing Kerri.

Kerri straightened to her full height. "I'm Kerri Middleton."

McNulty's eyebrow angled upward slightly. "And your relationship to Ms. Diller?"

"Work colleague. And friend."

"Right," he said. "Would you mind stepping inside my office for a moment?"

• • • •

I SAT ON A HARD BENCH in the corridor of the police station for half an hour, watching what passed for humanity come and go through the front door. But who was I to talk? I was a stranger in a strange town, and had just been declared a murder suspect! I'd never felt so small and lost and afraid.

I was about to start bawling when Kerri finally returned, escorted by McNulty. She looked pale.

"Keep my card handy," McNulty said, then shot me a dubious look. "You may need it."

"What did he say to you?" I asked as he walked away.

Kerri leaned close and whispered, "Not here. Come with me."

"Where are we going?" I whispered back. She didn't answer.

I followed Kerri down the corridor like an orphaned puppy. "McNulty told me not to leave town," I whispered. "I guess I need to find a place to stay for a few days."

"I'm sorry, but you can't go back to the beach cottage," Kerri said as we walked past a line of people sitting in the front lobby. "Marshall called and said it's a crime scene now. It's swarming with police investigators. I guess that just leaves my place."

I cringed. "I know it looks bad for me, Kerri. And you barely know me. If you don't want to take me into your home, I totally understand."

Kerri turned and put a hand on my shoulder. "Look. Being a news anchor taught me that people are capable of just about anything." Her eyes darted around. "This place is living proof."

"I hope you don't count me in this lot," I said.

Kerri looked into my eyes. "Let me tell you this, Doreen. You don't work in the business as long as I have and not learn how to tell a good guy from a bad guy. You just don't strike me as a murderer."

My knees nearly buckled from relief. "Thank you!" I cried. "Thank you for believing me. I only wish Sergeant McNulty did."

"Come on," Kerri said. "Let's get out of here before the news channels pick up on this and all hell breaks loose."

She swung open the door to the police station.

A barrage of blinding lights flashed in our faces.

A crop of microphones crackled to life.

Then a pack of reporters fell upon us like ambush predators closing in for the kill.

Chapter Twenty-Three

I stood, mouth agape, and stared in utter shock and awe at the crowd of reporters racing toward us like Kerri and I were the finish line. I'd often dreamt of being chased by the paparazzi—but that had been for winning an Oscar, not for being the prime suspect in a celebrity murder.

Not quite the same thing.

"Are you involved in the Tad Longmire case?" one of the news crew shouted from the gathering horde.

"Crap," Kerri hissed. "The word is out."

She shoved me back inside the police station, snatched a magazine from a table in the lobby, and said, "Here, cover your face with this."

"Got it," I said. Mimicking all the celebrity duck-and-cover videos I'd seen, I tucked my head and buried my face behind the magazine.

"Here we go," Kerri said, grabbing my hand to guide me. She kicked open the door and yelled, "Run!"

Then she nearly yanked my arm off.

Together we raced toward the parking lot, worming our way through the gauntlet of reporters' elbows and the cameras and microphones they jammed into our faces. Somehow, we made it to Kerri's Jaguar. We scrambled inside and locked the doors. Hands and faces filled the windows like a scene from *The Twilight Zone*.

"Now what?" I asked, confused and out of breath.

"Get down," Kerri said calmly.

She motioned for me to crouch down onto the passenger-side floorboard. I obeyed. A second later, she punched the gas and peeled out of the lot, trailing a ragtag parade of news vans and sketchy vehicles behind us.

• • • •

CRAMMED INTO THE SPACE between the passenger seat and the dashboard, it wasn't long before my left calf began to cramp. I looked up from Kerri's Gucci pumps mashing the gas pedal and said, "I think my foot is turning gangrenous."

The tension in Kerri's face relaxed a notch. "Sorry. Looks like we've lost most of the press. You can get up now. We're almost there."

"Thanks for saving me," I said as I extricated myself from the floorboard of the Jaguar and slowly straightened my body up and into the passenger seat.

To my surprise, Kerri was pulling up to an impressive, stucco guardhouse surrounded by tropical foliage. A huge iron gate blocked our entry into what appeared to be a hoity-toity paradise for the rich and famous.

"Ms. Middleton," a man in uniform said, smiling at her as she rolled down the window. "Nice to see you. Who's your guest?"

"Hi, Charlie. She's an old friend. Hey, I'm in a bit of a hurry today. No time to chat."

Charlie nodded and scribbled something onto a clipboard. "No worries. You two have a nice day." He reached over and punched a button. The massive metal gate swung open. Kerri sped inside, then stopped. She watched in the rearview mirror until the gate closed and locked back into place.

"Whew," she sighed. "Looks like we lost them."

"Thank you again," I said. "Without you, I'd be on the front page of every tabloid still in print."

"Bad news travels fast," Kerri quipped.

I glanced around. "Wow. This place is really posh!"

All around, lush tropical palms and flowering bushes formed oases in the sea of emerald-green grass. A fountain spouted water in a scallop-shell pattern from the middle of a small lake.

"It's all right," Kerri said, hitting the gas. "But the best part about Scallop Lake is that it's safe." She blew out a breath. "You know, I never was one for gated communities until I landed the job as a news anchor. Once you get a little famous, the psychos seem to come out of the woodwork."

"I know what you mean," I said, gawking at the elegant, Spanish-style mansions lining each side of the road. Everything—even down to the length of the grass blades—was perfect.

"The general public is bad enough," Kerri said, pulling into the driveway of a two-story Mediterranean house covered in swirly, pink stucco. "But give somebody a press pass and a microphone, and you have the makings of a petty dictator."

"Whoa. I never thought about it like that."

Kerri cut the ignition and turned to me. "Be careful what you ask for, Doreen. Take it from me. Fame, no matter how fleeting, can be a real bitch."

* * * *

SAFE INSIDE KERRI'S beautiful home, I'd spent Monday afternoon making phone calls to friends and associates back in L.A. to let them know Tad was dead. Oddly, none of them seemed that surprised—especially Tad's attorney, Ralph Steinberger.

"I was expecting something like this," he said.

"You were?" I asked. "Why?"

"Let's just say Tad knew how to irritate people."

I grimaced. "I can't argue with that. I guess that means I'm freed from my contract?"

"Yes. I'll send you a letter to that effect. Email okay?"

"Yes. Thank you. Will I get paid any kind of severance?"

"Don't worry, Ms. Diller. I'll make sure you get what's coming to you."

"Uh ... thanks."

"Good day," he said, then clicked off the phone.

"Who was that?" Kerri asked as I hung up.

"Tad's attorney. He's going to make the arrangements for his body to be shipped back to L.A. once it's released from the coroner's office."

"Will there be a funeral?" she asked.

I shook my head sadly. "No. Just a memorial service. He said Tad was too famous to have a funeral. What did he mean by that?"

"Too many nut jobs," Kerri said. "Like I told you, fame can be a mixed blessing. You hungry? I ordered pizza."

I suddenly realized I was famished. "Pizza sounds great!"

The doorbell buzzed. Kerri smiled. "I told Charlie to let the pizza guy through. That must be him now." She walked over to the front door and looked through the peephole. She frowned, then she mashed an intercom button. "Who's there?"

"Pizza guy," a voice sounded through the speaker.

Kerri's nose crinkled. "Take off the hoodie. Let me see your face." She shook her head. "Nice try, Brad. But I'm not opening the door."

"Come on, Kerri," the man said. "Just five minutes. That's all I'm asking."

"Not happening. Leave the pizza on the steps and I won't report you to the guard *or* your boss." Kerri stared through the peephole for another minute or so, then opened the door. She grabbed the pizza, and quickly shut and locked the door behind her.

"Who was that?" I asked.

"Brad Teller from Channel 7," she said. "Just your typical second-string reporter willing to sell his soul to make it to the next rung."

I nodded. "That was a pretty clever trick."

Kerri laughed. "Yeah. Can't say I haven't done the same thing myself. As a former reporter, I know all their sleazy tactics. I also know they have the upper hand on me."

"What do you mean?"

"They know where I live."

"Oh. So, what do we do now?" I asked.

"Keep the drapes pulled and we should be okay."

I followed Kerri into the living room. She put the pizza box on the coffee table in front of the sofa. "You want a Coke?"

"Sure. Let me help."

"Nothing to it. Help yourself to a slice before it gets cold."

"Thanks." When Kerri came back with the sodas, I hung my head.

"I'm so sorry about inconveniencing you like this, Kerri. I'd leave on the next plane out, but Sergeant McNulty told me I couldn't. I think I'm his main suspect. They found me with Tad's blood on my hands. It doesn't look good for me."

"Don't give up on yourself just yet," she said.

I tried to look nonchalant, but I was dying to know. "What did he ask you about back at the station?"

Kerri opened the pizza box and took a slice. "He asked me what I knew about Tad's and your relationship."

"What did you say?"

Kerri winced. "I had to be honest with him, Doreen. I told him the afternoon before the murder, I'd offered to put you up in a hotel, but you wanted to stay at the cottage."

"That's fine," I said. "It's true."

"I also had to tell him that the last time I saw Tad alive, you were screaming in his face that you were going to kill him."

My jaw dropped. "I'm doomed."

"Not if you're innocent."

"I am! But the evidence doesn't look good. I was in the room next to him when it happened. I slept through him being stabbed! Why didn't they stab me, too?"

I shook my head. "My hands were bloody from touching the knife in his chest, Kerri. And the only alibi I have is that I was watching Netflix, drunk. The media is going to crucify me!"

Kerri scrunched her face sympathetically. "Maybe not. Let's turn on the news and see what they know."

She clicked the TV remote. The screen blinked on, revealing a news desk with the emblem Channel 22 on it. A guy with a walrus moustache and matching waistline was sitting next to a stunning young blonde.

"That's anchorman Paul Fenderman," Kerri said, disdain marring her usually serene face. "I used to occupy the seat next to him until I aged out. Did I tell you his breath smells like sardines and day-old coffee?"

"Police report they have suspects, but they're not saying who," Fenderman's voice boomed from the screen. "What have you been able to find out, Tegan?"

"*Tegan?*" I said as if it were a curse word. "Ugh."

"Exactly," Kerri said.

"Yes, Paul!" Tegan gushed. "What was Tad Longmire, bad-boy heartthrob of *Days of Our Lies* doing in St. Pete?" Her voice squealed with naughtiness. "Some are specul ... speca ... *thinking* he was here on a secret rendezvous."

Kerri turned to me. "Could Tad have been meeting someone in secret while you were here?"

"Hardly," I said. "Tad had plenty of uh ... *rendezvous*, as you no doubt bore witness too. But Tad didn't keep secrets. He never thought anything he did was wrong, so where was the need? That's the reason he lost his last job, you know. He was caught boning the director's wife in broad daylight."

"I heard," Kerri said. "I'll be honest with you, Doreen. You sound angry. And perhaps even a bit jealous. Are you being straight with me when you say you and he didn't have something going on?"

"Yes," I said. "I'm angry because the guy ruined my life! Why would you even *think* that I'd sleep with him?"

"Well, I saw your hand on his knee once. Then Tad was naked on the front porch the other morning. Not to mention the constant barrage of innuendoes he kept flinging at you. Then there was the punched nose. The black eye ..."

"You think ... I never *hit* Tad!" I shook my head, bewildered. "Look. Sure, I had a crush on him at one time. But it took me less than an hour to figure out Tad was a horn-dog. For him, getting lucky with the ladies is just a numbers game. I felt like punching him out plenty of times. But I never acted on it."

Kerri nodded. "Okay. So, explain to me why you were screaming that you wanted to kill him last night?"

I crumpled back onto the couch. "I've been waiting *fifteen years* for someone to offer me a part in a movie. Last week, someone called Tad asking him for a recommendation for me. It was for a part in an action flick being filmed right now in Hollywood called *Breaking Code*. That part could've been my big break, Kerri. Maybe my only chance to hit the big time. But Tad blew them off, saying I wasn't interested."

Kerri blanched. "What a jerk! Why would he *do* that?"

"Out of spite, maybe. Or jealousy."

Kerri shook her head. "I don't understand."

I looked up at Kerri. "Tad was peeved that I was getting more attention from you guys than he was."

Kerri blew out a breath. "Men."

"There's no way I'd sleep with Tad. Like you said, he was a jerk. Besides, keeping Tad out of my pants was job security insurance number one."

Kerri's eyebrow rose. "Usually in this business it's the other way around."

I locked eyes with her. "I didn't say he didn't *try*."

"Well, once you reach my age, you won't have to worry about that anymore."

"As beautiful as you are? I'd say I find that hard to believe, except I've done the math."

"The math?"

"Yeah. Did you see the latest movie by Paramoral Films, *Baby my Baby*?"

Kerri shook her head. "No."

"Don't bother. Here's the gist. Gorgeous, blonde, 29-year-old hottie falls for 58-year-old barely passable gasbag twice her age. He's a lout and a loser, but she can't get enough of him."

Kerri groaned. "Not another one."

"Yep." I shook my head in disgust. "Ugh! I'm *so sick of it*! If the roles were reversed, the guy would have to date someone *116 years old*. We're talking *Tales from the Crypt*, here!"

"Typical misogynistic bull crap," Kerri sighed.

"Exactly. Tad's 40. I'm 39. I'd be lucky to get a part playing his mother!"

"You're right. But take my advice. *Let it go.*"

"Let it go? Why?"

"Because, in case you forgot, we have bigger fish to fry at the moment. You look worn out. Why don't you try and get some sleep?"

"Who can sleep with this going on?"

"I know," Kerri said. "But we're all exhausted from four days of nonstop filming. We can't think straight. I realize things look bad right now, but don't forget, you have an ace in the hole."

I blanched. "I *do*?"

"Yes," Kerri said. "You're innocent."

Oh. Right.

"You *are* innocent, aren't you?" Kerri asked.

I smiled weakly. "Of course. Of course I am!"

Chapter Twenty-Four

"Who would want to kill Tad?" I asked Kerri, putting voice to the question that had been silently plaguing both my thoughts and my dreams since finding my boss stabbed to death yesterday morning.

Kerri was perched on a barstool at her spotless granite kitchen counter, sipping coffee and tapping away on her laptop. Even though it was barely dawn, she was glamorously put together in a matching pink-satin loungewear ensemble. By comparison, I was dressed in rumpled sweatpants and T-shirt, looking as if I'd just tumbled out of a dirty clothes hamper at a homeless shelter.

"The question is who *wouldn't* want to kill him?" Kerri asked, looking up from her computer.

"What do you mean?" I reached for the cup she'd set out for me on the counter next to the coffee machine.

"Come look at this." She spun the laptop around so I could see the screen. "There's an entire AboutFace page dedicated to *Tad's a Cad*—a fan page for Tad Longmire haters."

I gawked at an image of Tad in an unflattering, leering, drunken pose. "Geez. There's like, over a thousand members!"

"Yes," Kerri said, her eyes darting up to mine. "See? Fame cuts both ways." She grimaced. "Sorry. I didn't mean to make a pun."

"Huh? Oh. It's okay." I shook my head. "I still can't believe Tad's really dead."

"Me, either. Well, he certainly won't be starring in any more episodes of *B&L*."

"Oh my gosh!" I blurted. "I completely forgot. What about the edits for the series finale? Weren't they due yesterday?"

"Yes. But don't worry. Marshall said he took care of it." Kerri looked away and smiled wistfully. "You know, that's one advantage of being young ... and a man. Ambition can overcome emotion. If it had been up to me alone, I'm not sure I could've gotten through the edits yesterday."

"I don't think I could either," I said, pouring myself a cup of coffee.

Kerri smiled wistfully. "Anyway, I'm proud of Marshall. He supervised Tommy through the entire editing process. The two of them got the project delivered to Channel 22 all on their own."

She let out a small laugh. "Maybe I'm not the only grownup in the room after all."

I smiled and touched her arm. "Thank you again for saving me yesterday. I'm sorry you missed out on supervising the final episode."

"It's fine, really. I was there for the first part of it."

"And?" I asked.

Kerri shrugged. "Honestly? It was just like the others. A bit hokey, a bit sexy, and no brain cells were harmed in the making of it."

I laughed. Kerri smiled at me. "You know, Doreen, without the wry humor we wrote into your killer's lines, to me the whole project would be ultimately forgettable. But do you think that you or I will get any credit? I, for one, am not holding my breath."

I crinkled my nose. "Maybe it's just as well if *B&L is* forgotten. Without Tad, the series is dead anyway, whether the station offers to pick it up or not."

Kerri's hazel eyes found my mismatched pair. "That's what happens when you kill off the heartthrob, Ms. Killigan."

Even though I was pretty sure Kerri was just joking, her words jabbed at my heart, rekindling the panic I'd felt yesterday after Sergeant McNulty had insinuated I was responsible for Tad's death. I didn't do it. But who did?

I needed to figure that out in order to save my own skin. So far, the only other lead I had was sitting across from me. If Kerri did away with Brent, she could certainly do-in Tad as well. It felt weird to even entertain the thought. Kerri had been so nice to me. But then again, according to the documentaries I'd watched, serial killers could seem absolutely normal.

"You know," I said, "I've been meaning to ask you about the guy who Tad replaced. Brent something? Whatever happened to him?"

Kerri pursed her lips. "Well, I—"

My cellphone rang. "Hold on," I said as I grabbed it up. The screen showed it was the St. Petersburg Police Department. "I better get this."

Kerri nodded. "Go ahead."

"Hello?" I said into the phone.

"Ms. Diller? Sergeant McNulty here. I need you to come in today at one o'clock for more questioning."

"Uh ... sure. Have you found something else?"

"Like what?"

I cringed. "I don't know. That's *your* job, isn't it?"

"We're working on it. So, I'll see you at one?"

"Sure. Anything I can do to help."

"Good. When you come, bring any receipts you have with you. Travel vouchers, airline tickets, and the like. We'll need to verify your whereabouts on Monday afternoon through Tuesday morning."

"Uh ... sure thing."

McNulty clicked off. I looked up at Kerri. Her face was lined with worry.

"What's wrong?" I asked.

"Look, I'm sorry to ask, but have you got anywhere else you can go?"

"I ... uh ... I guess so," I said.

The look on Kerri's face knocked the wind from my sails. I'd begun to worry she might be Tad's murderer. Now I was afraid she thought *I* might be. Geez. Tad had been dead for barely a day and suspicions were popping up everywhere like toadstools after a rain.

"Are you worried that I killed Tad?" I asked.

"What? No!" Kerri said, shaking her head. "We just need to get you out of here. While you were on the phone, Charlie at the front gate called. The entire entrance is overrun with news vans."

"Oh." I cringed. "What are we going to do? They know your car. And I don't have one."

Kerri's lips twisted in thought. "How do you feel about bagels?"

• • • •

IT WAS ANOTHER CLEVER idea from Kerri. She called a food delivery service. Twenty minutes later, a guy who barely spoke English came to the door with a bag of bagels. Tempted by a crisp fifty-dollar bill, Paco was more than happy to smuggle me out of Kerri's place in the trunk of his car.

"Message me when you get there," Kerri said as I lugged my suitcase into the junk-filled trunk of Paco's light blue Chevy Caprice.

"I will," I said. I handed him a slip of paper with an address, then climbed into the trunk next to my bag.

Kerri waved goodbye. As Paco closed the trunk lid, I saw her note down his license plate—in case she never heard from me again.

The address I'd given Paco was the only other one I knew in St. Petersburg. As he took off, I bounced around inside the dark, smelly trunk, chewing on a mouthful of onion bagel. The absurdity of my situation made me laugh, albeit with a tinge of hysteria.

To calm myself, I used my phone light to search through my *Hollywood Survival Guide*. I wanted to see if it offered any advice on what to do when trapped inside the trunk of a car.

Surprisingly, it did.

Tip #84 read: *When forced into a car trunk, call 9-1-1. No phone? Search the crevices for a weapon to whack your abductor with when he lifts the lid.*

I found a weapon, just in case. Then, in lieu of 9-1-1, I dialed the number Ma had texted me a week ago. As it rang, I crossed my fingers and said a short prayer.

Hopefully, Aunt Edna would be a lot more accommodating than my own mother had been.

Chapter Twenty-Five

I t was nearly ten o'clock when Paco's Chevy Caprice came to a lurching halt. Uncertain if I'd just been driven to Aunt Edna's place or to a serial killer's lair, I followed the advice in the *Hollywood Survival Guide* and armed myself with a rusty old wiper blade.

Fortunately, I didn't need to use it. True to his word, Paco opened the trunk and helped me out, no questions asked. As he drove away, I texted Kerri the code we'd agreed upon if all had gone according to plan.

The chick has hatched.

My phone pinged immediately with her reply.

Hope the new coop is nice. Keep me posted.

After being unceremoniously dumped from Paco's trunk, I glanced around. The neighborhood looked decent enough. Not nearly as posh as Kerri's place, but it was well-kept.

I could see the top floors of some high-rise condos at the end of the street and realized it was an older, mixed-use suburb near downtown St. Pete. On either side of the road, two-story block apartment buildings sat tucked amidst rows of cute, wood-frame bungalows in various states of renovation.

As for the address Aunt Edna had given me, it turned out not to be a house at all, but a collection of four small, single-story cottages encircling a common courtyard. A small, wooden sign by the walkway read, *Palm Court Cottages. No Solicitors.*

When I'd talked to her over the phone, Aunt Edna had said she was number one. I thought she'd been bragging or telling some kind of joke that had gone over my head. Now, seeing the place, I figured she must've meant she lived in cottage apartment number one.

Not wanting to show up on her doorstep toting luggage like some transient hobo, I stashed my suitcase behind an azalea bush. That sorted, I tugged the hem of my shirt to straighten out the wrinkles I'd gotten from lying next to a bag of kitty litter in Paco's trunk. Then I took a deep breath and poked my chin up.

Here goes nothing.

As I walked through the courtyard past a huge mango tree, I wondered if Aunt Edna looked like Ma. She'd sounded a lot like her when she'd invited me to tea and cookies. Funny thing was, besides the ancient postcards, I couldn't remember Ma ever talking about her sister Edna.

I wonder why.

"You must be Doreen," a woman's voice sounded from somewhere nearby.

A movement caught my eye. At the end of a rectangular table in the center of the courtyard, a filigreed metal chair swiveled around. A thin, older woman was sitting in it. She eyed me carefully from behind a pair of wrap-around sunglasses. Her face was narrow, punctuated by a large, pointy nose. Her head was capped with curly short hair the color of pewter.

"Aunt Edna?" I asked.

She laughed. "Lord, no. I'm Jackie Cooper. I live here. Come on, I'll take you to your aunt."

"Thanks." I followed Jackie to the first cottage on the right. Apartment number one. Jackie banged on the door with a boney fist and yelled, "She's here!"

The door flew open. A woman who looked like Shirley MacClaine in *Steele Magnolias* eyed me up and down. "So you're Doreen, are you?"

"Uh, yes ma'am. Thank you for seeing me on such short notice."

"Not at all. Come on in," Aunt Edna cooed. Slightly plump and wearing a flower-print house dress, she stood to the side and let me pass. "I made snickerdoodles. I hope you like them."

"I do," I said, shooting her a smile. It was a good sign. Ma *never* made snickerdoodles. "But you didn't have to go to any trouble."

"No trouble at all," Aunt Edna said. "Hey, Jackie. You want a snick-erdoodle?"

"Yeah, sure," she said, and followed me inside.

The apartment was neat as a pin. But it looked as if it hadn't been updated since VCRs were invented. Harvest gold appliances filled the kitchen. The couch was avocado green velveteen. Three gold chenille cushions on the sofa matched the urine-colored glass of the lamp bases flanking either side of the couch. The lamps sat atop knobby-legged end tables straight from a vintage Sears catalog.

"Have a seat," Aunt Edna said. I took a step toward the couch. "No. Take the easy chair. It's the best seat in the house."

"Thank you," I said, then settled into the huge, overstuffed vinyl recliner. I stared at the gold tassels on the green velour curtains while Aunt Edna poured the tea. "Uh ... nice place you've got here."

"Glad you like it," she said, handing me a dainty teacup. "I put two sugars in it. That's how Maureen ... uh, your *mom* likes it."

"Yes. Thank you," I said, taking the cup.

"Have a snickerdoodle," Jackie said, shoving a plateful at me.

"Thanks." I took a cookie and set it on my plate.

"How about a toast?" Aunt Edna said, raising her teacup.

"Yeah, a toast," Jackie said.

"Sure," I agreed. I smiled and raised my cup.

"To new acquaintances," Aunt Edna said, then drained her cup in one gulp. She shot me a crooked smile. "Come on, drink up. It's a Diller tradition."

I grinned. "Okay. Here goes nothing." I downed my cup.

A moment later, Aunt Edna's huge balloon hand reached out and took the empty cup from me.

She grinned.

The room began to spin around her.

My mouth fell open.

I tumbled forward.

Then I got an up-close-and-personal look at Aunt Edna's green, sculptured-shag carpeting right before the world went black.

Chapter Twenty-Six

I woke up in a strange bed with my arms over my head. I tried to move them but couldn't. Then I realized my hands were tied to the bedposts.

I guess it was true—what goes around comes around.

"She's awake," I heard someone say.

I flinched in fear as Aunt Edna came into the room and stood over me, studying me with narrow, accusing eyes. I spotted a rolling pin poking from her apron pocket. A knot the size of a fist formed in my throat. I was beginning to see why Ma and Aunt Edna had lost touch ...

"Who are you *really*?" Aunt Edna asked, her head cocked sideways at me like an angry parrot.

"Huh?" I stuttered, still recovering from whatever she'd drugged me with. "I ... I'm your *niece*, Doreen Diller."

"Yeah, right." She plucked the rolling pin from her pocket. "You usually travel around inside the trunk of a Chevy Caprice?"

"Uh ... no."

"Spill it. Who sent you?"

"*Ma* gave me your address. Your sister. Maureen Diller?"

Aunt Edna eyed me with suspicion while her friend Jackie took up position by the door, armed with a flyswatter and a can of Raid.

"Huh," Aunt Edna grunted. "From what I hear, my niece Doreen is living in L.A. And she's a lot fatter than you."

I was suddenly wide awake. "Ma told you I was *fat*?"

"I got my sources," Aunt Edna said, folding her arms across her chest.

I frowned. "I'm not fat. I'm big-boned. And nobody sent me. I'm here in town because I'm doing a film out at the beach."

"Uh-huh. I ain't buyin' it toots." Aunt Edna began to slap the rolling pin in her left palm like she was warming up to slam a homerun through my right temple.

I flinched. "I *swear* I am! How can I prove it to you?"

Aunt Edna sneered. "If you was really my niece, you'd have a bum eye."

I gasped. "How do you know about that? Ma told *nobody*!"

"I was there for Doreen's birth," Aunt Edna said.

"You were?"

"Yeah. Scared the poop outta the doctor. Pulled her out and nearly dropped the child on her head. Me and Maureen knew right then we had to hide the eye if the poor girl was gonna have a chance at a normal life. We'd both seen what it did to Sammy."

"Sammy?" I asked.

"Our cousin, twice removed. Sammy the Psycho. He had them crazy eyes, too. Made his childhood miserable. Turned him mean. Nuts, even. Last I heard, Sammy was a serial killer up in Wisconsin."

"He always did love cheese curds," Jackie said.

Aunt Edna smiled wistfully. "Yeah, he did."

I blanched.

Is that why Ma had home schooled me until I learned how to wear a contact lens?

"Look, Aunt Edna. Untie me and I'll show you my eye."

"Ha," she laughed. "You're a slick one. Just like Sammy." She motioned to her accomplice who was still standing guard by the door. "Jackie, you check her eye. I'll hold the pin on her."

"You got it." Jackie set the flyswatter and bug spray down on a white-and-gold French provincial vanity. Then, with two boney fingers, she pried open my right eye and clawed at it with a fingernail.

"Ouch!" I cried out. "No. It's in my *left* eye!"

"Oh. Sorry." Jackie let go of my eyelids and tried the left side. She peeled off my contact lens and gasped.

"Well, I'll be damned," Aunt Edna said. "Sorry, Dorey. A girl can't be too careful these days."

Says the woman who just drugged me, kidnapped me, and nearly clawed my eye out!

"Yeah, right," I said.

"So what'd you say you're in town for?" Aunt Edna asked, as if she'd just sat down next to me on a bus. "Some kind a film?"

"Yes." I blinked my watery eyes, hoping there was no corneal damage. "It's called *Beer & Loathing*. What time is it?"

She frowned. "Quarter to two. You got someplace to go?"

"The program," I said. "It'll be on soon. On Channel 22. Untie me and I'll show you."

Aunt Edna gave a quick nod. "Okay, go ahead Jackie. Untie her. I'll turn on the boob tube." She took a step toward the door, then turned back. "Wait a minute. Is that the one that bumped *Gilligan's Island* off the air? The one with Tad Longmire in it?"

"Yes," I said. "You *saw* it?"

"Hubba hubba," Jackie said. "That Tad Longmire's a real dish!"

"Stop!" Aunt Edna shouted, slapping Jackie's hand away from my restraints. "Don't untie her. The girl's working with Sammy!"

"What?" I gasped. I tried to tug my arms free. They wouldn't budge. I closed my eyes.

Dear god! Aunt Edna's bingo-wing crazy!

"The old guy in the bingo cap," Aunt Edna said.

"What?" I repeated. I opened my eyes and nearly gasped again. Aunt Edna's face was hovering inches above mine. She was so close I could make out the thin, black hairs sprouting above her upper lip.

"The guy in the bingo cap," Aunt Edna repeated. "He looks a lot like Sammy. Admit it. You two are in cahoots to kill us, aren't you?"

"No!" I cried. "That's *me* in the mask."

"Ha! I knew it," Aunt Edna said. She turned to Jackie. "See how I tricked her into confessing?"

"Nice work," Jackie said, pulling my restraints tighter.

"So it's *you* who wants to kill us," Aunt Edna said.

"What?" I cried. "No. I'm not a criminal. I swear!"

"No?" Aunt Edna pulled a cellphone from her pocket. "Well, how about I call the cops. Just in case."

"No!" I yelped.

"Why not?"

"They're ... uh ... kind of looking for me."

Aunt Edna nodded smugly at her partner in crime. "See? What'd I tell you, Jackie? That cop line works every time."

Chapter Twenty-Seven

I was trapped inside the plot of a Steven King movie. I couldn't decide which was worse—being held captive by deranged relatives, or knowing that I was floating along beside them in the same gene pool ...

"I knew it!" Aunt Edna said. "You *are* a criminal."

"No, I swear!" I said, tugging at the restraints binding my hands to the bedposts.

"Then why'd you say the cops are after you?" Aunt Edna asked.

"I didn't *say* that." I tried to sit up, but couldn't. "I mean ... the cops want to *question* me. I have an interview—" My jaw went slack. "Aww, crap! I *had* an interview at the police station at one o'clock. Thanks to you two, I missed it. Now the whole force is probably out looking for me!"

Aunt Edna's eyes narrowed. "So, what do they want to *question* you about?"

I cringed. "Uh ... somebody murdered Tad Longmire."

"In the movies?" Jackie asked.

"No. For real," I said. "And they think it was me."

"That don't surprise me none," Aunt Edna said, shaking her head. She stared at me. Suddenly her hard face softened and went pale. She wobbled on her feet, then collapsed onto a chair beside the bed. "I was hoping we'd saved you, Dorey," she said. "But I guess not."

"Saved me?" I asked.

"Yeah. Me and your ma. We tried to hide the eye. You know, so nobody knew you were cursed. Who do you think told Maureen to dress you like a pirate in all your baby pictures?"

"Huh?" I shook my head. "Wait. I'm *cursed*?"

"Yeah," Aunt Edna said. "You got the Diller Killer Curse, honey. You're doomed to be a serial killer, just like Sammy the Psycho. You can't help it. It's in your genes. You inherited it along with the Psycho Eye."

"Psycho Eye?" I gasped. A wave of indignation shot through me. "Look. I just have a genetic disorder, see? *Heterochromia iridum.*"

"Look out!" Jackie said. "She's trying to put a curse on us!"

"No, I'm not!" I yelled. "That's the Latin name for my eye condition. Lots of folks have it."

Jackie screwed up her face and stared at me. "Oh, yeah? Like who?"

"Uh ... Demi Moore," I said. "Dan Aykroyd. Christopher Walken. Kiefer Southerland. Look it up yourself if you don't believe me."

"Those are all actors," Aunt Edna said. "So, you're saying psychopathy and acting are related?"

Huh. I never thought about that.

"You're missing the point," I said.

"So, what *is* the point?" Aunt Edna asked.

"The point is, I was born with an eye condition. Otherwise, I'm perfectly normal."

My aunt's eyebrow shot up. "Except for this little 'killing Tad Longmire' thingy?"

I winced. "I didn't do it. I'm not lying!"

"Huh," Jackie grunted, looking up from her cellphone. "The girl's tellin' the truth, Edna. All them actors have this hexachromia thing. Even that guy Benedict Arnold Cucumber Patch."

"Benedict Cumberbatch," I said.

Jackie nodded. "Yeah. That's the one."

"So, will you untie me now?" I asked.

"Not yet," Aunt Edna said. "You still have to pass the sniff test."

I blanched. "The *sniff* test?"

"Yeah. Jackie, go get Benny."

"Benny?" I grimaced in horror, imagining some liver-spotted old man with a nose like Burgess Meredith smelling me from head to toe. *Ugh!*

"Here we go," Jackie said, returning to the room. Tucked in her arms was an ancient, gray-faced pug with googly, mismatched eyes and a gap-toothed underbite.

"What are you gonna do with *him*?" I asked.

"*Her*," Jackie said, shooting Aunt Edna a knowing smile. "This here pooch has a talent a lot of folks would kill for. You see, ol' Benny here smells dead stuff."

I blanched. "What?"

"You know. Like that kid in *Sixth Sense*," Aunt Edna said. "The one that saw dead people."

I winced in confusion. "Wha ...?"

Aunt Edna tapped a finger to her temple. "Benny here is like that. Only she can smell deadbeats."

Jackie dropped the dog onto the bed by my feet. It wandered up to my crotch and had a good sniff. Then the pooch ambled up to my head. It smelled my mouth, then tried to French kiss me with a tongue that stunk like roadkill.

"Ugh!" I grunted, pulling my face away.

"Well, what do you know?" Aunt Edna said. She grinned at me. "I guess you're okay after all, Dorey. Untie her, Jackie."

• • • •

"SO, YOU WANT ANOTHER cup a tea?" Aunt Edna asked as I rubbed my wrists and stared at the little dog who'd just tried to get to second base with me.

"No thanks."

Aunt Edna chuckled. "Guess I can't blame you there." The dog barked and wagged its stub tail. "Benny likes you."

"Benny?" I asked. "How'd she get that name?"

"On account a she looks like Dolores Benny," Jackie said, setting down her teacup. "You know, that actress who played Danny DeVito's ma on *Throw Momma from the Train*."

"That was Anne Ramsey," I said.

"Ha!" Aunt Edna laughed. "Told you, Jackie. You owe me fifty bucks."

Jackie scowled. "Crap."

"But you're right," I said. "That pug *does* look like Dolores Benny."

"You *know* her?" Jackie asked, her eyebrows almost to her hairline.

"Yes," I said smugly. "I was her personal assistant."

For four whole days.

"No kidding!" Jackie scooted to the edge of her seat on the couch. "You gotta tell me. Is that mole on her cheek real?"

I shook my head. "Nope. Drawn on with eyeliner."

Jackie scowled. "Crap!"

Aunt Edna laughed. "Looks like you owe me another fifty, Jackie."

"I can't win for losing." Jackie hauled herself up off the sofa and headed for the kitchen. "Hey Doreen, too bad we missed your TV show. We'll catch it tomorrow, okay?"

"No worries about that," Aunt Edna called after Jackie. "I recorded it on the VCR. We'll take a look at it after my niece here finishes her important call." She smiled at me and winked. "By the way, I got a spare bedroom if you need a place to stay. You'll be safe here. And it'd be nice to catch up on the family gossip."

There it was. The offer I'd come here looking for. But after being run over by Aunt Edna's version of the "welcome wagon," I was a tad dubious. Still, I'd survived. And things could only get better from here on out, right?

"Thanks," I said. "I appreciate that."

My aunt handed me my cellphone. "Here you go. Better call that cop and reschedule before he sends out a search party." She turned and cupped a hand to her mouth. "Jackie!" she yelled. "Be a doll and go get Doreen's suitcase she stashed in the azaleas!"

"You got it," Jackie said, filing out of the kitchen.

I followed Jackie out into the tropical courtyard, hoping to find a quiet spot to speak with Officer McNulty in private. As Jackie jerked my suitcase out of the bushes and rolled it back toward Aunt Edna's apartment, a thought clicked in my mind.

Wait a minute. I'll be safe *here? What did Aunt Edna mean by that?*

Chapter Twenty-Eight

I found a secluded spot in the tropical courtyard beside a palm tree and tried calling Ma. I wanted to thank her for not bothering to tell me our family was a bunch of lunatics. I also was keen to find out if Aunt Edna's brand of crazy was the harmless or the lethal kind.

I counted off ten rings. Ma didn't answer. I blew out a breath, then checked my recent calls in search of McNulty's number.

"Which cop you calling?" Aunt Edna's voice sounded from behind me, startling me so badly I jumped.

"Uh ... McNulty," I said, whirling around to face her.

Her lips snarled. "Ugh. McNutsack. He's a real ball buster. You should ask for Brady. He's a good cop. Try to switch to Brady."

"I don't think I get a choice here," I said.

"Then you better get your story straight before you say another word to McNulty."

My eyebrows rose an inch. "How do you know all these cops, Aunt Edna?"

She shrugged. "Eh. We go back a ways. Hey, when you're done, come back inside. It's half past three. I gotta get dinner going. You like linguini with clams?"

"As long as the clams aren't laced with arsenic."

"Ha!" Aunt Edna threw back her head and laughed. "You know, I like you, kid."

Jackie grinned. "Don't worry about dinner, Dorey. If Edna wanted you dead, you'd already be sleeping with the snitches."

"It's *fishes*, Jackie," Aunt Edna said, shaking her head. "How many times I gotta tell you that?"

"As many as it takes." Jackie shot me a wink. "You already passed the sniff test. You've got a shoe in, hun."

I glanced over at my aunt. She was pinching her nose like she felt a migraine coming on. "It's *shoe-in*, Jackie."

"That's what I said!" Jackie shot back.

"*You're* a *shoe-in*," Aunt Edna said. "Not you've *got* a shoe in."

Jackie cocked her head. "That don't make no sense. How could Doreen be in a shoe? She ain't exactly an old lady with a bunch a kids, like in that nursery rhyme."

Aunt Edna sighed and locked eyes with me. "What am I gonna do with her?"

"Don't look at me," I said. "I just got here."

• • • •

"SO, WHAT'S THE PLAN?" Aunt Edna asked, setting a plate of linguini on a wobbly TV tray in front of me.

While she'd made dinner in the kitchen, Jackie and I'd sat in the living room drinking Cokes and listening to the grandfather clock tick. According to Jackie, dinner was always served at 4:00 p.m. on the dot, and Aunt Edna preferred to cook alone—as in, "Enter the kitchen at your own risk."

"I have an appointment with McNulty in the morning," I said, taking the plate from Aunt Edna.

She scowled. "Not Brady?"

"No. I felt weird about asking McNulty. I mean, what could I say to him? My aunt thinks you're a nut sack?"

She shrugged. "I see your point." She turned and headed back toward the kitchen.

"I guess I could've told him you tried to kill me," I called out after her. "Maybe he'd go easier on me."

Jackie elbowed me. "Like we told you, if we wanted you dead, hun, you'd be dead already."

"Really?" I grimaced. "Were you really gonna kill me with a flyswatter and bug spray?"

"Jackie could make it happen," Aunt Edna said, setting a plate of linguini on Jackie's TV tray. "Dorey, you don't know it, but you're looking at the last crumbs of the Cornbread Cosa Nostra."

"The cornbread *what*?" I asked.

"Cosa Nostra," Jackie said. "It's mob lingo for *The Family*."

My nose crinkled. "*Whose* family?"

Jackie grinned. "The Dixie Mafia."

Aunt Edna searched for a glimmer of recognition in my eyes. "Come on. The Biloxi Brigade, Dorey." She shook her head and sighed. "How soon they forget, Jackie."

"Forget *what*?" I asked as my aunt's backside disappeared into the kitchen again.

"The women," Jackie said.

"The *women*?" I asked.

"Like me and Jackie," Aunt Edna said, emerging from the kitchen again with her own plate of pasta. "We're the gals the gangsters left behind. All the dons and made-men and hotshots. They're either dead or spending the rest of their days at Parchman Farm."

"Huh?" I grunted.

"MSP," Aunt Edna said. "Mississippi State Prison?"

"It ain't fair," Jackie said. "The guys get free room and board for life, but nobody ever thinks about the women they left behind."

"That's us," Aunt Edna said, sticking a thumb in her chest. "The Collard Green Cosa Nostra."

My mouth fell open. "Ma never said a word to me about *any* of this."

Aunt Edna's eyebrow shot up. "And for good reason. We're the original *Fight Club*, Dorey. Rule number one? You don't talk about the Collard Green Cosa Nostra."

Jackie crossed herself.

Aunt Edna locked eyes with me. "From now on, it's the CGCN. Got it?"

"But what about Ma—" I began.

"Enough said." Aunt Edna ran a finger across her neck. "You need to know more, I'll tell you. But only if there ain't no other choice."

"We operate on a need-to-know basis, hun," Jackie said. "And right now, you don't need to know nothin' else."

I poked a fork at some green stuff on my plate. "What's this?"

"Collard greens," Aunt Edna said.

"I have to eat this?" I asked. "Why? Is this some kind of club initiation?"

"No," Aunt Edna said. "Collard greens are good for you. They've got tons of calcium. No need for any of us to catch osteoporosis like your poor cousin, Marcie."

"Oh." I eyed the greens with a smidgen less disgust.

"Plus, they stink when you cook them," Jackie said. "Good for covering up the smell of blood and stuff."

I stifled a cringe. "So, uh ... how'd you ladies end up here in St. Petersburg?"

"Florida's a nice, warm place to die," Aunt Edna said. "Plus, it offers almost as good a cover as the moon."

"Huh?" I asked.

Jackie winked. "With so much weird stuff going on around here all the time, it's easy to live under the rainbow."

"Under the *radar*," Aunt Edna corrected.

Jackie's nose crinkled. "Who'd wanna live under a freakin' *radar*?"

"Forget it," Aunt Edna said. She grabbed the TV remote and clicked on the old set. "Okay, everybody. Put a sock in it. We're gonna take a look at this fakakta show of yours, Dorey."

"Fakakta?" I asked.

"Sorry," Aunt Edna said. "I picked that up from Morty. This guy I used to date."

• • • •

THE PASTA WAS IN OUR stomachs and the show credits were rolling on the TV screen. Episode three of *Beer & Loathing* had made its world debut.

"Huh. You're a regular wise guy," Jackie said, grinning at me.

I nearly blanched. "I am *not* a mobster."

She laughed. "No. I meant with the *jokes*."

"Oh."

"Sammy always did like a good joke," Aunt Edna said, a faraway smile on her lips. Suddenly, she pointed to the TV. "Ha! There's your name on the credits, Dorey. But it don't say what for. Unless your stage name is Miss Cellaneous."

"That's because the killer's supposed to be a secret," I said.

Aunt Edna crinkled her nose at me. "That was really you in that rubber mask? Your voice didn't sound right."

"They digitally enhanced it to sound gender neutral," I explained.

"Yeah?" My aunt snorted. "Well that Honey Potter's been enhanced too, but I wouldn't say it's gender neutral."

Jackie scrunched her face in disgust. "If you ask me, that blonde bimbo had it coming." She elbowed me. "If I were you, I'd a stabbed her, too."

I nodded and sniffed.

"Hey. You crying?" Jackie asked.

"No." I blinked hard. "It's my eye. It hurts pretty badly. I think it got scratched."

"Oh." Jackie winced. "Sorry about that." She scooted closer to me on the couch and patted my back. "We'll put some Mercurochrome in it. It'll be good as new tomorrow. You'll see."

Horrified, I glanced over at Aunt Edna. She smiled and shook her head. "I think Visine should do the trick. So, Doreen, what other movies have you starred in?"

"Did you see *Trailer Trash Mama*?" I asked.

"Oh my gawd!" Jackie yelped. "That's my favorite movie of all time!"

I blanched with surprise. "Seriously? Uh, do you remember the character Darla Dingworth?"

"Of course. Wait. That was *you*?"

"No. I was the stunt double. That was me in the dumpster with my head cut off."

"Wow," Jackie said, beaming at me. "You really *are* a movie star!"

Chapter Twenty-Nine

"How'd you sleep?" Aunt Edna asked as I dragged myself into her harvest gold time-warp of a kitchen.

I shot my unpredictable aunt a wary glance.

With the door locked and a chair wedged under the doorknob, just in case. That's how.

"Fine," I said. "I can't believe I went to bed at 7:30 last night. I must've been exhausted. Or did you put a little something extra in the peach cobbler?"

"Around here, you never can tell," Jackie said with a laugh. She was sitting at the kitchen table dishing sugar into her coffee cup. She turned to face me and smiled dreamily. "But you know, there's something about watching *Wheel of Fortune* that can wear a girl out. That Pat Sajak is one hot number."

Seriously?

Feeling slightly disoriented by my new surroundings and possibly mild sedatives, I glanced up at the ornate, gold-leaf clock on the wall. Like a prop from a *Godfather* film, it was a Rococo relief of a fat-cheeked cherub. It stared down at me accusingly. According to the clock dial wedged in its chubby-armed embrace, it was ten minutes past eight.

"Coffee?" Aunt Edna asked, holding up the carafe.

"Yes, please," I said with a grateful groan.

"So, what's your story?" my aunt asked as she poured me a steaming cupful.

My brow furrowed. It was way too early for twenty questions. "What do you mean?"

"You know. What's the story you gonna tell Sergeant McNutsack today?"

"Oh. I'm not sure yet."

"Well, then, we need to work on that." She handed me the cup of coffee.

"I say it was one of those bimbos on the show who killed Tad," Jackie said.

"She's got a point," Aunt Edna said as we sat down with Jackie at the dining table. "Who would want to frame you for murder, Dorey?"

"Nobody that I can think of," I said. "Besides, no one needed to. I did a pretty good job of doing that all by myself."

"What are you talking about?" Jackie asked.

I drummed my nails on the coffee cup. "Well, for one, I was alone with Tad at the cottage the night he got stabbed. Then I was the one who found him dead in his bed the next morning."

"So?" Jackie said. "That don't sound too bad."

I cringed. "When I found Tad, I panicked and tried to pull the knife out of his chest."

"Oh, crap," Aunt Edna said, shaking her head. "Amateur move."

"It gets worse," I said. "The last time Tad was seen alive he was with me. And I was stabbing him with a fake knife and screaming that I wanted to kill him."

My aunt grimaced. "Any witnesses to that?"

"Yes."

She blew out a breath. "Geez."

"Can we make them go away?" Jackie asked.

"Huh?" I asked. "Who?"

"The witnesses."

I blanched. "What? No. Besides, they've already told the cops."

"Bad break," Aunt Edna said.

"Did I mention that they found me with Tad's blood on my hands and a one-way ticket to L.A. for ten in the morning?"

"Okay, okay. We get the picture. It looks bad," Aunt Edna said. "Let's go through your alibi."

"Yeah," Jackie said. "When did these deadbeat witnesses leave you alone with Tad?"

"I guess it was about four o'clock Monday afternoon," I said.

"Gotta be more specific," Jackie said. "Cops like specific."

"How?" I asked. "Oh, wait. I remember the sun was going down."

"Aha," Jackie said, scrolling through her phone. "Sunset on Monday night was 4:23 p.m."

"Good," Aunt Edna said. "Let's start the timeclock there. What did you do next?"

"I left Tad at the cottage and went and bought a bottle of wine at the liquor store a couple of blocks away."

She nodded. "Okay, the cashier can back you up. You got a receipt?"

"Yeah. In my purse."

"Okay, so then what happened?"

"I went back to the cottage, packed my suitcase, and locked myself in my bedroom. Then I drank the bottle of wine watching *Bridget Jones*."

"So there you have it," Jackie said. "Just call this Bridget girl and get her to vouch for you."

Aunt Edna pinched her nose. "*Bridget Jones* is a movie, Jackie."

Jackie winced. "Oh. So then what happened?"

I threw up my hands. "*Nothing*. I stayed in my room all night until the alarm went off at six a.m."

"You didn't even get up to pee?" Jackie asked.

"No."

Jackie shook her head. "Lucky duck."

"Not *so* lucky," Aunt Edna said. She locked her earnest eyes with mine. "Doreen, are you *sure* you didn't kill this Tad guy?"

"Yes." I stiffened with indignation. "Why would you even *think* such a thing?"

"Because I've heard Sammy give pretty much the same alibi," she said. "Except his program of choice was *The Ed Sullivan Show*."

I blanched. "What?"

"Don't get me wrong. Sammy was a nice guy," she said. "Until he got angry. If something really pissed him off, he'd get drunk. But for Sammy, that one-two combination was bad news."

"What do you mean?" I asked.

Aunt Edna pursed her lips. "That mixture of anger and alcohol turned Sammy into a raging psycho. You know, kind of like Bill Bixby in *The Incredible Hulk*. Sammy'd get mad, then he'd get soused. Then he'd disappear for a while to sleep it off. Next thing you know, somebody got murderized. Sammy always swore he didn't know nothing about it."

Jackie bared her teeth. "Geez. That don't look too good for you, Dorey."

I winced. "Are you saying you think the same thing happened to *me*?"

"Huh?" Jackie grunted. "No. I mean your eye. It's all bloodshot."

"Oh. Yeah, right," I said, sitting up straight. "That's what I meant, too." I glanced over at Aunt Edna. Her lips were still pursed. "I can't wear my contact lens today. It hurts too much."

"I'll get you an appointment with the eye doctor for this afternoon," Aunt Edna said. "In the meantime, you can't go see McNutsack with your eye looking like that."

I chewed my lip. "You think they'll figure I injured it fighting with Tad?"

"I dunno about that. But if they get a good look at that pale blue marble rolling around in your head, they could get a bad vibe about you."

"Yeah," Jackie said. "We don't need any more bad juju around here."

"So, what can I do?" I asked.

"Hold on," Aunt Edna said. "I think I got something that'll work." She got up and ambled out of the dining room.

"What am I gonna tell McNulty?" I asked, turning to Jackie.

She shrugged. "The truth. They always find it out anyways."

"Here you go," Aunt Edna said, tossing something onto the kitchen table. One look at it made me question her sanity—yet again.

"Are you serious?" I asked.

"It's just a suggestion," she said. "Or you can show up at the police station looking like Sylvester Stallone at the end of *Rocky IV*, then explain to the cops how you couldn't hurt a fly."

Chapter Thirty

"You okay to drive like that?" Aunt Edna asked, chewing her bottom lip and giving me the once-over as I prepared for my meeting with Sergeant McNulty at the police station.

"Sure," I said. "I'm used to driving in L.A. traffic."

"No, I meant in that getup," Aunt Edna said.

I glanced over at Jackie. "Well, I don't have much choice, do I?"

Jackie grimaced. "Sorry, I owe you one for the laundry thing."

After breakfast, while I was taking a shower, Jackie had taken it upon herself to gather up every stitch of clothing I'd brought with me and dump it into Aunt Edna's washing machine. I'd stepped out of the bathroom to discover that the only things I owned that weren't sopping wet were my sandals, a pair of pumps, and my fuzzy bedroom slippers.

With no time to dash to a 24/7 Walmart, I'd been forced to don an orange terrycloth robe and follow Jackie to her apartment. There, we rifled through her closet in search of something I could wear to my interview with Sergeant McNulty.

Given the sketchy alternatives Jackie had on offer, I'd settled on a pair of black yoga pants and a leopard-print pullover shirt with open shoulders and elbow sleeves. (It'd been a toss-up between that or a souvenir "WTF"—Welcome to Florida—T-shirt.)

Afterward, Aunt Edna had pumped my eye full of Visine and helped me put on her solution for hiding my 'Psycho Eye' problem.

It was a child's black Petey the Pirate eyepatch.

"I better get going," I said, taking the car keys from Jackie. Like a pair of stray cats, she and Aunt Edna followed me out of the apartment all the way to the street.

"Which car is yours?" I asked.

"The green Kia," Jackie said, pointing to a vehicle almost identical to The Toad, the POS car I'd left back in L.A.

Dear lord. Maybe I really am *related to these people.*

"You know how to drive one?" Aunt Edna asked. "That thing's kind of tricky."

"Yeah," I said. "I got this." I opened the driver's door. "Where's the socket wrench to beat on the solenoid?"

I glanced over at Aunt Edna. She was beaming at me like I'd just graduated from Harvard. "It's under the passenger seat, Dorey."

I nodded and climbed in. "Thank you ladies. Wish me luck."

"Good luck, hun," Jackie said.

"Don't forget to stop by Dr. Shapiro's on your way back," Aunt Edna said. "I put his number and address in your phone."

"How did you unlock—? Never mind."

"The last thing you need is a tardy slip to go with your demerit for skipping school yesterday," Aunt Edna called out as I fastened my seatbelt.

Right. I only hope McNulty isn't the evil headmaster I fear he might be.

"Gotta go," I said, and shifted into drive.

As I pulled away, I glanced back in the rearview mirror. Aunt Edna was waving at me like Aunt Bea in *Mayberry RFD*.

An odd wave of nostalgia, either real or imaginary, made me wave back hesitantly. The last 48 hours had seemed like a surreal blur. But as I rounded the corner and headed for my second-ever police interrogation, I had a feeling things were about to get *very real*—very soon.

* * * *

JACKIE AND AUNT EDNA had shooed me out the door early, ensuring I had plenty of time to make my 10:00 a.m. appointment with Sergeant McNulty.

As I cruised down 4th Street, I glanced in the rearview mirror at myself. Between the eyepatch and the leopard print shirt, I looked like a one-eyed cougar on the prowl. I grimaced and adjusted the Petey the Pirate eyepatch. Somehow, my effort made it look even worse.

How is that even possible?

I sighed, hit the gas, and headed for my showdown with McNulty.

It was just 9:25 when I spotted the police station on the corner of 1st Avenue North and 13th Street. I was 35 minutes early. Not wanting to be arrested for loitering or solicitation, I drove on past and looked for a place to kill half an hour.

A few blocks down, I spotted a coffee shop with a drive-thru. I pulled up to the window and ordered a latte. "It'll be a minute," the young woman said. "Pull on into the lot and I'll bring it to you."

I drove Jackie's old Kia into a parking spot and turned off the ignition. As it coughed its way off, I practiced saying *McNulty* in my head. Thanks to Aunt Edna, I now kept stumbling over the sergeant's name, just like my pal Bridget Jones had with Mr. Fitzherbert-Titspervert.

McNutly. McNulty.

"Good morning, Sergeant McNutly," I said to my reflection in the rearview mirror. "Crap! I mean, good morning, Sergeant Mc*Nulty.*"

"Nice eyepatch," a voice sounded beside my open car window. Startled, I realized it was the girl from the coffee bar drive-thru window.

"I bet my kid would love one of those," she said. "Where'd you get it?"

"It was a gift," I said, my face suddenly as hot as the cup of coffee I took from her hand. "I gotta go." I rolled up the window and turned the key in the ignition.

Nothing happened.

Then, like a punchline on a bad joke, a fat raindrop hit the windshield.

Seriously? What next? A freaking asteroid?

On the bright side, at least I was close enough to walk to the police station.

I pulled the lever to pop the hood on the Kia, and grabbed the socket wrench from under the passenger seat. I flung open the door, got out, and pried open the hood. As I was about to beat the solenoid to death, a flash of movement caught my eye.

I looked up to see someone dressed in black dive headlong into the open driver's door of the Kia. Before I could utter a sound, he scurried back out of the car and took off for the alley, my purse tucked under his armpit.

"Come back here, you scumbag!" I screamed and hurled the socket wrench at him.

It missed and bounced onto the asphalt. I ran over and picked it up. As I tried to take aim at the robber again, somewhere behind me, a cop-car siren blasted out a single, soul-crushing note.

I froze, then slowly raised my hands over my head. As I turned around, a patrol car containing a man and a woman lurched to a stop in the parking lot beside me. The man, a uniformed officer, jumped out of the driver's seat.

"You okay?" he asked.

"I just got robbed!" I screeched. "He stole my purse. A guy in a black hoodie. He ran that way!"

The cop bolted in the direction I'd nodded. With my arms still raised like a criminal, I watched him disappear into the alley as the drizzling rain melted my hair like wet cotton candy.

"Hey you," a woman yelled.

"Huh?"

I turned around, wild-eyed, socket wrench still firmly in my raised right hand. The woman who'd been riding in the patrol car's passenger seat was now hanging halfway out the door. She had a video camera trained on me.

"What the?" I said.

"Shirley Saurwein, *Beach Gazette*," she said from behind the camera. "Nice eyepatch, cougar. You going to entertain some old men in the hospital in that getup?"

"What? No. It's ... uh ... a long story. One I'd prefer didn't end up in your newspaper."

"Ooo," she squealed. "That's even more attention-grabbing than that sexy leopard-print shirt of yours. What's your name?"

I grimaced. "I don't have to tell you, do I?"

"Sorry. Looks like he got away," the officer said, huffing as he sprinted up to us. He looked to be about forty, and in good shape. Impressive biceps pulled at the fabric of his short sleeves, and there was no hint of a donut paunch.

"I see you met Shirley," he said.

"Uh ... yes."

"And you are?" Shirley asked again. She lowered her camera, revealing a hard, suntanned face. Her ice-blue eyes took notes while she chewed a thin bottom lip covered in bright-red lipstick.

"I'm nobody," I said.

"You want to file an incident report?" the cop asked. "I can take it down back at the station. It's just down the block."

"Yeah," Shirley said, smirking at me. "It's no problem at all."

"Uh ... no, that's okay," I said. "There wasn't much of value in there anyway."

"You sure?" he asked. His face, almost boyish, seemed genuinely concerned. "Looks like you've got car trouble?"

"No, it's all fixed." I unlatched the hood and let it freefall with a loud *clang*. "I really need to go."

"Sounds like she's got a prior engagement," Shirley said to the cop. "I can't wait to see where she leads us next."

"Leave her be, Shirley," he said, "or this is the last time I let you ride along on patrol." He turned to me. "Here's my card. I'm Officer Gregory Brady. If you change your mind about filing a report, give me a call."

"Thanks, I will." Out of habit, I reached toward my side to tuck the card into my purse.

The purse I no longer had.

I smiled weakly, then waved and climbed into the Kia. Thankfully, the keys were still in the ignition. I tucked the socket wrench back under the seat, and watched the patrol car cruise down the street. Once it was out of sight, I tried the Kia's engine again.

Nothing.

I scrambled out of the car, slammed the door, and ran for all I was worth in the rain toward the police station and my meeting with Sergeant McNutly.

Argh! McNulty!

Chapter Thirty-One

It was 10:00 a.m. on the dot when I burst into the police station. Dripping, I ran up to the reception desk. "Help!" I yelled, then remembered where I was and tried to compose myself. "I mean ... uh ... hello, there. I have an appointment to see Sergeant McNutly."

"You mean McNulty?" she asked.

Argh!

I poked my chin higher. "That's what I said."

"Diller?" a voice sounded behind me.

I whirled around to see Sergeant McNulty eying me like Damon Wayans in *Major Payne*.

"Yes, sir!" I said, stopping short of saluting.

"You nervous?" he asked.

"No, sir!"

"Then why are you all sweaty?"

"I ... uh ... it's raining out."

"And what's with the eyepatch?"

"Scratched cornea, sir."

"Really. Let me see."

He reached for it. I stepped back.

"Can't," I lied. "Doctor's orders. It's all gooped up with salve."

"I see," he said. "Which doctor?"

"No, sir. An ophthalmologist. Dr. Shapiro."

The hard edges around McNulty's eyes softened slightly. "On 12th?"

"Central."

"Okay. Follow me."

McNulty led me back to the same interrogation room as before. I assumed the position on the hard metal chair. He stood across from me, leaning over the table on his knuckles, just like last time.

"So, here's what we've got so far," he said. "We found your prints in blood in the hallway and on the driver's shirt."

"I told you—"

He held up a finger to silence me. "But curiously, there was no blood in the shower. Not even a speck of a Luminal hit. That means you couldn't have cleaned yourself up in there after the attack. So you were being truthful in that statement."

A glimmer of hope flickered inside me. I nodded eagerly. "Like I told you, why would I shower and then go incriminate myself by getting bloody all over again?"

"I can think of one reason. To make the crime seem fresh," McNulty said, extinguishing my hope he was on my side. "But that wouldn't have worked. According to the initial crime scene reports, all the blood samples collected were coagulated. That means Tad Longmire was murdered hours before you allegedly 'found' him."

I blanched. "*Allegedly*?"

"Unfortunately, all the evidence still appears to point to you, Ms. Diller. Help me out here. Besides the blood evidence, you're the only one in town who actually *knew* Longmire, right?"

"Uh, as far as I know, yeah."

"And you admitted to being livid with him over ruining your chances at a movie role." He shot me a sympathetic smile. "Missing your big break after fifteen years of auditions must've stung pretty hard."

I sighed. "You have no idea."

"The night before his death, you were seen fighting with Longmire, threatening to kill him. There are witnesses to you actually stabbing him with a fake knife. And you were the last known person to see him alive. I'm sure you can appreciate why this would make you our prime suspect."

"Appreciate being called a murderer? No, I don't appreciate that! Come on. I was just angry and venting my frustrations. I ... was just play-acting when I stabbed him."

"The first time, perhaps," McNulty said. "Maybe that was just practice for the real thing?"

"What? No! I swear!"

"According to the autopsy, Mr. Longmire was killed with a single stab to the heart. The blade cut his aortic valve clean through. Do you have medical training, Ms. Diller?"

"No."

"Then that was one lucky stab, I'd say."

I shook my head. "Give me a break. Do I look *lucky* to you?"

McNulty's dark eyes moved from my black eyepatch to my goosepimply shoulders sticking out of Jackie's secondhand leopard blouse. The cruel smirk on his lips evaporated.

"Surely I'm not your *only* suspect," I said.

"Okay, fine. Care to name another for us to investigate?"

My mind raced.

Kerri? No. She's been so nice.

"Uh ... there were like a *dozen* other people working with me on the set. What about the other cast members?"

"They were at an after-party," McNulty said, pulling out a metal chair and sitting down across from me. "I've got the pictures and bar bill to prove it. I'm curious. Why didn't you and Tad attend the party?"

"He didn't want to. And we had tickets to leave for L.A. in the morning."

McNulty's eyebrow rose. "Tad Longmire didn't want to party? That doesn't sound right, from what I heard about him. Maybe he didn't go because *you* wouldn't let him."

"Well ..."

"Kerri Middleton told me that's what you said. That Tad couldn't go because you didn't want him to. She also told me Tad showed up on the set the first day with a swollen nose. Then later in the week with a black eye. Ms. Diller, do you like to punch men who don't do as you say?"

I gasped. "What?"

McNulty smiled cruelly. "Let me tell you what I think. You and Tad had a thing going. But he couldn't keep his hands off the beach bunnies on the set. Let's face it, you can't exactly compete with a twenty-three-year-old silicone sister."

"How dare you!"

"What are you going to do? *Punch me* in the face?"

"No." I crumpled into my chair. "But I swear, I didn't hit Tad. He got that swollen nose in L.A."

"How?"

"He'd just been fired from filming *Breaking Code* for 'having relations' with the director's wife. That's why he took this job in St. Petersburg in the first place. That director in L.A. is the one who punched Tad. You can ask anybody working on the set that day."

"This director have a name?"

"Yes. Victor Borloff."

"That certainly was on the tip of your tongue."

"You don't forget the man who derailed all your hopes and dreams."

"I thought Longmire did that."

"He *did*. For *me*. But Borloff was the one who ended *Tad's* dreams."

"You don't say." McNulty leaned back in his chair.

"Wait," I said. "Maybe *Borloff* flew here and killed Tad. Or maybe he sent a hitman to do his dirty work!"

"Right," McNulty said. "You've been watching too many mafia movies, Ms. Diller. That kind of thing rarely happens in real life."

I bet my Aunt Edna would disagree.

"Come on," I begged. "There's got to be *somebody* else you can investigate besides me. What about the person who gave Tad the black eye?"

"That makes more sense. Whoever punched him had to be local. So, who did it?"

I cringed. "I have no idea." I slumped back in my chair. Then I remembered something Kerri told me. "Hey. Did you check on About-Face? There's a whole pile of people who hate Tad on there. It's called—"

"Tad the Cad," McNulty finished. "Yes, we're aware of it. Our cyber forensics crew is combing through the list for leads now. But from what I hear, the group is based mainly in Hollywood."

"So?"

"Again, the murder took place *here*, Ms. Diller. Hollywood is over twenty-five hundred miles away, on the other side of the country."

With the last lead I could think of summarily debunked by McNulty, I let out a defeated sigh.

I wonder if there'll be worms in the prison food, like in Shawshank Redemption ...

"Ms. Diller?"

McNulty's voice burst my thought bubble.

"Yes?" I gulped. Then I laid my hands on the table so McNulty could cuff me. But to my surprise, he offered me an olive branch instead.

"You've been helpful," he said. "So I'll share something with you. We *do* have a couple more leads we're following up."

I perked up a bit. "You *do*? Who?"

"That's confidential information. But be assured, just like with you, we're gathering evidence that will either exonerate these individuals or incriminate them."

"Good," I said, feeling a tiny wave of relief. "Let me know if I can help."

"You can," he said.

"How?"

McNulty's raven eyes locked on mine. "By taking a polygraph."

"Oh. Uh ... sure. When?"

McNulty smiled. "As they say, there's no time like the present."

Chapter Thirty-Two

Flop-sweat dribbled down my temples. It pooled along the black elastic band that secured my Petey the Pirate eyepatch to my head.

I was strapped into a chair, six clothespin-like sensors clipped to my fingers. I was trying to remain calm and focus on my breathing, but Jackie's borrowed bra was itching my left boob, and her leopard-print shirt was casting a weird reflection off the metal base of the polygraph machine.

I closed my eyes and sighed.

This is so not how I pictured the final scene going down in The Life & Times of Doreen Diller ...

"Okay, that's it," the technician said. "You can relax. We're done."

"Really?" I asked. "Did I pass?"

The woman's lips smiled, but the rest of her face must've missed the cue. She glanced down and said, "I'll leave that to Sergeant McNulty to discuss with you."

"But—"

"I have to go," she said, ripping a sheet of paper from the polygraph machine. She scrambled for the door, nearly tripping over her chair. She flung open the door, raced out, then quickly pushed the door shut behind her. It closed with an ominous *click*.

I sat there stunned.

Was she afraid of me?

It seemed pretty clear the polygraph technician hadn't believed my version of events. I could barely blame her. After what Aunt Edna had told me about Psycho Sammy, I was beginning to question it myself.

I thought back to all the murderous thoughts I'd had. Like the time I'd considered putting arsenic in Dolores Benny's latte. And when I'd tied Tad to a bed and threatened him with the cuticle scissors. Good grief! I'd even been prepared to stuff socks down his throat if he'd hollered! To top it off, three nights ago, I'd actually stabbed Tad with that fake knife!

But they'd all been nothing more than idle threats. Jokes, even. Right?

Geez, Louise. What if they hadn't been? What if they'd all been steps leading me down a slow progression toward psycho-eyed homicide?

My eyes grew wide at the thought. I struggled in the chair, wanting to break free and run. But from whom? And to where?

What if there's some evil killer twin living inside me? What if I stabbed Tad for real in a drunken, Hulk-like rage like Sammy the Psycho?

Suddenly, the door to the polygraph room cracked open. I stifled a gasp. McNulty entered, gave me a solemn nod, then sat down across the table from me.

I smiled sheepishly. "Everything turn out okay?"

"According to the technician, you've been truthful," he said.

I nearly fell out of my chair. "Thank god!"

"With one exception," he added. "When asked if you had any involvement in Tad Longmire's death, the results came back inconclusive."

I closed my eyes.

Dear God. I'm a psycho killer. This can't be happening.

"What do you think would cause an inconclusive result?" I asked, my voice squeaking as it squeezed through my tight throat.

"Guilt, for one," McNulty said. "But it could be due to a conflicting memory relating to a prior incident."

"Prior incident?" I gulped.

Dear god! How many people have I killed that I don't know about?

"Yes," McNulty said. "When you stabbed Longmire with the fake knife, the memory of that could have caused you to react, thus registering a false positive on the polygraph. Or perhaps there was yet another incident involving Tad? Tell me, have you ever threatened Tad Longmire with a *real* weapon?"

I gulped. "Uh ... do cuticle scissors count?"

"This is no time for jokes." McNulty said. "In case you're not aware, you're in serious trouble, Ms. Diller."

"Believe me. I'm aware."

McNulty shook his head. "Still, something doesn't add up. Why would an otherwise law-abiding citizen such as yourself suddenly decide to stab a man to death? Stabbing is usually a rage killing. And highly personal. In my line of work, murder motives usually fall into three categories—sex, drugs or money. You say there was nothing sexual going on between you and Mr. Longmire."

"That's right."

"Regarding drugs, you've openly admitted to alcohol abuse."

"Wha?"

"But one bottle of wine rarely leads to homicide. Do you take prescription drugs?"

"No, sir."

"Street drugs?"

"Absolutely not!"

"So if we took a blood sample from you right now, it would come back clean?"

I opened my mouth, then snapped it shut. Aunt Edna had put something in my tea yesterday. Would it show up on a blood screening? I didn't want to lie to Sergeant McNulty, but I didn't want to get my aunt in trouble, either.

"I don't give myself drugs," I said.

"Okay." Sergeant McNulty studied me carefully. "That leaves money. What were your financial arrangements with Tad Longmire?"

I sat up primly. "I was his personal assistant. So when you think about it, it makes no sense for me to kill him. I'd be out of a job."

"So, you enjoyed working with Mr. Longmire?"

I grimaced. "I've had worse assignments."

"I see." McNulty pressed his fingertips together. "Then explain something to me. Why, on the very same day after you were hired, did you place a call to Longmire's attorney asking if you could be released from working with him?"

My throat went dry. "You spoke to Ralph Steinberger?"

"Yes. He told me you two had quite an interesting conversation at three in the morning." McNulty flipped through a notebook full of scribblings. "Here it is. You'd called him asking if you could quit. Steinberger explained there were three circumstances in which you could be released from the contract."

"Yes," I said. "Tad tricked me into—"

"Hold on," McNulty said, reading from the notebook. "Steinberger said, and I quote, 'One, by mutual agreement to end it. Two, if Mr. Longmire fails to pay you. And three, if either party dies.'"

"I remember the terms," I said. "What's your point?"

"Steinberger also said he explained to you that the probability of Tad agreeing to let you go was extremely low. He said you might be able to get Longmire to do so if you found a replacement willing to engage in sexual relations with him."

"Yes, that's right," I said.

McNulty frowned. "Longmire sounds like a real creep."

I nearly blanched. Could McNulty be softening to my side of the story? "Uh ... yes. Tad was definitely no choir boy."

McNulty leaned in toward me, his eyes narrowing. "Steinberger said you then made a joke about Tad Longmire's impending death."

I gasped. "I did *not!*"

"No?" McNulty leaned back and picked up his cellphone. "Let me refresh your memory. Steinberger sent me a recording of your actual conversation."

"He did? Is that *legal?*"

McNulty hit a button on his cellphone. Steinberger's voice came through clearly on the speaker.

"Are you having sexual relations with him?"

"What?" I heard my voice say. *"No!"*

"Good. My advice? Don't. Find a replacement who will. It's your best hope."

"Unless he dies."

"Excuse me?"

"Nothing."

"I thought so. Good luck, Ms. Diller."

"What about if I—"

The recording cut off.

"What about if you *what?*" McNulty asked, his dark eyes staring right through me. "What about if you *stab him to death with a butcher knife?*"

Chapter Thirty-Three

I raced out of the police station, my heart thumping in my ears. I was both terrified *and* hopping mad. First Kerri had ratted me out. Now Steinberger. God only knew what Marshall and the others had said about me during *their* interviews! Even my Aunt Edna thought I was a chip off the old psycho. Geez. I was beginning to question the possibility myself.

Not knowing where to turn for help, I shuffled back toward where I'd parked Jackie's ugly green Kia. At least the rain had stopped harassing me. And, for the moment at least, all the evidence McNulty had against me was still circumstantial. Merely he-said, she-said stuff. He had no solid motive for me to murder Tad Longmire, other than the guy was a complete douchebag.

I think even *McNulty* was beginning to realize *that.*

Why else would the sergeant have freed me on my own recognizance? Still, I knew my freedom might not last. Once the DNA results came back, they'd show for sure that I'd touched the knife sticking out of Tad's chest. Unless I could prove that somebody else stabbed Tad, that DNA was going to be game over for me. Do not pass go. Do not collect two-hundred dollars.

Go directly to jail.

I thought about wormy porridge in *Shawshank Redemption* again and nearly heaved. Where was Morgan Freeman when you needed him? I walked back to the car, just another broken-spirited woman wearing an eyepatch and an old lady's man-catcher clothes.

Cut me a break, universe! Who else around here would want Tad Longmire dead?

My cellphone rang. I fished it from my shirt pocket. It was an L.A. number.

I nearly choked on my own spit. Could Dolores Benny finally be calling me back about that part in *Breaking Code*? Was my career in show business about to be resuscitated from the dead?

"Hello?" I said, trying to sound cheerful. I *was* an actress, after all.

"Ms. Diller?" a man asked.

"Yes. This is Doreen Diller. How may I help you?"

"It's Ralph Steinberger."

"You!" I hissed. "Thanks for throwing me under the bus. Are you recording *this* conversation, too?"

"Look. The police called asking about you. I sent them the tape. I didn't record it with the intent to harm you. I *always* tape conversations that come in between midnight and five a.m. It's the only way I can remember them clearly."

"Yeah, right," I grumbled. "What do you want?"

"I just got into town last night to make Tad's um ... travel arrangements. I'd like to meet with you, if possible."

"What for?"

"It's nothing I want to discuss over the phone."

"Too incriminating?" I sneered.

"No. Too *important*. Can we meet?"

"Right now?" I asked.

"Yes, if possible. I've got a tight schedule. I need to catch a plane back tomorrow night. Where are you staying?"

Somewhere between a patch of collard green crazies and the trunk of a Chevy Caprice ...

"I'm out at the moment," I said. "Pick me up at the coffee shop at the corner of 1st Avenue North and 15th Street?"

"Perfect. I'm only a few blocks from there now. See you in a minute."

I ambled back to Jackie's beat-up Kia and leaned against the dented hood. A minute later, a white Mercedes convertible pulled into the lot.

A burly man with a full head of salt-and-pepper hair and a beard to match waved at me.

"Doreen Diller?" he asked.

I adjusted my eyepatch and walked over to his car. "Maybe I am. Maybe I'm not."

"Look, lady," he said. "I'm not in the market for a hooker right now. I'm meeting someone."

"Hooker!" I growled. "I'm Doreen Diller!"

"Why didn't you say so?" He looked me up and down. "Wow. You sure don't look like your headshots. I guess it was the eyepatch that threw me off. What's up with that?"

I scowled. "Long story. Can we just skip it and you tell me *yours*?"

"Sure. Climb in. Hey, did you drive that Kia all the way here from L.A.?"

"Are you crazy? No. It's a loaner."

He smirked. "If I were you, I'd loan it to somebody else."

"Hilarious," I said as I settled into the plush leather seats.

Damn, this car is nice.

Steinberger fished around in his briefcase. "Here, hold this for a minute." He handed me a fistful of papers. The one on top was a rental car agreement.

"Geez," I said, reading it. "Two hundred bucks a day? That's ridiculous."

"I know. Good thing I only need this baby for three days. I take her back tomorrow."

I picked up a cardboard tube rolling around on the floorboard at my feet. "What is this? Generic oatmeal?"

"Tad. I had him cremated."

"Oh." Then it dawned on me what I was holding. "Eew!" I laid Tad back on the floorboard. "I thought Tad wanted to be buried in Hollywood Forever Cemetery, next to Rudolph Valentino."

Steinberger shook his head and laughed. "He *would*."

"Pompous jerk," I said to the container.

"Well, life doesn't always turn out like we planned, does it?" Steinberger said.

I blew out a breath. "You can say that again."

Steinberger pulled a folder from his crammed briefcase. "Here we go. This is the paperwork regarding your remuneration for the dissolution of the contract between you and Tad Longmire—"

"*This* is what you wanted to meet me about?" I said, annoyed at the inconvenience. "I thought you were going to email all that stuff."

"Yes, well, that was before I came across a stipulation in Tad's will."

"A stipulation?" I shot him a dirty look with my good eye. "Are you trying to screw me out of my severance money?"

Steinberger looked taken aback. "No. Just the opposite, actually. I thought you knew, Ms. Diller. Mr. Longmire recently changed his will to provide $25,000 to his personal assistant at the time of his demise, whoever that may be. Which, according to my records, is you."

My stomach sank. "How recently did he make the change?"

"The day before he died," Steinberger said. "He faxed me the paperwork himself."

I grabbed the paper and studied it. There it was, in black and white, just as Steinberger said. Tad Longmire, bane of my existence, had managed to gut punch me one final time right before he kicked the bucket.

Somehow, even from beyond the grave, Tad had found a way to deliver a crystal-clear motive for me to murder him.

For the money.

Chapter Thirty-Four

At least at the ophthalmologist office, Dr. Shapiro couldn't tell I'd been crying. I'd blamed my tears on my scratched left eye. (The *real* reason—that at any moment I could be snatched by the cops and hauled off to jail for murder—had seemed rather off-topic.)

After removing my Petey the Pirate eyepatch, Dr. Shapiro had diagnosed me with a pretty nasty corneal abrasion. He'd cleaned my eye and given me a little plastic bottle of ocular lubricant, along with instructions not to wear my contact lens until my cornea had completely healed.

On the way out the door, Dr. Shapiro told me to give his regards to Aunt Edna. He also informed me that the Visine and eyepatch she'd given me had probably saved my eye from getting infected and possibly ulcerated.

Gee. Maybe Aunt Edna and her Collard Green Cosa Nostra aren't out to get me after all …

As I drove back to my aunt's apartment with a sterile bandage the circumference of a grapefruit covering my left eye, my cellphone buzzed.

It was Sergeant McNulty.

My gut lurched. I envisioned him and Tad's stupid attorney Steinberger sitting around like a pair of villains in a *Batman* movie, rubbing their hands together and laughing maniacally at my twenty-five thousand new reasons to kill Tad Longmire.

Unnerved, I let McNulty's call go to voicemail. As I steered Jackie's Kia down 4th Street, I finally spotted a friendly face. A liquor store. Like a responsible citizen, I turned on my blinker.

Then I pulled into the lot.

It was time to stock up while I still could.

I PARKED THE KIA ON the street in front of the Palm Court Cottages and grabbed the canvas tote from the liquor store. As I ambled toward Aunt Edna's apartment, I grunted under the strain of hauling ten bottles of wine.

"I see you traded in your eyepatch," Jackie said, spying me from her usual spot in the shade of the umbrella-covered table in the center of the courtyard garden. "How'd it go with Dr. Shapiro?"

"Not so great. He cleaned my eye out and put some drops in it. He says I might have posterior uveitis."

Jackie's eyebrow arched. "That dirty old man did a pelvic exam on you?"

"Huh? No. Posterior uveitis means swelling in the back of the eye."

"Oh. So your peeper's gonna be okay?"

"Probably, yeah." I set the heavy tote full of wine on the table. "He said I've got to be careful, though. If I get uveitis, it could last for years. I might not be able to wear a contact lens ever again."

"That'd be a tough break," Aunt Edna said, coming up the path with a garden hose. "How long do you have to wear that bandage?"

"Just overnight. Then I have to protect my eye from bright light while it heals for the next couple of days."

"Uh-huh." Aunt Edna aimed the hose at a patch of flowers. "Jackie, don't you have a pair of those wraparound glaucoma sunglasses?"

"Sure do."

"No offense, ladies, but I look old enough as it is," I said, tugging at the hem of Jackie's leopard-print shirt. "Anyway, keeping my eye a secret probably won't matter soon, when the cops haul me off to jail."

"What?" Aunt Edna gasped. "What did McNutsack say to you?"

I grimaced. "He had me take a polygraph."

Aunt Edna scowled and shook her head. "Damn. You should've called me, Dorey. You should *never* take a polygraph!"

"Why not?"

"Because if it comes back clean, the cops don't believe it. If it comes back dirty, they never quit riding your ass."

"So were you clean or dirty?" Jackie asked.

"Clean," I said.

"All right!" Jackie cheered.

"Uh ... except for when they asked if I stabbed Tad," I said sheepishly. "That came out inconclusive."

"Ha! I can tell you why that happened," Aunt Edna said.

I cringed. "Because I really *did* go psycho and stab Tad like Sammy the Psycho?"

Aunt Edna's face puckered. "Huh. Well, I was gonna say it was because your mind got all confused about stabbing Tad with that fake knife the night before. But what you said could work, too."

I shook my head and flopped into a chair across the table from Jackie. "Believe it or not, that's not the worst thing that happened while I was out."

"No?" Jackie asked. "What could be worse than failing a polygraph?"

"I ran into Tad's attorney," I said. "He told me Tad changed his will the day before he died. He left me $25,000 in the event of his death."

Jackie whistled. "That's a lot a dough. Congratulations!"

Aunt Edna squirted Jackie with the hose. "That ain't good news. Now she's got even more reason to have murdered him."

"Oh," Jackie said. "Tough break."

"What's in the bag?" Aunt Edna asked.

I sighed. "Wine. Lots of wine."

"Amateur move," Aunt Edna said. "This obviously calls for gin."

● ● ● ●

WHILE AUNT EDNA MADE dinner, I sat at the table in the courtyard and got busy opening the first bottle of cabernet.

"Thanks for lending me the clothes," I said, pouring Jackie a glass. "I should probably go finish up my laundry before I'm too drunk to do it."

"It's all done, hun. Washed. Folded. Hanging in your room."

"Seriously? Wow. Thank you. I mean, Ma stopped doing that for me when I was ten."

"When you're retired like me, you got time. Hey, what's your ma have to say about all this Tad business, anyway?"

"I don't know." I set down my glass. "I haven't been able to get ahold of her on the phone."

Jackie chewed her lip. "I was afraid this would happen."

"What do you mean?"

Jackie did a sharp little inhale. "Oh. Nothing." She glanced over toward Aunt Edna's cottage. "Better talk to your aunt about that. But not now. Not while she's cooking veal parmigiana."

"She might get angry?" I asked.

Jackie shook her head. "She might screw it up. She makes the best I've ever tasted."

"Oh." I played with my glass. "I wish I knew what to do."

"Hey, I know," Jackie said, her face brightening. "It never hurts to have some character witnesses. What about your friends here? You got anybody who can vouch for you?"

"Besides you two?" I asked.

"Yeah. About that. I don't think we'd be much help."

"Because you don't know me," I said.

"Well, besides that. Let's just say when it comes to the local cops, we got a little trouble with credibility."

"Why? Because of the Collard Green Cosa—"

Jackie's face flashed in horror. She raised a finger to her lips. "Don't say it. And no, that ain't it."

"Then what?" I asked.

"It's on account of our neighbor Wanda. She ain't quite right in the head. She calls the cops every other day about something. She's like, you know, the boy who cried wharf."

"Wolf?"

"No. *Wanda.*" Jackie's brow wrinkled. "Hey, what about that lady who put you up? The one who sent you here in the trunk of that Caprice?"

"Kerri Middleton," I said. "Last time I talked to Ma, she thought something was sketchy about her."

"Like what?"

"Well, I told Ma I thought Kerri was a real professional. She had everything so organized, you know? But then Ma said if that was true, why did Kerri call us at the last minute to work on the project here in St. Petersburg."

Jackie nodded knowingly. "Your Ma always was one to spot the files in the ointment."

Flies.

"Anyway, I asked Kerri about that. She told me she'd called on a whim after reading about Tad Longmire getting fired, figuring he might be available. I thought, okay, that makes sense. But later, when I talked to Marshall, the studio director, he told me the guy who had the role before Tad was a friend of his, Brent Connors. He said Brent quit right after talking to Kerri."

Jackie shrugged. "So? Maybe Kerri thought Tad would be better, so she fired this other guy."

"Maybe. But Marshall said he hasn't been able to get ahold of Brent ever since. He said it was like he disappeared off the face of the earth."

Jackie's eyebrow shot up. "You don't say. Maybe that's what was supposed to happen to Tad, too. But you interrupted her before she could get rid of the body."

"What?" I gasped. "You think Kerri might—"

"What does this Kerri lady say happened to this Brent guy?"

I frowned. "I don't know. I've tried to ask Kerri a couple of times, but she keeps evading me. Or something happens and we have to drop the topic."

"Uh-huh," Jackie said, obviously unconvinced. "So, what's stopping you from picking up the topic right now? Go on, give her a call."

My back straightened. "You're right, Jackie. I'll do that right now."

I pulled my cellphone from my pocket and unlocked the screen. It was one minute to four. Kerri was probably still in the office. I moved my thumb to the dial icon for Sunshine City Studios. I was about to press the button when the door to Aunt Edna's apartment flew open.

She stuck her head out and yelled, "Dinner's ready!"

Chapter Thirty-Five

"Here," set these on the table outside," Aunt Edna said, handing me a stack of melamine dinner plates covered in a daisy pattern. "And Jackie? Go inside and get the nice placemats. The ones with the manatees on them."

"Why are there four plates?" I asked, setting them down on the table beside the tote full of wine.

Aunt Edna shrugged and turned back toward the apartment. "Eh. I invited a friend."

"A friend?" I asked.

"That's right," she said, turning back to face me. "From what I hear, you don't have too many around. So I thought I'd help you make some. You'll like him. He's a nice fella."

"He?" I asked. "You're not setting me up on *a date* are you? Right in the middle of a murder investigation? Look, I'm trying to keep a low profile here—"

"Aww, would you look at that," Aunt Edna said, looking past me over my shoulder. "Here he comes now."

I turned to see a fit man in jeans and button-down shirt walking toward us carrying a bouquet of daisies.

Coincidence, or has he eaten with these ladies before?

I realized his face was oddly familiar. Then the bulging biceps gave him away. It was Officer Brady, the cop who'd tried to run down the guy who stole my purse earlier today.

"These are for you," he said, handing Aunt Edna the flowers. He offered me a warm smile—one without a glint of recognition.

I sighed.

It's official. I really am *totally forgettable.*

"This is my niece, Doreen," Aunt Edna said. "She's new in town."

"Nice to meet you," I said, grateful that at least I'd had the chance to change out of Jackie's cougar shirt and into a pink tank top. Then I remembered I was wearing that big honking bandage over half my face. *Argh!*

"Nice to meet you, too," he said, lingering a little too long over the bandage. "Are you here visiting a medical clinic?"

"No," Jackie said. "That's my fault. I nearly scratched her eye out. But it's gonna be all right. Right Doreen?"

"Sure." I smiled tightly, feeling my face heat up. "Oh, gee. I think the red wine is giving me rosacea." I cringed, realizing Brady must've thought I was either a hypochondriac or decrepit and falling apart at the seams.

Desperate to divert attention off myself, I turned to my aunt. "Aunt Edna. The food smells fabulous."

"It always is," Officer Brady said, smiling over at my aunt. "What can I do to help?"

"Sit down by Doreen," Aunt Edna said, patting the back of a chair. "You two have a nice little chat while Jackie and I bring out the food."

I objected. "But—"

It was no use. Two women were already giggling and scampering back toward Aunt Edna's cottage. I turned back to Officer Brady, feeling a bit like a trapped animal. At least it wasn't a *cougar* this time.

"Please. Allow me," he said, pulling out a chair and motioning for me to sit.

"I can do it," I snapped. "I'm not old or infirm."

"I'm sure you're not," he said. "You know, I almost didn't recognize you without your leopard shirt and Petey the Pirate eyepatch."

I flopped into the chair and groaned.

Brady laughed and sat down beside me. "It appears you failed to inform them that we've already met."

I grabbed his arm and whispered, "Please, let's keep that our little secret. I don't want them to know that I got robbed. I've already given them enough to worry about."

He eyed me coyly. "What do you mean?"

I shook my head, then noticed Aunt Edna coming out the door with a plate loaded high with veal parmigiana. "It's a long story," I said. "Maybe I'll tell you later."

"So," Aunt Edna said, putting the platter down on the table. "Did my niece Dorey tell you about how she might end up in the slammer for murder?"

• • • •

AFTER LAYING OUT THE whole story between mouthfuls of the best veal parmigiana in the entire history of the world, Aunt Edna turned to Officer Brady and asked, "So, can you help our girl?"

He let out a low whistle. "I'll ask around and see what I can do. But McNulty usually likes to run the ship his way."

Aunt Edna frowned. "And that's fine, just as long as he doesn't shipwreck our niece here."

"You got to help our girl," Jackie said. "Look at her. She's a delicate flower. She won't last a day in the hoosegow."

"And the way she put away my veal, she's an eater," Aunt Edna said. "She'll starve in prison. I hear the meatballs in there are as tough as Titleist golf balls, but what do I know?"

"I'll see what I can do." Brady turned to me. "I agree with McNulty. It makes sense the murderer would be someone who held a grudge against Tad. Most likely a lover. Or one of the cast or production crew he might've pissed off. Did he tell you when the murder took place?"

"No. But he said it had to have happened quite a few hours before I reported finding Tad at six-thirty that morning. So probably sometime around midnight? Maybe three a.m. at the latest."

"Okay, good."

"Oh, and McNulty said the night of the murder, all the cast and crew were at an after-party at the Birchwood downtown. He said he had evidence to substantiate their claims."

"Is the evidence their *word*, or surveillance tapes?" Brady asked.

"I don't know."

He nodded. "Okay. Get me a list of everyone involved in the production of this *Beer & Loathing* project. I'll see if I can find out from forensics the exact time of death. Once we know that, I'll see if I can get my hands on any surveillance footage from the Birchwood and see if anyone's missing. Or if anyone left in time to commit the murder."

My jaw went slack. "You'd do that for me?"

Brady glanced over at Aunt Edna, who was busy pretending not to be listening. "For you and Edna. She and I go way back. But that's a story for another day." Brady cleared his throat. "Thank you for a lovely dinner, ladies, but I best be on my way."

"Always a pleasure," Aunt Edna said. "Dorey, walk the nice man out to his car."

Too grateful and embarrassed to object, I did as I was told. As we reached Brady's car, I said, "Thank you for anything you can do to help. My aunt means well, but I know you can't get involved in someone else's investigation."

"No, but I can volunteer my time. No cop ever turned down free help with paperwork."

I smiled up at him, and was surprised to see he was smiling back. "I appreciate it," I said. "What can I do to help, Officer Gregory Brady?"

"Two things, to start. One, call Kerri Middleton and see what she has to say about Brent Connors. I'm curious about her."

"Okay." I watched him climb into his Ford pickup. "And the second thing?"

"Brady," he said, climbing into the seat. "Don't call me Gregory. Call me Brady. I only use my full name for official *Brady Bunch* business."

I grinned. "Yes, sir. I can do that. Brady it is."

• • • •

LOVERS.

For some reason, my conversation with Officer Brady—or just Brady as he'd asked me to call him—had me thinking about Tad and his many lovers. I shivered at the thought of what perverted horrors awaited the police techs who had to wade through the lecherous text messages on Tad's cellphone.

Victor Borloff had punched Tad in the nose over his wife Bonnie. I wondered if another jealous husband was the cause of the black eye I'd found Tad with on Thursday morning.

Thursday was the same day I'd caught a glimpse of Tad canoodling with a red-headed woman on a lounger on the porch of the beach cottage. At the time, I'd assumed it was Candy Leibowitz from the shoot.

Could the mystery red-head have been Bonnie Borloff, back for more?

I shook my head.

Love is such a ridiculous thing. Who needs it? All it does is drive people crazy.

Drive ... Hold on a second!

If Bonnie had flown to Miami and rented a car, she could've driven it anywhere. Including right here to St. Petersburg for another rendezvous with Tad. And who's to say Victor wasn't hot on her heels?

Chapter Thirty-Six

"I thought you said you were trying to keep a low profile," Aunt Edna said, tossing a newspaper on the breakfast table beside my coffee and onion bagel.

"What's this?" I asked, staring at the top half of a folded newspaper called the *Beach Gazette*.

The front-page article featured a shot of two dolphins swimming beside a boat being captained by a couple of bearded, shirtless, beer-bellied guys with herniated navels. The headline read, *Another Day in Paradise.*

Well, that's one *version of it, anyway.*

"You know these guys?" I asked.

"The other side," Aunt Edna said.

I flipped the paper over. The bottom right quarter panel was taken up with another large photo. A picture of a woman in a leopard print shirt wielding a socket wrench. A Petey the Pirate eyepatch covered her eye. A maniacal expression covered the rest of her face. The caption read, *Cougar Pirate Robbed During Booty Call.*

"So," Aunt Edna said. "It says a local streetwalker got robbed yesterday. Were you not going to mention this?"

I cringed. "Somebody stole my purse, that's all. With everything else that's going on, I ... uh ... I forgot."

"You forgot you got mugged? Or you forgot you were a prostitute?" Aunt Edna shook her head. "Geez. Life in L.A. must be tougher than I thought."

"I'm not a hooker!" I said, then wilted. "I only played one on TV. Once. A headless one ... in a dumpster."

Aunt Edna kept shaking her head.

"Look," I said, trying to explain. "Compared to failing the polygraph and then Tad leaving me $25,000 worth of rope to hang myself with, somebody jacking my purse yesterday didn't seem like such a big deal."

"Okay, I get it. Sort of. But why aren't you eating your onion bagel? I thought you liked them. You reeked of one when you first got here."

"I actually prefer cereal for breakfast. Lucky Charms."

Aunt Edna smirked. "Oh yeah? And how's that been working out for you so far?"

My shoulders stiffened.

Ouch. Point taken.

My aunt flicked a hand at the newspaper on the table. "That Shirley Saurwein is a piece of work. At least she had the decency not to use your name."

"Only because I didn't give it to her," I said sourly. "That's probably the only thing that went *right* yesterday."

"Besides meeting hunky Officer Brady, you mean," Aunt Edna said, smirking.

"More like besides tasting your *veal parmigiana*. One bite and I felt like I'd wasted the last forty years of my life without it."

Aunt Edna beamed. "Eh. I do what I can."

"I see you two survived the bathtub gin party," Jackie said, sailing into the kitchen.

Funny. I never even heard her knock.

"Bathtub gin?" I asked. "Are you saying you made that stuff we drank last night *in a tub*?"

"Oh, no. That's just something my father—" Jackie's voice trailed off, obliterated by the lasers shooting from Aunt Edna's eyes.

"Never mind," Jackie said. She walked over and stood behind my chair and put her hands on my shoulders. "Looks like you're a regular celebrity, Doreen. First I seen you kill off that bubble-headed blonde girl yesterday on Channel 22. Now you're gracing the cover of the *Beach Gazette*. So, which bimbo do you murderize today?"

"Shirley Saurwine," I hissed. "If I can find her."

"Eh. Shirley? Don't worry about her," Aunt Edna said. "By this afternoon, every copy of that rag she writes for will be wrapped around fish guts or lining a bird cage."

"Yeah," Jackie said. "Besides. That picture's no good for business. You ain't even showing any cleavage."

I blanched. "What?"

"It's boobs what sells, Doreen," Jackie said. "Socket wrenches? Not so much. I figured you'd know that, given your line of work."

I opened my mouth to explain. My cellphone rang. I gave up and checked the screen. It read *McNutsack*.

I said a silent prayer of gratitude that the cops had already examined my phone for evidence. Then I glanced over at Aunt Edna. "Seriously?"

I'd already blown off McNulty yesterday. I didn't dare piss him off again. "I gotta get this." I got up and sprinted back to my bedroom and clicked the answer button. "Hello?"

"Is that you on the front page of the *Beach Gazette*?" McNulty asked.

I cringed. "I'd hoped nobody would notice. How did you figure it out?"

"I saw you in that outfit, remember? And, in case you forgot, I'm a detective."

"I didn't forget. Are you calling to tell me I'm under arrest?"

"No. Not yet. I wanted you to know I checked out your lead on Victor Borloff. Nobody by that name flew from L.A. to Tampa. At least, not within the three days prior to Longmire's murder."

"Maybe Borloff didn't use his real name."

"That's pretty tricky to pull off these days," McNulty said. "Plus, it seems like a longshot that a Hollywood director would take the trouble to fly all the way across the country to kill Longmire. Why not just wait until he got back to L.A.? You said you were heading back there the following morning, correct?"

"Yes. But I don't think Victor Borloff would've known that. Actually, I don't even think he knew Tad was here in St. Petersburg. Not unless someone told him."

"How could he have found out?"

I scratched my head. "Maybe my roommate Sonya? But I doubt it. Wait a second. The first episode of *Beer & Loathing* aired on the Friday before Tad was killed."

"How is that relevant?" McNulty asked.

"In that episode, Tad hooks up with a redhead who looks an awful lot like Victor Borloff's wife, Bonnie. Sonya told me last week that after Borloff caught Bonnie with Tad, he sent her to Miami to keep her off the set."

"I'm still not following you."

I sat down on the bed and chewed my lip. "What if Victor thought Bonnie had traveled from Miami up to St. Petersburg for another rendezvous with Tad? If they started up their affair again, that'd be motivation enough for Victor to catch the first plane out, wouldn't it?"

"It would be for me," McNulty said. "But I've already checked the commercial flight manifests. No Borloff."

"What about a private charter? Borloff could certainly afford it. Or he could've flown into Miami to surprise her, but then the surprise turned out to be on him."

"Hmm. Okay. I'll look into it."

"Really? Thank you. I ... I appreciate that."

"This is an investigation, Ms. Diller. Not a witch hunt. I follow all leads."

I nodded, even though he couldn't see me. "I'm glad to hear that, Sergeant McNulty. Because somebody's got to have killed Tad—besides me, I mean."

"Your willingness to cooperate speaks well of you," McNulty said. "And to be frank, I'm finding it hard to see sufficient motivation on your part for such a gruesome murder."

"Uh ... thank you," I said hesitantly.

"I sense a 'but' coming," McNulty said.

I cringed. I was finally making headway on my public relations campaign with Sergeant McNulty. And now I was about to blow that ship out of the water. I didn't want to say what I was about to say, but not saying it would make it even more incriminating if McNulty heard it from somebody else.

"Uh ... did you happen to talk to Steinberger lately?" I asked.

"Longmire's attorney? No. Should I?"

"He told me yesterday that I'm in Tad's will. I just found out I stand to inherit twenty-five grand."

McNulty cleared his throat. "I see. And you didn't know about this until yesterday?"

"That's right. I swear. I know it looks bad. But Borloff still looks worse than me, right?"

"I'll refrain from commenting on that for now."

Crap.

"Okay, I understand. But what about other leads? What about all those Tad haters on AboutFace?"

"We've skimmed through the profiles. Not a single one lists St. Petersburg as their home address."

"So?" I said. "As we were just discussing, people travel."

"Yes. For business or pleasure. But not usually to commit crimes. They tend to do those in familiar places."

"What about Tad's phone?" I asked. "Were there any leads on that?"

"We haven't been able to open it yet. We're still trying to crack the code."

"Oh. Well, if you need the password, I know it."

"Why would you know his phone code?" McNulty asked, his tone taking a turn for the worse.

I winced. "Uh ... we exchanged codes in case of emergency."

"I'd say this is an emergency, wouldn't you?"

"Yes, sir."

"So, what's the code?"

"T-A-D-1."

"Thank you, Ms. Diller. I'll get the techs on it right now. Perhaps you're correct and there are some incriminating messages on it. Or do you already know that?"

"Huh?" I gulped. "No. I never snooped on his phone. It wasn't like that."

"I'll take your word on that for now. But I still think we're looking for someone with the proximity to perpetrate."

"What does *that* mean?" I asked.

"It means that for now, our suspect list remains local and short."

I bit my lip. "How short?"

"Very short. Look, Ms. Diller. I appreciate you being forthcoming with information about the phone and your pending inheritance. And I'll check the private air charters for Borloff's name. But I'm fairly certain this will all sort itself out when the DNA results come back tomorrow."

"Right. Tomorrow," I whispered, suddenly out of breath.

What hope remained inside me fluttered in my stomach like a battered moth.

Unless I can figure out who did this by tomorrow, I'm toast.

Again.

Chapter Thirty-Seven

"Kid, you look like you just saw a ghost," Jackie said after my call with McNulty.

"Pretty accurate, considering I'm fairly certain I just dug my own grave." Like a zombie, I flopped down at the table in front of my cold coffee and bagel and stared at them listlessly.

Jackie eyed me funny. "What are you talking about?"

"I told McNulty about Tad's will. Like you said, Jackie, they're gonna find out the truth anyway."

Jackie picked up my cold coffee. "Why don't you just not take the money? That'd show them you weren't gonna get nothing from Tad's death."

"Too late. It's already been deposited into my account."

"How's that possible?" Jackie asked, pouring my cold coffee down the drain and rinsing the cup.

"Tad paid me by direct deposit."

"Oh."

"But that's not the only nail in my coffin," I said. "McNulty thinks the killer has to be somebody who *knew* Tad. But besides the *B&L* cast, who else would've even been aware Tad was here in St. Pete? We kept it pretty hush-hush. After all, this was supposed to be a low key project. Almost a vacation."

"Well, it ain't no vacation no more," Jackie said, handing me a fresh cup of coffee. "Tad's been all over the news ever since he went and got himself killed."

"Right," I said. "But all that publicity didn't start until *after* he was already dead."

"Hmm. Maybe McNutsack's wrong," Aunt Edna said, joining us at the table. "Maybe the killer *didn't* know who Tad was. They could've hated this creep just the same. I mean, you said Tad was a first-rate jerk, right?"

I frowned. "I suppose so. But what if McNutsa—McNulty's right? What if I really *am* the killer? What if I'm just like Sammy the Psycho and I turn into a raging green Hulk without knowing it?"

Jackie stood over me and put a hand on my shoulder. "That ain't possible, hun."

"It's not?" I asked, a smidgen of hope glimmering in my good eye.

"Naw. You can't be the Hulk. You ain't got the biceps. The most you could turn into is Gamora. That green lady on *Guardians of the Galaxy.*"

I wilted. "Thanks, Jackie. I feel a lot better now."

Jackie patted me on the shoulder. "Any time, kid."

I turned to my aunt, who was busy working a crossword puzzle in the newspaper. "Aunt Edna, I've been trying to reach Ma. She's not answering. Jackie said to ask you about it."

Aunt Edna looked up from her puzzle and shot Jackie a look. "Maureen's probably busy right now." She turned her gaze to me, her expression switching to a soft smile. "What about that Kerri lady? You reach her yet?"

"No. I left a message for her to call me." I hung my head. "What's going on? Why doesn't anybody want to talk to me?"

"*We* do," Jackie said. "What's on your mind, hun?"

I nearly blanched.

Seriously?

"Well, for starters, when the DNA results come in tomorrow, I'm finished. My prints are all over the knife." I slumped into my chair. "Honestly, maybe I really *did* kill Tad in a drunken rage."

"Nah," Jackie said. "I think you're innocent."

I looked up at her. "Really?"

She shrugged. "Yeah. If you'd a killed Tad like Sammy the Psycho, you'd a stabbed him at least a dozen times."

"Gee, thanks."

"Jackie's right," Aunt Edna said. "If you turned into that green lady from Gamora, you'd have been outta your gourd, right?"

I grimaced. "Uh ... I suppose so. Is this supposed to be helping my case?"

"Yes," Aunt Edna said. "So listen up. If you were nuts, Tad's murder would've been a crime of passion. One lousy stab seems more like a business transaction to me. A calculated hit." She rubbed her chin. "If you ask me, whoever killed Tad with one jab either got really lucky, or they knew exactly where to stick him. In other words, this was no amateur move."

I wanted to ask Aunt Edna how she knew about where to stab someone, but then again, I wasn't sure I really wanted to know.

"Uh-huh," I offered as a form of non-committal response.

"Either that, or they hired a killer," Jackie said. She eyed me slyly. "Hey, Dorey, this driver who just happened to be at the cottage when you found Tad. Who hired *him*?"

"Uh ... Kerri did. Why?"

"Again with the Kerri lady," Aunt Edna said, her eyes narrowing. "Any reason *she* might want Tad dead?"

I shook my head. "Not that I can think of."

"You sure about that?" Jackie asked. "I mean, how well do you know these studio folks, anyway? Could they be blowing sunshine up your ass?"

My face suddenly went slack. "Publicity." The word leaked from my mouth like a slippery secret. I jumped to my feet. "Oh my lord. That's *it*!"

"What's it?" Aunt Edna asked.

"Marshall and Kerri told me we needed *publicity* for the series. Something that would go viral!"

"But Tad didn't die of no virus," Jackie said. "Unless the stab wound got infected. Or he had the flu and they gave him the jab wound just for show."

"Go viral on *social media*," I said.

"Ah! *Murder*," Aunt Edna said, shaking her crossword newspaper in the air. "Now *that* sells papers!"

I stood beside the table motionless for a moment, frozen by a mixture of elation and horror. I was elated at the prospect of someone else besides me being the murderer. I was horrified that it could be Kerri and Marshall.

I shot a desperate glance at Jackie and Aunt Edna. "So, what should I do now?"

The two women exchanged knowing glances. Then Aunt Edna turned to me and said, "Sounds to me like it's time to hire a limo driver."

Chapter Thirty-Eight

I reached for my imaginary purse again. "Crap. Darryl's card was in my purse that got stolen."

"Who's Darryl?" Jackie asked.

"He's the limo driver Kerri hired. The one who found me with Tad."

"Well, ain't that a coincidence," Aunt Edna said. "He's there at the crime scene, gives you a business card, and then your pocketbook goes missing."

I blanched. "You think Darryl stole my purse so I wouldn't have his phone number anymore? That doesn't make sense. I mean, if that's the case, why would he have given it to me in the first place?"

"Criminals make mistakes all the time," Jackie said, shooting Aunt Edna a knowing glance.

"But the police interviewed him," I said. "Plus, all I have to do is call Kerri to get his number again."

"Maybe that's why she isn't answering your calls," Aunt Edna said. "She's still trying to get her story straight."

"I dunno," I said. But Aunt Edna's reason made more sense than anything else I could come up with.

Aunt Edna shrugged. "I'm only saying, it all sounds kind of hinky to me, Dorey."

"Yeah," Jackie said. "Hinky dinky."

Aunt Edna locked eyes with me. "Okay. You listen to me, Doreen Diller. I think it's time you gave that studio woman another call. And don't take no for an answer this time. But also, you know, don't let on like you're suspicious she hired a hitman. Capeesh?"

"Hitman?" I swallowed hard and picked up my phone. "Uh ... okay. I'll try."

Aunt Edna smiled like I'd just earned a gold star. "You do that, Dorey. In the meantime, I think I'll bake some cookies."

• • • •

"DOREEN!" KERRI NEARLY shouted over the phone. "It's you!"

"Uh ... is this a bad time?" I asked.

"No. It's *perfect*. There's um ... there's something I need to talk to you about. Urgently."

"What?" I asked.

"I don't want to discuss it over the phone. Can we meet face to face?"

Why? So you can stab me to death, too?

"Uh, sure," I said. "But not right this minute. I'm in the middle of something."

"Okay. How about at noon? I can pick you up. Give me your address."

No way I'm telling you where to find me.

"Um, I have another idea," I said. "Why don't we meet for lunch downtown?"

"Too many prying eyes," Kerri said. "The media's in a frenzy. How about the boat launch at Coffee Pot Park?"

Should I bring my cement shoes with me?

"Sure, Kerri," I said, trying to sound breezy. "Hey, you wouldn't happen to have Darryl the limo driver's number, would you? I can't find his card."

"Oh. Sure. Hang on a second. I think I have it here handy."

I bet you do.

I'd no sooner hung up with Kerri when McNulty called.

"Yes, sir?" I answered.

"I want to ask you about a curious phone message on Longmire's cellphone."

"Just one?"

He sighed. "I'll admit, there's plenty to curl your toes on there. But only one that looked truly suspicious."

"What did it say?"

"It's a text message from someone asking to meet up with Tad on Sunday night. Do you know anyone with the initials BS?"

"I most certainly do," I said. "Victor Borloff's wife. Her name is Bonnie Sutherland."

Chapter Thirty-Nine

"I know desperate times call for desperate measures, but this is not what I signed on for," I said, staring in wide-eyed horror at the latest felonious scheme baked up by Jackie and Aunt Edna.

Jackie laughed. "Hey, like Yogi Bear says, 'It's déjàvu all over again."

"That was Yogi Berra," Aunt Edna said. "The manager of the Yankees."

"Oh. So who's in charge of the Confederates?"

"Ladies, could we please *focus*?" I asked, teetering on the edge of hysteria.

"Oh. Sorry," Jackie said.

"Thank you." I turned back to Darryl, the limo driver. He'd been knocked out cold by Aunt Edna's tea. Sprawled on my bed, we'd zip-tied him to the same bedposts I'd been lashed to on Tuesday, a mere three days prior.

It seemed like another lifetime ago.

"Geez Louise," I muttered, checking the zip-ties. "You two must spend a fortune on these things."

"Nah," Jackie said. "They come free with the garbage bags. And you can't beat 'em for tensile strength. Flexible nylon polymer's the best. Right, Edna?"

"Right," Aunt Edna said. "Here, Dorey. Wake him up with this. She opened the lid on a small, brown bottle. Suddenly the air smelled like a chorus of dead frog farts.

"Whew! Smelling salts?" I asked.

"Fermented collard green juice."

I grimaced and stuck the vile brown tonic under Darryl's nose. He bolted awake like Frankenstein's monster.

"What the hell?" he yelled. He took a second to surveille his surroundings, then began pulling at the restraints like a hog about to be branded.

"Calm down and keep quiet," Aunt Edna said. "Unless you wanna drink some of that stuff in the bottle."

Darryl went slack and silent. With what sounded like a mixture of terror and curiosity, he whispered, "What do you want from me?"

"Who hired you?" I asked.

Confusion flashed across his face. "*You* did."

I winced. "No. I meant Sunday morning, when you came to pick me up."

"Uh ... *you* did."

"Tsk-tsk. Amateur," Aunt Edna clucked. She grabbed the bottle of collard green juice from me, shoved me aside, and plopped down on the edge of the bed. "Look, Darryl, if that *is* your real name, we just want to know how you know Marshall and Kerri."

"Uh ... I give them rides. I'm a limo driver."

Aunt Edna blew out a breath. "We *know* that, genius. But why, of all the Uber and Lyft drivers in the world, do they use *you*?"

Relief registered on Darryl's face. I wasn't sure if it was because he thought he was out of the woods now, or because he finally knew the answer to one of our questions.

"Oh," he said. "I went to school with Marshall. We're high-school buddies."

Aunt Edna grinned wickedly. "Buddies enough to *kill* for each other?"

Darryl gasped. "What?"

"Doreen said you had blood on your shirt when Tad got murdered."

"Yes, ma'am." Darryl looked my way. "That woman there got it on me when she ran into me."

"Uh-huh," Aunt Edna grunted. "But she says when you took that shirt off, you had a T-shirt on underneath it."

Darryl looked at Aunt Edna like she was crazy. He was probably aping the expression on *my* face.

"Yeah, so?" he said.

"Get real," Aunt Edna said. "Nobody from Florida wears a T-shirt under their shirt. It's too hot. Who are you really? Some kind of Yugoslavian hitman?"

Darryl's eyes grew wild. He glanced up at me, most likely in search of a sane voice in the wilderness.

Yeah. Good luck with that.

"Look," I said to Darryl. "I'm in big trouble. Everybody thinks I killed Tad, but I didn't."

At least, I hope I didn't.

"Oh, I get that," he said, trying to appease his captors.

"Thanks," I said. "Look. Do you think Marshall or Kerri would be capable of killing Tad?"

"What? No," he said. "But hey. I'm no great judge of character, as you can see." He eyed Aunt Edna. "What'd you put in those cookies lady?"

"Forget the cookies," I said. "It was the tea. Anyway, did you pick up anybody else for Marshall and Kerri the Sunday night before Tad was killed?"

Darryl shook his head. "No. I swear."

"Okay. Did you pick up anybody before you came to my place Monday morning?"

"No. Geez, lady. I wasn't even supposed to *do* your job Monday morning. I just swapped fares with another driver because I was already at the beach."

My brow furrowed. "Why were you at the beach?"

"Why do you think?" he said. "I had a fare."

"An affair?" Jackie asked. "With who?"

I groaned. "He said, 'A fare.'"

"Oh," Jackie said.

I turned back to Darryl "But you just told us you didn't have any customers that night."

"No. I said I didn't pick up any fares for Marshall and Kerri."

"That's true," Jackie said. "Semantically, that's what you asked him."

"Okay, thank you for the clarifications, everyone," I said, trying to hide my rising frustration. "So, Darryl. Who was the customer you took to the beach Sunday night?"

He shrugged. "I don't know. Some guy. I dropped him at the Crooked Conch around midnight. He asked me to wait around for him, but he never showed up again. I ended up falling asleep in the parking lot. Woke up when one of the other drivers Kerri uses buzzed me about picking you up."

"This guy you dropped off at midnight. Was he young? Old? Fat? Skinny?"

"An old guy. At least forty."

I stiffened with indignation. "Was it Tad Longmire?"

"The guy who got stabbed? No. This guy was no movie star."

"What did he look like?"

"I dunno. I wasn't exactly keeping score."

"This is important," I said. "My life may depend on it."

"Okay, okay." Daryll closed his eyes tightly and licked his lips. Suddenly, his eyes flew open. "Uh ... I think he had dark hair. And was packing some extra pounds. He kind of looked like an ancient Seth Rogen."

O.M.G! That sounds suspiciously like Victor Borloff!

"Hold on a second," I said.

"Like I got someplace to go?" Darryl said, pulling on the zip-ties.

I grabbed my cellphone and google-searched the director's name. I shoved a headshot of Borloff at Darryl. "Is this the guy?"

"Yeah, sure. That was him."

"Ha! *Bingo!*" I yelled.

Jackie cocked her head. "Is it Friday night already?"

"Look," Darryl said. "Can I go now?"

"Oh. Sure." I turned to my aunt and whispered, "We're *are* going to let him go, aren't we?"

"Of course," Aunt Edna said.

I turned back to Darryl. "Sorry about the unconventional interview tactics."

He scowled at me. "That's what they're calling kidnapping these days?"

"Look, Darryl," I said as I cut off the zip-ties. "The cops are on my ass for killing Tad. If you were in my shoes, what would *you* have done to find out the truth?"

"I dunno," he said, rubbing his wrists. "Asked nicely?"

I winced. "Here's a hundred bucks for your troubles. Hope there's no hard feelings."

"Worth every penny," Aunt Edna said. "You're a prince, Darryl. You just helped clear my niece of murder."

Darryl's shoulders straightened. "Oh. Thanks. You know, I guess I'd have done the same thing to get out of a murder rap." He pocketed the money. "Funny thing. I always thought about becoming a detective myself."

"You'd be a natural," Aunt Edna said. "I'll put in a good word next time I see Officer Brady."

To my amazement, Darryl actually smiled.

"Really?" he beamed at Aunt Edna. "You'd do that? Thanks." He turned to me. "But I'd rather you put in a good word with Kerri and Marshall at the studio. Maybe they have a part for me?"

Why do I suddenly feel like I'm back in L.A.?

"I'll do that," I said. "You know, as long as they don't turn out to be murderers or anything."

"Snickerdoodle?" Aunt Edna asked, holding out a paper sack.

Darryl eyed the bag. "No thanks."

I took the sack from Aunt Edna and shoved it into Darryl's hands. "Go ahead. Take them. Like I said, it was the *tea*."

Darryl grabbed the bag reluctantly. "Can I go now?"

"Oh. Sure." I stepped aside. He scurried toward the door.

As I unlocked it and let him go, Darryl whispered, "Does this kind of stuff happen a lot in your house?"

I winced. "I'd like to say no, but I've never been a very good liar."

Chapter Forty

I called McNulty's office to inform him about what Darryl had just told me regarding dropping Borloff at the Crooked Conch, but his voicemail said he was out of the office. Pinning a murder on someone didn't seem like the type of thing to leave on a recorder, so I asked McNulty to call me back instead.

It was fifteen minutes to noon. If I hurried, I'd have just enough time to get the Kia started and make it to the waterfront park to meet Kerri. After what Darryl had told me, I was fairly confident Kerri wasn't planning on sending me to a watery grave. Even so, I reached under the passenger seat, grabbed the socket wrench, and tucked it away in my back pocket, just in case.

Following doctor's orders, I still had a bandage over my eye, but it was smaller, and mostly hidden by Jackie's glaucoma sunglasses. They weren't fashionable, but at least this time I got to wear my own clothes.

Even though things were looking up a bit, as I drove to the park, my desperation rose again about the impending DNA evidence. McNulty had made it clear that the results would most likely be the deciding factor in the case.

And that factor was most definitely *not* in my favor.

If the evidence I'd gathered so far failed to implicate Borloff, I'd still be on the hook for Tad's murder. But then again, so would whoever else was on McNulty's suspect list. Including Kerri Middleton.

I drummed my thumb on the steering wheel. It was literally do or die time. I needed to gather every incriminating fact I could on Kerri, no matter the risk. Emboldened by desperation and the socket wrench in my back pocket, I decided it was time to go for broke and confront Kerri about Brent Connors, the young man who was cast to star in *Beer & Loathing* before Tad and I ever got involved in the project.

If Kerri got rid of Brent, maybe she got rid of Tad, too.

. . . .

"DOREEN!" KERRI YELLED when she spotted me pull up in the parking lot of Coffee Pot Park.

I took a deep breath and set my jaw to determined mode.

Here we go.

I climbed out of the Kia and waved at Kerri. Then I picked my way toward her across a wide patch of grass where a set of swings and a slide stood at the ready for neighborhood kids to play on.

Kerri was at the opposite end of the park, on a sidewalk that ran along the edge of a waterway called Coffee Pot Bayou. She sprinted toward me, a smile on her face. Hopefully there was no knife behind her back to go with it.

"Hi, Kerri," I said as she drew near. "What a crazy week, eh?"

"You said it. I've been trying to shake the press since Monday. What a nightmare! So far, the police have kept your name out of the papers, thank goodness. But I saw that photo of you with the eyepatch in the *Beach Gazette*. What happened there?"

I shook my head. "Long story. And not that interesting, relatively speaking. I'd rather talk to you about Brent Connors, if you don't mind."

"Brent?" Kerri eyed me funny. "What about him?"

I swallowed hard and went for it. "Marshall says you had a meeting with him after his audition. And that he quit the project after it, and was basically never seen again."

Kerri's face went dark. "Oh."

"What's up with that?"

She winced and locked eyes with me. "You don't think Brent got jealous and stabbed Tad, do you?"

Whoa. I did not see that coming.

"Not until you just mentioned it," I said.

"Well, I don't think he'd do it," Kerri said. "Brent was a nice kid."

"You said 'was.' Is he dead?"

"What?" Kerri seemed startled. No. It's just that ... he left the project due to 'artistic differences.'"

"Kerri, I'm from L.A. That can mean *anything*. Can you give me more details? My life is, you know, kind of at stake here?"

She grimaced. "Okay. But this is just between you and me, okay?"

"Okay."

"This could take a minute," Kerri said, leading me to a picnic table. She sat down and motioned me to join her. I sat down across from her, at a distance I hoped was out of stabbing range.

"Brent is a friend of Marshall's," Kerri said, nervously twisting her thumb in her palm. "He's a nice looking young man. So when he wanted to audition for *B&L*, I let him. I had him take a few quick scenes with Candy Leibowitz."

"The red-headed rocket scientist," I said.

Kerri smiled wryly. "That's the one. Anyway, after he shot a scene with her in bed, I pulled him aside and asked him to wear a cup. He refused."

"A cup?"

"Yes." Kerri looked down. "To hide his uh ... *masculine enthusiasm*."

"Oh."

"Well, Brent got embarrassed and stormed out. I never saw him in the studio again."

"That explains him leaving," I said. "But why isn't he returning Marshall's calls?"

Kerri's nose crinkled. "I don't know. But I can look into it."

"Thanks. And thanks for sharing that with me."

Kerri reached out and took my hand. "Sure. Anything to help."

I smiled, relieved that Kerri hadn't killed Brent, Tad, or me. "So, you said you had something you wanted to tell me?" I said.

Kerri winced. "Yes. It's about the series."

"*Beer & Loathing*?"

"Yes." She swiped at an errant lock of gleaming silver hair. "You may not be aware of this, but since news of Tad's death hit the press, the ratings have sort of ... *skyrocketed.*"

Part of me was elated. Part of me was mortified. I could tell Kerri's feelings were mixed as well.

"I wasn't aware," I said. "I've been tied up—uh, working on trying to clear my name."

She nodded, a sympathetic smile on her face. "I know it's morbid, but Tad's death has been good for us. Can you see that?"

"Good for you. Not so good for me. I'm the one people think murdered him."

Kerri bit her lower lip. "Um ... that's what I want to talk to you about."

"I didn't do it, Kerri!" I blurted. "Geez! Why won't anyone believe me?"

"No!" Kerri said. "I believe you! What I meant was, well, with Tad dead, we had to make some adjustments to the final episode. He won't be coming back for another season, you know?"

"Not unless there's some parallel dimension I don't know about," I said.

Kerri shot me a tight smile. "Of course, due to the unfortunate circumstances, we couldn't get any new shots of Tad, so we had to rework the ending with stock footage."

"I get it. You did what you had to do."

Kerri let out a huge sigh of relief. "Thanks for understanding. Anyway, I wanted you to see the final episode before it airs today. I meant to do it sooner, but it's been such a crazy week."

"I totally understand," I said. "And I appreciate you taking the time. To be honest, I've been so busy with my ... uh ... *relatives* ... that I haven't had time to think about it."

"They showing you the sights?" Kerri asked as she reached into her purse and pulled out a small laptop.

"Uh ... in a manner of speaking, yes."

She fired up the tablet. "You've already seen most of this before. I'll skip through to the last five minutes. That's where we had to make the biggest changes."

"Okay."

Kerri found the spot on the video she wanted me to see, then turned the laptop around so I could see the screen. The first thing I saw were Fanny Tight's breasts bouncing as she ran for her life from an as yet unseen psycho killer. She tripped and fell in the sand, of course, right on cue.

I grimaced with expectation at what I knew would come next. I was about to catch up with Fanny in the cottage bedroom, stab her in the chest, and deliver my "You're a real pain in the ass," line. But to my surprise, suddenly Tad was there, helping Fanny to her feet.

"What?" I said as the camera cut to a shot of Fanny running up the steps of the beach cottage and through the French doors. The camera cut again to an image of Tad sprinting toward the camera. Suddenly, the angle went wonky. The shadowy image of two figures scuffling in the sand came into view.

Suddenly, to my utter horror, my face appeared on the screen—my completely unmasked, recognizable, crazy-eyed face.

I glanced up at Kerri. "What's going on? That's the shot I did to make Fanny quit giggling!"

Kerri nodded, her lips pursed into an apologetic grimace. "This is where we had to write Tad out," she said.

I looked back down at the laptop screen to see my image say, "You know, Taddy dear."

I gasped. The studio had dubbed in "Taddy" for the name "Fanny."

"Wha?" I said, staring at the rewritten scene. I watched myself raise the knife above my head.

"You can be a real pain in the ass," my psycho-killer persona said. "I won't be the butt of your jokes anymore."

And then, there it was. The coup de grâce.

I was standing next to Tad on the front porch of the cottage, red-faced and screaming, "Tad Lovemire, I could kill you!"

Then I plunged the fake knife into Tad's bare chest.

Chapter Forty-One

O h my god! *Tommy must've filmed Tad's and my fight that night when he was outside getting shots of the cottage at sunset.*

And those creeps used it in the final episode!

The stabbing had looked so real on the screen. Stunned, I watched the shot switch back to my maniacal, cackling, weird-eyed face. A squirt of fake blood splatted across my cheek in a perfect line.

The screen went black.

I thought it was over, but then up flashed an outside shot of the beach cottage—complete with crime scene tape and cop cars with blue and red lights blazing.

Finally, mercifully, the credits started rolling.

I slowly looked up at Kerri. "What did you do?" I gasped. "You can't ... put that on the air."

Kerri cringed and snapped the laptop closed. "Tommy and Marshall pieced this together without us, Doreen. It's already been approved by Bob Johnson at Channel 22. We can't change it."

"But it makes me look even more guilty!"

"I know it wasn't what you were expecting," Kerri said, putting the laptop back into her purse. "But you have to admit it works. And this surprise ending could send the show off the charts!"

And me to jail.

"Kerri, please. I'm begging you. Don't air this."

Kerri shook her head. "I can't stop it, Doreen. It's too far in motion. It airs in like, an hour and a half from now."

Anger shot through me. "I could sue you for character defamation!"

"No. You can't," Kerri said coolly. "According to your contract, Sunshine City Studios has the right to use stock footage as they see fit for programming and publicity purposes."

Damned contracts!

"But ... I thought we were friends," I said.

Kerri cringed. "We are. And I'm sorry, Doreen, I truly am. I had no idea about this until it was already too late."

"But don't you see? This makes me look like Tad's murderer! Did Tommy and Marshall do this on purpose to frame me?"

Kerri blanched. "On *purpose*? What do you mean?"

I stood up and leaned over the table on my fists like I'd seen McNulty do. "I mean, are *they* the real murderers? Are they trying to point the finger at me and disguising it as some horrible publicity stunt?"

"How could you say that?" Kerri gasped.

"Because I'm desperate! I'm being accused of murder, Kerri. *Murder*!"

"I know. And I'm sorry."

The tears in Kerri's eyes took the steam out of my sails. I flopped back down onto the picnic bench. "Are you absolutely sure they didn't have a hand in killing Tad?"

Kerri shook her head. "I've learned you can never be absolutely sure about anything, Doreen. Even so, I can't imagine those two being involved in a real-life murder."

"Only a fake one on screen."

Kerri nodded.

I blew out a breath. "Okay. Call me if you hear anything that could exonerate me. The sooner the better."

A tear streamed down Kerri's cheek. "I will. I promise."

• • • •

STILL REELING FROM Kerri's death blow, I was dragging myself back to the Kia when my cellphone rang. It was Sergeant McNulty.

"I think I know who killed Tad," I said before he could get a word in edgewise.

"Ms. Diller?"

"Yes."

"You don't sound like yourself."

"I've had a long day."

"It's lunch time."

"Whatever," I said. "Look, I think Borloff really could be the killer. If Tad met Bonnie on Sunday night, he'd have blown his stack. I've seen the man in action."

"Okay. But right now, all we have to go on is circumstantial at best."

"Not anymore. I've got a witness."

"To the murder?" McNulty asked.

"Not exactly. You remember Darryl, the limo driver you guys interviewed?"

"Yes."

"He told me he dropped off a guy who fit Borloff's description at the Crooked Conch around midnight the same night Tad was killed. It's just a short walk to the beach cottage from there."

"Interesting. Can you get Darryl to come in and make an official statement to that effect?"

I envisioned Darryl fleeing Aunt Edna's apartment with a hundred dollar bill and a bag of snickerdoodles, compliments of his kidnappers.

"Uh, sure," I said.

"Good. I'm in my office all afternoon waiting on the DNA results. They're supposed to be here anytime now."

I hung up the phone. "Easy peasy," I muttered to myself. Then I raised the hood on the Kia and beat the life out of the poor solenoid.

Chapter Forty-Two

"I'm doomed," I said, then took a savage bite of the humongous sandwich Aunt Edna had waiting for me when I got back from talking with Kerri at the park.

"Why do you think you're doomed?" Aunt Edna asked, heaping pastrami on rye bread for her own sandwich.

"If the DNA comes back as a match, I know McNulty's gonna arrest me today for probable cause."

"Hmm." Aunt Edna took a bite of pastrami and chewed it while she talked. "Better if you turn yourself in before they come and haul you away. Trust me on this one."

"Thanks for the vote of confidence," I said sourly.

Aunt Edna slapped her sandwich together. "I was joking. Don't lose hope yet, Dorey. DNA is just a piece of the puzzle. It doesn't tell the story. Like they say on those cop shows, 'It's not the whole narrative.'"

"It isn't?" I poised mid-bite. "What do you mean?"

"If you have a good reason for your DNA to be on the knife, then that can introduce reasonable doubt."

"Yeah," Jackie said, fixing her own sandwich after Aunt Edna was through. "And you have to be proven guilty *beyond a reasonable doubt.*"

"I touched the knife because I thought Tad was pulling a prank on me," I said. "Does that sound reasonable enough?"

Jackie shrugged. "I'd buy it, maybe."

I turned to Aunt Edna. "What about you?"

She shrugged. "Eh. But you were living there, right? So your DNA could've been on the knife before the killer touched it, eh?"

"Yeah, I suppose so." I sighed and set down my sandwich. "But now McNulty wants me to try and get Darryl the limo driver to come with me to the police station and testify he saw Borloff. How am I gonna do that? Since we tied him to the bed and threatened him with collard green juice, I doubt he'll come anywhere near here again."

"Some people are touchy that way," Jackie said.

"I don't know if any of that matters anyway," Aunt Edna said. "From what I remember, Darryl didn't exactly say the guy he saw was Borloff."

"Yes he did," I argued. "When I showed Darryl the picture of Borloff, he said it was him."

Aunt Edna laughed. "I saw that picture. I gotta say, Borloff looks like half the poor slobs in the world, Dorey." She sighed. "And, sadly, every man I've ever gone out with."

I wilted. "So, it really *is* like I said at the beginning. I'm doomed."

Aunt Edna walked over and wrapped her arm around my shoulder. "Not yet, you aren't. It ain't over until I've hit the high notes."

• • • •

AS MY BELLYFUL OF PASTRAMI digested, I contemplated whether to turn myself in to the police *now*, or wait and be hauled out kicking and screaming later. As for Aunt Edna, she was calmly thumbing through the tattered yellow-pages of a phone book that had to contain ads for Burma-Shave.

While she searched for an attorney she knew who wasn't already disbarred or taking an extended dirt nap, I fished a quarter from my pants pocket and walked over to the kitchen counter.

Heads I turn myself in. Tails I make a run for it in Jackie's Kia.

I tossed the quarter. It bounced off the counter, hit the floor rolling, and disappeared under the harvest-gold refrigerator.

Just my luck.

I sighed. I was officially out of time and out of ideas. McNulty would have the DNA results in his hands any second now, and then my fate would be sealed for good. Where else could I turn for advice?

Suddenly, I remembered my *Hollywood Survival Guide.* I sprinted to my bedroom, grabbed it off the dresser and thumbed through the pages. I stopped at Tip #48. *Whatever you decide to do, make sure you look fabulous doing it.*

That's it! If I'm going to jail, I'm going there in style.

I jumped in the shower, washed and blow-dried my hair, and slathered on my best body lotion. I slipped into my fanciest white silk shirt and gray slacks. Then I pulled out my cosmetic bag and prepared my makeup like I was going to the Emmy's. When I was done, I slipped on Jackie's glaucoma glasses and stared at myself in the mirror.

I barely recognized myself.

That's when the idea hit me.

Eureka!

I grabbed my purse. "Gotta run," I said to Aunt Edna and Jackie. Then I bolted out the door.

• • • •

FIVE MINUTES AGO, I'D sprinted out of Aunt Edna's apartment and over to Jackie's next door. There, I'd made a quick call on her landline using my best impersonation of Fran Drescher on that sitcom, *The Nanny.*

Now I was standing on the street corner five blocks away, waiting.

"Is that the Cougar Pirate of Penzance?" a man's voice sounded behind me.

I whirled around. Officer Brady was grinning at me. He was in uniform, straddling a ten-speed bicycle.

"What are you doing here?" I asked.

"I was headed to your aunt's to give you the update on the alibis of your cast and crew. You going to a Hollywood party? Or are you making a quick getaway?"

"Oh, this? Just didn't have anything else clean." I glanced around warily. "So, tell me what you found out. But do it quickly."

"You in a hurry?"

"Yes. And being seen with a cop right now could blow my cover. So, come on. What did you find out?"

Brady shrugged. "In a nutshell? Everybody's alibis check out."

I frowned. "What about Tommy and Marshall?"

"They left the party early, like you thought they might've. But surveillance cameras on Central have them entering Sunshine Studios at eleven p.m. They didn't leave until daybreak on Monday."

"Yeah," I said sourly. "Apparently, they had some editing they needed to finish up."

"Everyone else stayed at the party until three. They didn't have time to kill Tad."

Crap.

"Okay. Thanks for the info, Brady. Now, could you do me another favor?"

"Sure, what?"

"Beat it. Scram. *Now.*"

His eyebrow arched. "Yes, ma'am. You got it."

Officer Brady had barely rounded the corner when my target approached. I waved down the limo, crawled in the backseat, and laid on the Drescher accent. "Police station. And make it snappy."

"Okay," the driver said. He pretended to adjust the rearview mirror while he checked me out. Suddenly, his mouth fell open.

I'd been made.

"Hi, Darryl," I said in my normal voice.

"What? *You* again?" He slammed on the brakes. "Get out! *Now!*"

"Hear me out," I said. "No funny business this time. I swear. I just need a ride to an interview. Fifty bucks for a ten-minute ride."

"Geez," Darryl muttered. "Fine. But only if you promise never to call me again." He scowled for a moment. Then his face brightened like a lightbulb just went on. "I mean, unless it's about a part at the studio, I mean."

"Will do," I said.

Not wanting to aggravate the situation, I kept my mouth shut on the ride to the station. Once there, I handed Darryl the fifty bucks and said, "Come in with me."

He shook his head. "Not on your life."

"Come on. I thought you wanted to be a detective. You're here. Why not take a look around the place? Fill out an application?"

"No."

"What about taking a look around to get a feel for a movie role as a cop? My interview won't take long. And I hear there's free coffee and donuts inside."

He crossed his arms over his chest. "Not happening."

"How about for another fifty?"

He cracked open the driver's door. "Twenty minutes and I'm out of there."

"Deal."

We got out of the limo and headed into the station. Once inside, I latched onto Darryl's arm like a rabid Chihuahua.

"Let go of me!" he growled under his breath.

"No way. You're coming with me. It'll take you five minutes to corroborate my story about Borloff to Sergeant McNulty, then you're free as a bird and I'll never bother you again."

"Why should I?" he said.

"Because I'm desperate. Do you know how hideous I'd look in an orange jumpsuit?"

"Diller, is that you?" McNulty's voice rang out across the lobby.

"Yes!" I practically squealed. "And I brought the limo driver like you asked me to."

"The same one you accused of stealing your purse so you wouldn't have his card anymore?" McNulty asked.

I grimaced. "Uh ... no. I was wrong about that. I'm thinking now it was just a reporter trying to get the goods on me. Anyway, Darryl's here to back me up about Borloff."

"Right. Follow me." McNulty turned and headed down a dim hallway that was already way too familiar for my taste. Halfway down the corridor, Darryl tried to make a run for it, but I had him hooked by the elbow. I dragged him along behind McNulty, whispering, "It's too late to turn back now."

McNulty put us in a room slightly bigger than the original interrogation room. I hoped that it was where they put the nice, innocent people.

"So, what do you have for me?" McNulty asked as we took seats around a small, round table.

"Darryl here can confirm he picked up Victor Borloff late Sunday night and dropped him off around midnight at the Crooked Conch. It's just blocks from the beach cottage Tad was murdered in."

"Is that so," McNulty said. His eyes shifted to Darryl. "I'd like to hear the story in your own words."

The young man squirmed in his chair. "Look, I'm sorry, but I lied."

"You what?" I squealed.

"I ... I just said that the guy I picked up looked like the guy you showed me so you and your old-lady kidnapping crew would let me go. I mean, my *life* was at stake."

"But—" I muttered.

Darryl turned and glared at me. "You said it yourself. You'd do the same thing if you were in my shoes."

Something crumpled inside me. The way McNulty was glaring at me, I had a feeling that whatever had just crumpled would soon be ablaze.

"Kidnapping? Lying?" McNulty asked.

"I can explain," I said.

McNulty shook his head. "Don't bother, Ms. Diller. I've already spoken with Victor Borloff. He has an iron-clad alibi. He was in L.A. the entire weekend."

McNulty's eyes narrowed in on me. "But now I have a whole new lead. *You two.* How interesting that the only two people found at the scene of the crime should work together to point the finger at someone else." He laughed and shook his head. "I should've seen that coming."

"That's not how it is, sir," Darryl blurted. "I had nothing to do with that guy's murder. I just showed up and found this lady all bloody and screaming, just like I said before."

"And then you two bonded and became best pals," McNulty said. "How nice for you. And how convenient that you should remember picking up the guy she needs to pin this on. One of life's true miracles."

"It's true," I whimpered with so little conviction I barely believed it myself.

McNulty let out a tired sigh. "Let's start from the top again. Ms. Diller, you said you were here filming a TV series called *Beer & Loathing,* correct?"

"Yes, sir."

"What exactly is it about?"

I winced. "It's crap. A low-rent version of *Dude, Where's My Boat?* Only not as thoroughly thought through."

"Excuse me?" McNulty said, rubbing his temples.

"Um ... it's just a silly TV drama," I said. "A little beach murder-type thingy. It's hard to explain."

McNulty glared at me. "Try."

"Wait," Darryl said. "Marshall told me the final episode airs today, right?"

I grimaced. "Yes."

"What time?" McNulty asked.

"I think it's already over," I answered.

"No," Darryl said. "It's only 2:45. Actually it's on right now. Turn on that monitor, Sergeant. If you're quick, we can catch the tail end of it."

McNulty picked up the remote and switched the monitor on above our heads. "What channel?"

"Twenty-two," I said, feeling the life drain out of me.

Oh, please, God. Let the show be over already!

It wasn't. McNulty switched to Channel 22 just in time to see the train wreck that was my life jettison fully off the rails and into a giant cesspool.

There I was, in all my unmasked, crazy-eyed glory, grinning like Glen Close in the bathtub in *Fatal Attraction*.

Darryl gasped and withered in his chair.

McNulty stared at the screen, open mouthed. "Is that *you*?"

"You know, Taddy dear," my image on the TV screen said, raising the glinting knife above my head. "You can be a real pain in the ass. I won't be the butt of your jokes anymore."

My life flashed before my eyes, waiting for what I knew came next. And there it was. Me standing with Tad on the front porch of the cottage.

"Tad Lovemire, I could kill you!" The knife plunged into Tad's chest. Blood squirted across my maniacal, cackling, weird-eyed face. Then the beach cottage appeared—caught up in crime scene tape and flashing cop cars.

"Wait a minute," McNulty said. "That's footage of the real crime scene. Did you *plan* this all along? For *ratings*?"

"No!" I cried. "I promise. I had nothing to do with the ending!"

"That's not the way it looked to me," McNulty said.

"Me either," Benedict Darryl said.

Just when I thought things couldn't possibly get any worse, the TV crackled with a breaking news report. McNulty turned up the volume.

A hard-faced woman sporting red lipstick and a microphone leered into the camera like a vulture at a kill. "I'm Shirley Saurwein," she said. "And I'm standing in front of the beach cottage where soap-opera heartthrob Tad Longmire was murdered. In an eerie twist of fate, life imitates art here in St. Petersburg, Florida."

A picture of my crazy-eyed serial-killer mug flashed on the split screen while Saurwein continued her commentary.

"Los Angeles actress Doreen Diller, who played the serial killer Doreen Killigan in the local production of *Beer & Loathing*, has been accused of murdering Tad Longmire, the star of the—pardon the pun—*short-lived* daytime TV drama. Fans might recognize Longmire as Dr. Lovejoy in *Days of Our Lies*. As for Doreen Diller, this may be her first and last memorable role."

As the three of us sat there stunned, the door to the conference room cracked open. A cop stuck his head in. "Sarge, you've got a phone call."

"Take a message," McNulty said. "Can't you see I'm in the middle of something here?"

"Um ... I think you'll want to take this, Sarge. Someone on the line says they witnessed the murder of Tad Longmire."

"Did they name the perpetrator?" McNulty asked.

The cop's eyes darted to me. Then he leaned in and whispered, "She's sitting right across from you."

Chapter Forty-Three

D*id I really kill Tad in a psychotic, blackout rage?*
        As I sat there wondering if my only friend would be a blackbird I raised from a chick by feeding it the worms in my prison porridge, McNulty burst back into the interrogation room.

"I knew she did it!" Darryl squealed like a rat. "Don't leave me in here with a murderer!"

McNulty eyed him with disgust. "Save it," he said.

"Am I going to prison?" I asked.

"Not yet," McNulty said. "The witness was ... confused. She said she saw the murder ... ahem ... on Channel 22."

I couldn't tell if McNulty was blushing. I hoped he couldn't tell I'd just peed my pants a little.

As we sat there in awkward silence for a moment, another rap sounded at the door. The same cop poked his head back into the room. "Uh, Sarge, you've got a visitor. Says you've been expecting a package from him?"

"Finally," McNulty, letting out a long breath. "I had the DNA results couriered over."

McNulty glared across the table at me and Darryl. "Take my advice, you two. Sit tight. And keep working on that story of yours. So far, the plot is total garbage."

• • • •

"LADY, YOU ARE CERTIFIABLY nuts," Darryl said, turning on me as soon as McNulty left the room.

"Tell me something I *don't* know," I said, laying my head on the table. "Could you do me a favor and turn that stupid TV off?"

"We're both going to need good attorneys," Darryl said, clicking the remote.

"Correction. We're both going to need *fabulous* attorneys." I sighed and lifted my head. "The only one I know is Ralph Steinberger, Tad's lawyer. You think it would be a conflict of interest for him to represent me?"

"I dunno," Darryl said. "But maybe he'll represent *me*."

I gritted my teeth. "Lawyers. They'll do anything for money. Maybe we can talk him into a two-for-one deal."

"Seriously?" Darryl said.

"Either that, or I can call my Aunt Edna and see who she dug up from the 1965 yellow pages."

Darryl groaned. "Geez. So go ahead and call the guy already!"

I pulled out my phone. "Okay. Here goes." I rang Steinberger's number. He didn't answer.

"That's weird. This guy *always* answers his phone."

A phone rang out in the hallway. I hung up and tried Steinberger's number again, in case I'd gotten a bad line or something. Oddly, right on cue, the phone in the hallway rang again.

"Wait a minute," I said. I got up, cracked open the door, and peeked outside. Ralph Steinberger was standing in the hallway talking to Sergeant McNulty.

I nearly choked on my own spit.

"Mr. Steinberger!" I yelled. "Boy am I glad to see you!"

"Get back in there," McNulty said, reaching over to shut the door on me.

Before he could, Darryl pushed past me and burst through the opening. "Please, Mr. Steinberger. You gotta help us!"

Darryl took another step toward the two men and froze. His eyes grew large. "Hey, wait a minute. Aren't you the guy I picked up at the Don CeSar a couple of days ago?"

"Me?" Steinberger said, shaking his head. "No. Couldn't have been."

"Yeah," Darryl said. "I remember you because of the weird request. You wanted a ride to the airport, but you didn't want to catch a plane. You wanted to rent a car."

Steinberger shook his head. "Sorry, son. You've got me confused with someone else."

"No, I don't think so," Darryl said. "I asked you, 'Why go to the airport to rent a car when there's places at the beach to do it?' You told me it was the only place with white Mercedes convertibles in stock."

"What?" I said.

"When was this?" McNulty asked Steinberger.

"He told me he got here on Wednesday," I said.

"I did," Steinberger said. "You saw the car rental receipt yourself."

My eyes narrowed. "Yeah, I did. You made darn sure I got a good look at it, didn't you? You wanted me to think you didn't arrive in St. Pete until Wednesday. But you were already at the Don CeSar when Darryl picked you up."

"That's right. I'd just gotten in," Steinberger said.

"If you'd just gotten in, why didn't you simply rent a car while you were at the airport?" I asked. "Or did you drive all the way here from L.A. and then your car broke down?"

"I don't have time for this nonsense," Steinberger said, turning away from me. "McNulty, thank you for signing the paperwork. Now, I have a plane to catch."

"Not so fast," McNulty said. "Let's all go have a seat in the conference room. I want to hear what these two have to say."

· · · ·

MCNULTY SAT AND STUDIED the three of us like we were lab rats. I glared at Steinberger from across the conference table. Now that I thought about it, the guy really *did* look like an older, liver-spotted Seth Rogen.

"Hey Darryl," I said. "Could Steinberger here also be the guy you dropped off at the Crooked Conch on Sunday evening?"

"It's possible," Darryl said. "It was dark. And like I said before, the guy never came back. But one thing's for sure, whoever the guy was, he was a real cheapskate."

"Well, then, it couldn't have been me," Steinberger said. "I'm not cheap. I always go first class."

"Is that so?" Darryl said. "Funny. That's *exactly* what the guy told me who stiffed me Sunday night."

My eyes narrowed at Steinberger. "You told me that, too, when we were in your Mercedes." Suddenly a passage from the *Hollywood Survival Guide* popped into my head. Tip #62. *Where there's a will, there's an attorney.*

"Cardboard," I said, voicing a thought out loud.

"What?" McNulty asked.

I turned to the sergeant, the thread of a thought weaving into a tapestry in my mind. "Tad Longmire once told me he wanted to be buried in Hollywood Forever Cemetery. Next to Rudolph Valentino. But Steinberger over there had him cremated and stuck Tad's remains in a cheap, cardboard tube."

"I fail to see your point," Steinberger said. "There's nothing illegal about being cremated."

"Maybe not," I said. "But you're in charge of Tad's affairs, right?"

"Yes."

"So, if you can change his burial arrangements, why not change his will, too? Why not give me twenty-five grand?"

Steinberger blanched. "Why would I do *that*?"

"To make me look guilty," I said. "To throw some shade on yourself. Given what Tad told me about his trust fund, twenty-five grand would be chicken feed to pay."

McNulty's eyes narrowed on Steinberger. "You have a copy of Longmire's will in that briefcase of yours?"

"It's not public domain," Steinberger said, tightening his squeeze around the briefcase he held against his chest.

"Maybe not," McNulty said. "But with a warrant it will be. And I already have the airline manifests handy to check out passenger records for the past week. Do you spell Steinberger with an E or a U?"

"An E," I said. "And might I suggest you start with first class."

Chapter Forty-Four

As it turned out, a passenger manifest showed that Steinberger had flown to Tampa not on Wednesday as he'd claimed, but four days earlier. And, true to his word, the attorney had traveled first class. The registry at the Don CeSar hotel recorded Steinberger as checking in on Saturday, the day before Tad's demise.

While those points of evidence were circumstantial and could be explained away as a business trip or vacation, the DNA results proved to be a little trickier to deflect. While they confirmed my DNA on the murder weapon, they also detected an unknown male's DNA as well.

When Sergeant McNulty discovered Steinberger had been "in proximity to perpetrate," he'd insisted on fingerprinting Steinberger and collecting a DNA sample. After running the attorney's prints through AFIS, the Automated Fingerprint Identification System, no one was more surprised than me when they got a hit.

Steinberger's thumbprint was a perfect match to the bloody print found on the light switch in Tad's bedroom. DNA results are still pending, but let's just say it's not looking too good for poor old Steinberger.

It was kind of ironic, but we might never have identified Steinberger's thumbprint if he hadn't insisted on trying to pin Tad's murder on *me*. He could've handled the dissolution of my contract with Tad by email, like we'd discussed over the phone. If he had, there's a good chance we would never have known he'd even come to St. Petersburg.

But Steinberger's desire to provide a solid motive for me to murder Tad for the money was his undoing. The $25,000 inheritance document had been meant to seal *my* fate, not his. Instead, it helped us catch him in his web of lies.

As Aunt Edna says, that's the way the snickerdoodle crumbles, sometimes.

As for what the cops found in Steinberger's suitcase, it hardly matters now. Even if he forged more than that inheritance document he tried to snag me with and set himself up as Tad's sole beneficiary, no amount of money could save him from a murder rap. And dollars don't matter much when you're locked in the slammer.

I hear there's no first class in Sing Sing.

As for that note on Tad's phone from BS? It turned out that Steinberger's middle name was Brutus. Man, that guy just couldn't catch a break.

· · · ·

YOU MIGHT NOT BELIEVE this, but when McNulty let me and Darryl go, he actually smiled at me. What was even more unbelievable was that I was able to talk Darryl into giving me a ride back to Aunt Edna's in his limo.

There were terms, of course.

The main demand from Darryl was a stop at Sunshine City Studios on the way. He wanted me to chat him up to Marshall and Kerri for acting gigs. Considering I owed Darryl big time for helping put the spotlight on Steinberger, it was the least I could do.

"Doreen!" Kerri said as she opened the faded red door to let us into the studio. "I was just about to call you. I finally got in touch with Brent Connors' mother. She said he's been working on an oil rig in Texas. No phone reception out there. So all is well. He couldn't have killed Tad."

"It doesn't matter now," I said. "Darryl and I figured it out. It was Tad's attorney, Steinberger."

"Really? That's crazy," Kerri said.

"I couldn't have solved it without Darryl, here. He's got quite the talent for ... acting and stuff."

Darryl shot me the look of an unsatisfied customer. I upped my game.

"I mean, you should use Darryl in your productions," I said. "He's a real team player!"

Kerri eyed Darryl. "Are you interested in working here?"

"Yes, ma'am. I know a lot more than how to drive a limo."

Kerri smiled. "Okay. I'll see what I can do. In the meantime, Marshall and Tommy are in the editing suite, if you want to say hi."

"Thanks!" Darryl beamed, then took off down the hall.

Kerri turned to me. "You know, I can think of someone else I'd like to work here."

"Who?" I asked.

She grinned. "I could use another adult to play with. We can't offer you full-time work. Not yet, anyway. But I'd love to have you around for production jobs and acting parts, when it works out. I might even have something for you coming up next week. This local—"

"Gee, thanks, Kerri," I said. "But I need to get back to L.A."

She nodded. "I understand. Well, if you change your mind, my door is always open. I see your eye is healing up. No eyepatch today."

"No. Just these lovely geriatric glaucoma glasses."

Kerri smirked. "They're not *that* bad." She took me by the hand. "And Doreen? I wanted to say again, I'm really, truly sorry about how the final episode of *Beer & Loathing* turned out."

"I know it wasn't your fault. It was—"

"There she is!" Marshall said, coming toward me with open arms. Tommy and Darryl came trailing behind him. "The star of my show!"

I bristled, then decided to let my feelings go. What was done was done. "Hi, Marshall."

"Did Kerri tell you the good news?" he asked.

"What? No, I don't think so."

"The viewers are wild about the show! The station wants to air Beer & Loathing again during the summer, and maybe even pick up a new season in the fall!"

My mouth fell open. "Seriously? That's ... something."

Marshall laughed. "Are you kidding? It's *fantastic*! Hey, I saw that picture of you in the *Beach Gazette*. Kind of funny, eh?"

My nose crinkled. "What do you mean?"

"When you and Tad first got here, I showed you that pirate on Treasure Island. You know, the one with the oranges in the treasure chest?"

"Yes. But I—"

"And then you go and become a pirate for real! Where'd you get that Petey the Pirate eyepatch anyway? I've only ever seen them on vintage memorabilia sites."

"My aunt gave it to me."

"Man, she must've kept that in a drawer for like, forty years!"

"Yeah, I guess so. Well, Darryl, I guess we better get going."

"Let's keep in touch," Marshall said. "I may need you for the next season of *B&L*."

I grimaced. "Yeah, I don't know about that."

"Oh, come on. You were perfect for the role." He shot me a grin. "You know, not everybody's *cut out* to be a serial killer."

I cringed and shook my head. "Are you really gonna go there?"

Marshall cocked his head. "What? Too soon?"

Chapter Forty-Five

For the last time, I found myself being unceremoniously dumped in front of Aunt Edna's place—but at least this time I'd ridden there in a backseat instead of a trunk.

I waved goodbye to Darryl, then trekked through the tropical courtyard of the Palm Court Cottages up to my aunt's little bungalow.

As I reached the door to her apartment, I noticed the brass palm-tree door knocker below the peephole. A vague recollection overcame me. A déjàvu feeling—as if I'd been here and done this all before. A long, long time ago. When everything seemed, I dunno, *bigger* somehow.

"Is this the home of the Cougar Booty Call Lady?" a man's voice rang out behind me. I turned to see Officer Brady walking up the path toward me, a smile on his boyishly handsome face.

I smirked. "On that, I plead the fifth."

He studied me playfully, his eyes twinkling. "No eyepatch today, I see."

"Um, no. Just the glasses."

He grinned. "And boy, are they ever *fab-u-lous*!"

"They're for glaucoma."

Brady cringed. "Oh. Geez. Sorry. That would just ... uh ... I feel like a big jerk."

I let him squirm for a few seconds, stifling the smile eager to curl my lips. "Eh, you're not *that* big," I quipped.

The lines creasing Brady's brow vanished. He laughed. "I guess I deserved that. Hey, I heard you solved the murder of Tad Longmire. Congratulations."

"News travels fast around here."

He waggled his eyebrows. "You have no idea. McNulty told me. He said he never took you as a serious suspect."

"What?" I blinked hard. Twice. "That's not how *I* read him. What did he say to you?"

Brady shot me a devilish grin that kind of reminded me of Tad's. Whether that was a good thing or bad, I wasn't sure. "McNulty told me he knew from the start that you were too big a klutz to pull off a murder."

I folded my arms across my chest. "Well, what a relief to know *somebody* believed I was innocent."

"He also told me to tell you he prefers McNulty over McNutly. What's that all about?"

"Long story. Anyway, what are you doing here again?"

The question seemed to catch Brady off guard. "I ... um—" he stuttered.

Suddenly, the café curtains in Aunt Edna's kitchen window jerked to the side. Jackie's face peered at us from behind the bug screen.

"He's here because—" Jackie managed to utter before a hand clamped over her mouth and pulled her from the window like a cane jerking a bad act from the stage.

The curtains swished closed. Either Aunt Edna had shut Jackie down again, or some hapless kidnap victim had gotten loose from the zip-ties. Oddly, neither prospect seemed to bother Brady ... or me.

"Will you be staying here in St. Pete?" Brady asked.

I chewed my bottom lip. "I don't think so. I've got a career back in L.A."

Or do I?

Besides Sonya's Trailer-Trash Crew calls, I hadn't heard a peep from anyone in Hollywood for the three weeks I'd been in St. Pete. And as far as a paycheck went, my only remaining source of income was now quite inconveniently sitting in a cardboard tube in the police station's evidence room.

"Seems to me you've been putting down roots here," Brady said. "I know your aunt and Jackie are glad you're here."

My right eyebrow rose. "They said that?"

"Sure. In their own special way."

I laughed. "Well, I only hope nobody was harmed in the process."

* * * *

"WHAT WERE YOU DOING in the window?" I asked Jackie as I set my purse on the kitchen counter.

"About to blab a secret," Aunt Edna said.

"What secret?" I asked.

Jackie opened her mouth, then shut it again after getting a gander at the stern look on Aunt Edna's face.

Aunt Edna came over and put an arm around my shoulder. "Secrets are like character flaws, Dorey. You don't go blurting them out all at once. You gotta let them leak out here and there. Slowly. Like molasses in winter."

My nose crinkled. "What are you talking about?"

"Secrets," Aunt Edna said. "Pay attention! What I mean is, you've got to let a person *habituate to the information.* Let them ease into the concept until it becomes their new normal."

"Sounds ominous," I said, crinkling my nose. "What secret are we talking about here?"

Jackie laughed. "Oh, there's plenty more than just *one.*"

Aunt Edna shot Jackie a death ray, then turned back to me, her face transformed into a sunny smile. "Come into the living room, Dorey."

"Uh, okay."

Aunt Edna's arm dropped from my shoulder. I followed her down the hall and into the 1970s time capsule she called a living room.

"Sit in the good chair," Aunt Edna said, motioning to the big, over-stuffed vinyl recliner. As I settled in, she said, "Jackie, go get the box."

"The box?" I asked. "Uh ... what's going on here?"

"You like it here, don't you?" Aunt Edna asked, smiling down at me.

"Sure. But I need to get back—"

"Well, we like you here, too." She turned and yelled, "Jackie! Come on with the fakakta box already!"

Jackie stumbled out of Aunt Edna's bedroom carrying a shoebox and a pair of meat scissors. A shot of cold adrenaline surged through me.

Maybe I really am *in a Steven King movie.* Misery. *Come to think of it, Aunt Edna looks a bit like Kathy Bates ...*

I gulped down a knot in my throat. "What are you going to do with those meat scissors? Cut off my toes so I can't get away?"

"Huh?" Aunt Edna shook her head. "You been watching too many weird movies, Dorey."

"Then what's in the box? And what are those cutters for?"

"See for yourself," Jackie said, handing me the box.

I opened it slowly, bracing for a severed horse head or some gruesome body part. Instead, I was greeted by a pair of gleaming pink flip-flops.

"What the?" I asked.

"The scissors are to cut the tag," Jackie said. "I wasn't sure if you was a size six or seven. We might have to exchange them."

"Oh." I held up the plastic sandals. "I don't get it."

"It's a little celebration gift for beating the murder rap," Aunt Edna said. "Pink flip-flops are the official leisure footwear of the Collard Green Cosa Nostra."

"Seriously?" I snorted. "I mean ... uh ... *thanks.*"

"Don't tell me you haven't noticed," Aunt Edna said.

I looked down at the women's feet. Both were sporting a pair of flip-flops identical to the ones in my hands. "Uh ... sure. I just thought they had a sale on them at Walmart or something."

"*Walmart?*" Aunt Edna said with a huff. "These are high-class Gucci pinks." She shook her head. "We've got to work on your observation skills, Dorey."

My nose crinkled. "Why?"

"'Cause you got some big shoes to fill, that's why," Jackie said. "Go ahead. Try them on."

"Whose shoes?" I asked.

"Molasses," Aunt Edna said, handing me the scissors.

"Fine." I cut the zip-tie holding the flip-flops together and slipped them onto my feet. They fit perfectly. "Gee. I wonder if this is how Cinderella felt," I quipped.

"Ha," Jackie said, elbowing Aunt Edna. "Size seven. You owe me fifty bucks."

Aunt Edna opened her mouth to speak, but was interrupted by a sharp rap on the front door.

"That must be my fairy godmother now," I cooed. "Should I click these things together? Or take them off and slap somebody in the face with them?"

"Check who it is, Jackie," Aunt Edna said, ignoring me.

Jackie peeked out the peephole, scrunched her face, then unlocked the door and flung it open. "Ain't nobody here," she said, glancing around. "Oh, wait. Somebody left us a package."

"What is it?" Aunt Edna asked.

Jackie bent over, then stood up and showed us the small Styrofoam box she'd found. "It's a cooler," she said. "Did you order more pastrami, Edna?"

"No." Aunt Edna eyed the cooler warily. "Open it."

For the second time in under two minutes, I was afraid I was about to get a gander at a dismembered body part. I flinched as Jackie slid the top off the cooler and reached inside. She pulled out a clear plastic bag stuffed with globs of white, gooey-looking stuff.

"Oh my god!" I said. "What *is* that? Somebody's cerebellum?"

Jackie's face went as white as the stuff in the bag.

"No," Aunt Edna said. "It's cheese curds."

"Cheese curds?" I asked. "What's up with that?"

Aunt Edna motioned me toward the recliner. "Sit down, Dorey. We've got something we need to tell you."

THE END

Thanks so much for reading *Almost a Serial Killer*. It's book one in the *Doreen Diller Mystery Series*. If you enjoyed it, I'd be grateful if you took a minute to leave a review on Amazon. I appreciate every single one! Here's a handy link:

https://www.amazon.com/dp/B09XFDFV98

Ready for more Doreen? Awesome! *Almost a Clean Getaway* is the next book in the series. Check out the Sneak Peek included in the back of this book, or read the book description on Amazon by clicking here:

https://www.amazon.com/dp/B0B2W92N7Z

Want to stay in touch and get a laugh in your Facebook feed every day? Join my Facebook page at:

* Facebook: https://www.facebook.com/valandpalspage/

Want to reach me by email or join my newsletter and be the first to hear about new stories coming up? Here you go!

* Newsletter Link: https://dl.bookfunnel.com/fuw7rbfx21

* Website: https://www.margaretlashley.com

* Email: contact@margaretlashley.com

Thanks again. I appreciate you!

All my best,

Margaret

Sneak Peek at Almost a Clean Getaway

Chapter One

Molasses.

That's the word Aunt Edna used to describe secrets. Or, more accurately, how secrets should be *revealed*.

Slowly. Drip by drip.

She told me people needed time to soak in the bittersweet information. To acquire a taste for it. To adjust to the "new normal" that remained after their sugar-plum fantasies about reality had been blown to smithereens.

After hearing the secret Aunt Edna just laid on me, I totally got her point. In fact, a "new normal" sounded pretty good about right now. Actually, a new *planet* sounded even better.

I wonder if they've started that colony on Mars yet ...

• • • •

"CHEESE CURDS?" I ASKED as I flopped back into Aunt Edna's "good chair." The brownish-gold vinyl recliner had come off the assembly line well before I was born—and I was no spring chicken. Let me tell you, my aunt might've been an immaculate housekeeper, but she hadn't redecorated her living room since Disco Duck let out his last quack.

"Yes," Aunt Edna said, her gaze never wavering from the plastic bag full of gooey-looking white globs her friend Jackie was holding up like a goldfish she'd won at the county fair.

A sturdy, no-nonsense woman, normally my aunt was one tough cookie. But at the moment, it appeared as if she were about to crumble. She wiped her hands on her apron, then took a step toward me. Wobbling unsteadily, she grabbed ahold of the avocado-green couch for support.

"You okay?" I asked.

"Yeah," she muttered. "Jackie. Anything else come with those things?"

Jackie lowered the bag of curds and peeked inside a small Styrofoam cooler the clots of cheese had arrived in it mere minutes ago. Someone had placed the cooler by Aunt Edna's cottage door, rapped hard with the palm-tree doorknocker, then taken off before we could see who they were.

"There's a note," Jackie said, plucking a damp piece of paper from the cooler.

"Gimme that." Aunt Edna snatched the note from Jackie's hand. As she read it, her face took on a slack-jawed expression I couldn't decipher.

"What's the note say?" Jackie asked, beating me to it.

Aunt Edna's hand fell to her side. "It says, 'Atta girl.'"

"Who's Atta?" Jackie asked.

"Some kind of congratulations?" I asked, ignoring Jackie.

Aunt Edna pursed her lips. "That's *one* way to look at it."

My brow furrowed. "What's the other way?"

Aunt Edna bit her bottom lip, then whispered, "Sammy the Psycho *knows.*"

"Knows *what*?" I asked.

She locked eyes with me. "I dunno. Maybe nothing. Maybe everything."

"She *means*—" Jackie said, before Aunt Edna shut her down with a stare that could make birds forget to flap and tumble out of the sky.

"There's a lot you don't know about this family, Dorey," Aunt Edna said.

"No kidding." I sat up in the recliner. "I only found out last Tuesday that you guys even *existed.*"

My mother, Maureen Diller, never talked about her family. I wasn't aware she even had one until I'd mentioned to Ma that I was in St. Petersburg, Florida. I'd come here to film a TV serial starring my boss and soap-opera heartthrob, Tad Longmire.

Oddly, when Ma had found out I was in St. Pete, she'd informed me that I had an Aunt Edna who lived here. She'd given me her sister's phone number and told me to call her and drop by for a visit.

Surprised by the news, I'd scoffed at the idea. For me, *family* wasn't exactly a word that conjured up warm, fuzzy feelings. Ma was what some people would call a cold fish. Distant. Secretive. And hard to catch—especially in a good mood.

To be honest, ever since seventh-grade biology class, I'd been fairly certain that in a past life Ma had been one of those weird, sharp-toothed, big-eyed fish that lived in the darkest depths of the ocean. An angler fish, dangling a heart-shaped bioluminescent lure designed to ensnare and devour her hapless prey.

That would be me.

Ma didn't believe in hugging or sharing feelings. I guess she thought that was for weaklings. When she'd instructed me to visit my aunt, I'd figured that if what she had on offer was more of the same, I'd take a raincheck. No thanks.

But fate had stepped in, intervening in a way I'd never seen coming. The night Tad and I'd finished shooting the TV series on St. Pete Beach, someone had snuck into his bedroom and stabbed him to death.

Being pretty much the only person in town who knew Tad, the local cops had pinned me as the prime suspect. They'd also advised me to stick around while they conducted the homicide investigation. Unfortunately, their suggestion hadn't come with an offer to pay for my room and board.

Being that St. Pete was a tourist town, hotel prices were insane. Adding to my predicament, Tad, my only source of income, had been reduced to ashes shuffling around in a cardboard cremation tube.

Needless to say, I'd found myself a bit short on cash. So short, in fact, that staying at a relative's house had sounded like a good idea at the time.

So I'd rung up Aunt Edna. She'd invited me for tea and cookies. Over the phone, she'd sounded like a sweet little old lady—the granny type you see in the movies. But that wasn't exactly how our meeting went down.

Instead of Ellen Corby from *The Waltons*, I'd gotten Ruth Gordon from *Every Which Way But Loose*.

A mere week ago, in the very same vinyl recliner in which I now sat, I'd taken one sip of Aunt Edna's tea and fallen face-first onto her green sculptured carpeting. Sometime later, I'd awoken to find myself in a strange bedroom, tied to the bedposts.

Aunt Edna had interrogated me wielding a rolling pin, while her sidekick Jackie Cooperelli stood watch with a can of Raid pointed in my direction. The two hadn't believed I was Ma's daughter, Doreen. In their defense, I supposed arriving in the trunk of a Chevy Caprice had done nothing to add to my credibility.

Anyway, long story short, I managed to convince them that I was *indeed* family, and not a hit woman out to get them. But the deal wasn't sealed until their canine companion—an ancient pug named Benny that purportedly could smell deadbeats—had given me a good sniff—along with her signature tail-wag of approval.

Fun times.

Once the pair decided I was legit, they spilled the beans on why Ma never talked about her family. According to Aunt Edna, it had been against "Family" rules. Which Family? A little-known southern branch of the mafia referred to as the Cornbread Cosa Nostra.

My aunt explained that back in the 1970s and '80s, their entire limb of the mafia had been cut down by the long arm of the law. Nearly every single one of the Cornbread mob men had either been killed or were doing life sentences in maximum-security prisons.

But the mob *women* were a different story altogether.

For reasons that still weren't completely clear to me, the girlfriends, mistresses, and wives left behind had decided to ditch the Cornbread handle and dub themselves the Collard Green Cosa Nostra, or the CGCN.

Jackie and Aunt Edna were two such women. And although both of them were pushing 70, they still carried a healthy fear of mobsters.

One in particular.

Sammy the Psycho.

And he just happened to love cheese curds.

• • • •

KEEP THE FUN GOING! Get your copy of *Almost a Clean Getaway* here:

https://www.amazon.com/dp/B0B2W92N7Z

About the Author

Why do I love underdogs?

Well, it takes one to know one. Like the main characters in my novels, I haven't led a life of wealth or luxury. In fact, as it stands now, I'm set to inherit a half-eaten jar of Cheez Whiz...if my siblings don't beat me to it.

During my illustrious career, I've been a roller-skating waitress, an actuarial assistant, an advertising copywriter, a real estate agent, a house flipper, an organic farmer, and a traveling vagabond/truth seeker. But no matter where I've gone or what I've done, I've always felt like a weirdo.

I've learned a heck of a lot in my life. But getting to know myself has been my greatest journey. Today, I know I'm smart. I'm direct. I'm jaded. I'm hopeful. I'm funny. I'm fierce. I'm a pushover. And I have a laugh that lures strangers over, wanting to join in the fun.

In other words, I'm a jumble of opposing talents and flaws and emotions. And it's all good.

I enjoy underdogs because we've got spunk. And hope. And secrets that drive us to be different from the rest.

So dare to be different. It's the only way to be!

All my best,

Margaret

Made in the USA
Middletown, DE
05 June 2023

32090443R00151